MW00462064

INDEPENDENT LEGIONS
PUBLISHING

COYOTE RAGE
BY OWL GOINGBACK

ISBN: 978-88-31959-25-4
COPYRIGHT (EDITION) ©2019 INDEPENDENT LEGIONS PUBLISHING
COPYRIGHT (TEXT) ©2019 OWL GOINGBACK
FEBRUARY 2019
COPYEDITING: MICHAEL BAILEY
COVER ART: BEN BALDWIN

SPECIALTY PRESS AWARD RECIPIENT

INDEPENDENT
LEGIONS
PUBLISHING

SUMMARY

OWL GOINGBACK

COYOTE RAGE

INDEPENDENT
LEGIONS

CHAPTER 1

The Great Council did not begin for another moon, but already some of the old ones were making the journey to the house in the hollow mountain, following well-worn paths through ancient forests of tall trees and deep shadows, passing through the land of origin called Galun'lati. Some traveled in spirit form, mere wisps of vapor or orbs of light, dancing like fireflies upon the gentle evening breeze. Others traveled in manicured cloaks of fur or feathers, pausing occasionally to lift their voices to the night.

Once every seven years, in the season of green growing things, representatives from all the different tribes made the long, and often difficult, pilgrimage to the sacred gathering. Animals and men, little people and giants, they sat side-by-side in a circle, their features illuminated by the flames of a central fire. Even the tiniest creature had a place within the circle, and its voice heard, for all were considered equal.

Those who arrived early at the grounds, gathered in pairs or in small clusters, renewing friendships and sharing stories of long ago and far away. But there lurked one among them who spoke softly in the shadows, devising a plan that would do away with the rule of man in the New World.

Bear sat on a soft bed of leaves, his shoulders hunched, listening to the words Coyote whispered in his ear. Ordinarily, he would have swatted the Trickster away, scolding him for making suggestions that went against the Council's sacred rules, but Bear had grown soft and fat with age and he no longer saw things with clear eyes. Or maybe he also tired of seeing the New World ravished and polluted by the greed of humans. Had not his people also been hunted and killed for their coats, claws, and meat? Had not the clans of his brothers and sisters been whittled down to near extinction since the Council first formed many millennia ago?

"We must act quickly, before it is too late." Coyote spoke to Bear in sneaky coughs and whispers, suppressing the urge to bark and howl for fear of being overhead. "They have forgotten the old ways, turned their backs on the medicine and teachings of the Great Mystery, and now wander lost as babes in the forest."

Coyote's tongue dripped poison as he spoke out against man, for his people too had been relentlessly hunted for a hundred thousand years, their skins turned into clothing to protect the hairless ones against the winter cold.

When the original tribes left Galun'lati and migrated to the New World, the stronger animals of fur and fangs had been the rulers of the great forests and plains. But mankind had mastered tools, weapons, and technology, and soon even the mightiest creatures were at their mercy. Hunted for food and sport, the animals had hid in fear and watched helplessly as their homes were destroyed to make room for sprawling cities of stone and glass, testaments to the ever-increasing power of the human race.

Some of the animals who sat in Council wanted to punish people with diseases and physical afflictions for what they had done in the New World, but they were outvoted by those who looked upon men as allies. Even the tiny plants had sided with the hairless ones, courageously offering their bodies as cures for deadly ailments.

But the influence of man was finally coming to an end in the Great Council. Of the original seven places given to humans, only one still remained. And that place belonged to a man far too old and weak to make the journey to the gathering.

Coyote paused and looked about the darkness, searching for spies in the forest. He licked his lips and smiled, for he knew his words had gotten through to the Great Council's chief.

Bear turned and studied Coyote, wishing he had never agreed to the meeting. "And what do you propose we do?"

Coyote's grin spread wider. Bear had always been reluctant to hear his words in the past, often blaming him for dozens of things that had gone wrong with the world since its creation. It was a bad reputation, one he felt he did not deserve.

Leaning closer, Coyote whispered, "There is only one left to represent the original people, an old Cherokee man named Luther Watie. He is unfit to travel, and will never make it to the Council before the spring moon."

"What if he does make it to Council?"

"He will not!" Coyote snapped, his voice a little too loud and sharp. He looked around quickly, making sure he had not been overhead. But the others gathered near the house, well beyond hearing range. "If you agree to my plan, then I will make sure he does not arrive. His people will lose their voice at the Council, and the animals will again rule in the New World."

Bear mused over Coyote's words, silent for a moment in thought. Coyote had always been one for quick words and action, but he liked to think things through and take his time before making a decision. He waited a long time before speaking again, taking pleasure in the Trickster's restlessness.

"He has a daughter. By law, she will take his place at the Council. And her children will take her place."

"She has no children. She is the last of the bloodline. Get rid of her and her father, and we will be free of them once and for all."

"It would not be right," Bear said, shaking his head. "This is not how things are done."

Coyote leaned closer, his nose practically touching Bear's ear. "They have murdered your people. They have murdered my people. For a thousand moons we have sat back and allowed this to happen. Many of our old ones are no more, their homes taken and their tribes scattered to the four winds. We hide in caves, shivering with the cold, while the hairless ones sit fat at their tables and eat of our flesh. We can do away with them, put it back to how it was in the beginning. Those who have crossed over to the shadows will return again to the sunlight. Let me do this, I beg of you."

"And what do you expect in return?" Bear asked.

Coyote tried his best to look shocked. "Me? Why, nothing. Nothing at all. I do this for the betterment of those of fur and feathers. But if I am successful, then perhaps you will allow me to take my seat beside you at the next Council."

"Trying to improve your status in the circle. I should have known." Bear's paw shot out, grabbing him by the scuff of the neck, and holding him tight.

Coyote scratched at the soft earth but could not pull away.

Bear tightened his grasp, looking him straight in the eyes.

"I will let you do this, but heed my words. If you fail, you will find yourself sitting next to Rabbit. I have heard you are quite fond of eating his people, so I imagine you two will have much to talk about."

Bear smiled and released him.

Coyote, visibly shaken, smoothed his fur. "I will not fail. I have been to the land of men many times, and have no problem wearing my skin both ways."

With plans so made, the meeting came to an end.

Coyote and Bear went their separate ways in the darkn
looked up, or noticed Raven sitting on a branch above them.

Raven, also a Council member, had heard every word spoken in secret and was furious that such an evil plan be hatched against the original people. Unlike Coyote and Bear, he had nothing against mankind, and even looked upon cities and towns as places of shelter. Had it not been for the cornfields of men, and discarded pieces of bread and McDonald's French fries, many of his people would have starved during the harsh winter months.

Not wanting to return to the old ways of going hungry and shivering in a cold December forest, Raven decided to do what he could to stop Coyote and his followers. Besides, Luther Watie was his friend; he had watched over the old man and his daughter for many years. He would do anything to help the two of them, even if it meant traveling to the New World and wearing his skin inside out.

But even Raven could not be in two places at the same time, and would need help to stop Coyote.

Throwing back his head, he whistled his finest song and called out to the spirits of the night. He sang the song four times, for four is a sacred number, and then he sat back and waited.

A few minutes passed, and then an elemental spirit drifted up from the forest floor in the form of bluish mist.

The spirit hovered just above the branch where he perched, listening to his story and agreeing to help. And since it was not hampered by flesh and form, and could pass quickly between the two worlds without aid of magic or a portal, Raven sent the spirit on the longer of the two journeys that needed to be made. He would take the shorter route, traveling through the mountains to a place he had often visited.

Raven spread his wings and launched himself from the branch, flying up into the night sky. He flapped his wings with great urgency, hurrying toward a doorway that would take him to the world of men.

CHAPTER 2

Ray Talmage had achieved great wealth and power during his lifetime. A skilled trial lawyer, and successful business owner, he had served in the Florida State Senate for three consecutive terms. He was a man to be respected, and even feared in certain circles, but that didn't stop Sarah Reynolds from jamming a wad of cotton up old Ray's ass with a pair of stainless steel forceps.

Not that Mr. Talmage seemed to mind. He didn't move a muscle, utter a derogatory word, or even flinch. Of course, he had been dead for a little over forty-eight hours, his jaw wired shut, and his eyelids sealed with a small amount of dental powder.

Sarah set the forceps back in a jar of alcohol and grabbed a handful of paper towels to wipe up the small brown puddle of fluid that had leaked from Ray's rectum during the night. Her assistant should have already packed the dead man's anal cavity when he did the embalming yesterday, but he had left that last little chore for her. Not that she minded. Sticking something up a local politician's ass seemed a fair payback for all the taxes she had paid over the years.

Tossing the paper towels in a trash receptacle, she stepped back from the preparation table to examine her work. The late senator was properly embalmed and sanitized, his face shaved, and his thinning gray hair shampooed, dried and lovingly parted on the side. She had applied just enough makeup to bring out the color in his cheeks, and would administer a splash of his favorite cologne—supplied by Mrs. Talmage—once the corpse was dressed.

Ray's dapper gray suit and tie, socks, shoes, underwear, and a new white shirt, awaited in the adjoining dressing room, safe from the smells of embalming fluids and other chemicals that permeated the air in the preparation room.

Even though the prep room had its own air conditioning system, and a large exhaust fan vented to the outside, the smells associated with the embalming process and death could be quite overpowering during the brutally hot summers, or when a corpse had been dead for a long period of time prior to being brought into the funeral home.

The Lewis Powell Funeral Home had been an institution in the historic town of Sanford, Florida for over seventy years. Named for a Confederate soldier involved in the plot to assassinate President

Abraham Lincoln—and whose remains were buried just up the road in Geneva—the business occupied the first floor of a stately Victorian house, located five blocks west of the St. John's River on a quiet street lined with sprawling live oak and magnolia trees.

Sarah had owned the funeral home for nearly four years, buying it from her former boss when he retired. She thought about changing the name of the business, but decided against it. She was a thirty-two-year-old Yankee from a small Wisconsin town, had only lived in Florida for a little over six years, and didn't want to rub the locals the wrong way, especially when the entire city of Sanford seemed to be on a "save our history" kick with many of the older neighborhoods undergoing a much needed facelift.

So, the name had remained the same, the business continuing to operate on the lower level of the house, and with the rooms on the second floor serving as living quarters for Sarah and her husband.

Most husbands might object to living above a mortuary, but Jack was perfectly fine with the arrangement. Nor did he have a problem with his wife's chosen profession, for he was a sexton and managed Greenwood Cemetery in nearby Orlando, that city's oldest and largest burial ground.

Of course, living above a funeral home could put a damper on one's social life. But the two of them didn't have many friends to begin with, and those who occasionally dropped by were usually in the same line of work or had a twisted sense of humor—like the horror author they knew who spent nearly as much time exploring old graveyards as he did writing books.

Sarah glanced at her watch. Mr. Talmage's family had arranged for a private viewing to take place that afternoon in the funeral home's small chapel. While she wasn't pressed for time, there were still quite a few things that needed to be done before the service

After she dressed the corpse, she would place it in the expensive Batesville casket which had arrived earlier that morning. Seeing how she was alone, it would probably be quite a wrestling match to get the body properly positioned in the box. But it would not be the first time she had to wrestle a stiff all by herself. After all that, she would have to pop upstairs to shower and dress for the service, and bake a quick batch of chocolate chip cookies for those attending the viewing. Baking cookies was something she always did to bring a little comfort to the grieving loved ones of the dearly departed.

Unlocking the brakes on the wheels, she pushed the prep table with the body into the adjoining dressing room. She double-checked to make sure Mr. Talmage was no longer leaking, nor in need of rubber pants, then opened a package of new boxer shorts and began to dress him.

She had just finished putting socks and shoes on the late senator, and was about to hit him with a splash of cologne, when the corpse sat up on the table and opened its eyes, revealing the pink eye caps that were supposed to hold the eyelids in place.

"Jesus Christ!" she said, somewhat surprised.

While it wasn't all that unusual for a dead body to sit up, due to muscles tightening, she never had one open its eyes before and wondered if she had used enough denture powder. Perhaps the eyeballs had shrunk due to dehydration, and she needed to inject massage cream or tissue builder behind them. If nothing else, she could apply a few drops of adhesive to hold the lids down. Super Glue worked wonders.

"Now enough of that. Behave yourself and lie back down."

She stepped forward, and started to push the senator back down on the table, when he spoke to her.

"Fred Astaire ..."

Sarah jumped back, startled, the bottle of cologne slipping out of her hand and shattering on the tile floor. The overpowering scent of musk filled the room.

"Fred Astaire ..." he repeated.

At least that's what she thought he said, but it was rather hard to understand him because his jaws were wired together, his slightly protruding upper lip held in place with a small bit of restorative art wax to give it a more youthful appearance.

She was shocked as hell when he spoke. She didn't know what "Fred Astaire" meant, or why Ray Talmage's spirit had crossed back over from the hereafter, but she felt the message from beyond was important and listened carefully to everything he had to say.

"Fred Astaire ..."

Something about the late actor, or perhaps dancing. Maybe the senator enjoyed Fred's movies and wanted one played during his service.

"You want me to play a movie? Is that it?" she asked, afraid to step any closer.

The muscles in his jaw flinched. He forced his lips farther apart and spit out the flattened piece of restorative wax. It landed on the tile floor near her feet.

Forcing his lifeless lungs to inhale and fill with air, the dead man repeated what he had said with a loud hiss. His breath reeked of embalming chemicals.

"Beware ..."

She heard the word loud and clear. Not a message about a deceased movie actor known for his dancing skills. A warning.

"Beware ... beware of what?" she asked, recognizing the absurdity of talking to a corpse.

"Beware, Blue Sky Woman ..." he said, looking at her with unblinking eyes still covered by the pink eye caps.

It was definitely a warning, but what did the message mean?

Sarah inched closer to the table, trying to hear every raspy syllable.

"I don't understand. Who is Blue Sky Woman, and what should she beware of?"

The corpse stopped talking, a heavy silence falling over the room.

Sarah stepped back, already beginning to wonder if she had imagined the incident.

But then Mr. Talmage spoke once more. "Beware, Blue Sky Woman. Coyote's coming ..."

With that, he gave a final sigh and lay back down on the table.

She stood in stunned silence, staring down at the body, then turned to look around the room, searching for hidden cameras or microphones, thinking that what she had just witnessed was some sort of joke. But there were no cameras or microphones, at least none in plain sight.

Crossing the room, she searched through all the cabinets, even checked under the worktables, but found no recording devices of any kind—nothing to indicate a prank.

She turned her attention back to the corpse. The initial shock had worn off, and a small quiver of fear now passed through her body causing her hands to tremble.

"Mr. Talmage, did you just talk to me? Senator ...? Sir ...?"

He did not reply.

Taking a deep breath to steady her nerves, she walked over to the table and carefully closed his eyelids, fearful he would again sit up and speak. And had he done so at that particular moment, she would have screamed or maybe even wet herself. But the late senator remained quiet and still, looking no more unusual than the hundreds of other bodies that had passed through her care over the years.

Glancing down, she spotted the piece of wax on the floor. She started to pick it up, but could not bring herself to touch something spat from the dead man's mouth. She would get a new piece to set his lips again, but that could wait until later. Right now, she needed a hot shower, and a stiff drink to settle her nerves. Luckily, relief awaited in the rooms above.

Sarah turned off the overhead lights and left the dressing room. Had she looked back, she would have seen a slight smile form on the lifeless lips of Ray Talmage.

CHAPTER 3

Jack Reynolds saw a familiar flash of bright color enter the building, but didn't have time to duck out of sight or close his office door. A few seconds later, Sonny Harris appeared in the doorway, dressed in his usual tacky attire of cargo shorts, Hawaiian shirt, and collection of gold chains.

"How's it going, Jackie-boy?" Sonny asked, his speech heavy with a New York accent. "You's busy?"

Jack wanted to tell him that he was terribly busy, up to his neck in unwanted paperwork, but he didn't. As the manager of Greenwood Cemetery, he often had to put aside his work to console and comfort the grieving loved ones of the recently departed, even if they had been grieving for months.

Sonny had come to Greenwood every single day since his wife passed away six months earlier, sitting by her gravesite for hours at a time, talking, reading, even singing. He would always stop by the office first to visit with Jack for a few minutes, and often stop by again before leaving the cemetery. He was a lonely man, looking for reassurance that his visits were not in vain and that his wife could somehow hear his words and know she was missed, perhaps even seeking affirmation that he wasn't just talking to a corpse slowly rotting in the humid Florida soil.

"Never too busy for you. What's up?" Jack pushed a stack of paperwork to the far corner of his desk. His soft mid-western drawl was in complete contrast to Sonny's nasally northern pronunciation. Jack and his family had moved to the Orlando area over twenty years ago, from Logan, Missouri, but he still couldn't shake his accent. Not that anyone cared; central Florida was a land of immigrants with dozens of dialects and accents to be heard.

"Nuthin much." Sonny folded himself into one of the two chairs in front of the desk. "I came by to see my wife. I brung her some flowers. Daisies. Those were her favorite."

"That's nice," Jack said, trying not to be too obvious as he glanced at the clock on the wall. "I'm sure she'll appreciate it."

Sonny nodded, not saying anything for a moment, as if lost in his own thoughts. When he finally spoke, a sad little frown tugged at the corners of his mouth. "I tried to get my kids to come along, but they said they were too busy. They're always too busy. They don't even invite me over to their house no more. I think they hate me."

Sonny's daughter and son were both grown and had families of their own. Jack could understand why they didn't invite their father to visit anymore, because all he ever talked about was his dead wife. It was depressing and unhealthy. The kids had gotten over their grief and had moved on with their lives, but their father refused to let go of his sorrow and clung to the memory of his wife like a drowning swimmer.

"I'm sure they don't hate you," Jack said, forcing a smile.

"Yes, they do. They hate me. My daughter doesn't even invite me to dinner anymore."

Jack wanted to tell Sonny the truth, but had a feeling the man would break down and cry. Instead, he said, "They probably just have a full schedule. You know how it is with young people nowadays, all the time running around. Never have time to sit down and visit. Why do you think there are so many fast food places? No one has time for a sit-down dinner anymore, just grab a burger and eat while driving. Take it and go."

Sonny remained quiet for a moment, the silence stretching uncomfortably in the office. "Perhaps you're right. My kids have a lot of things going for them."

"See, I told you."

"But I do wish they would come here with me once in a while, show a little respect."

"Everyone has a different way of dealing with grief. Some put flowers on graves every day, others put the memory behind them and get on with their lives." Jack had aimed the last comment at Sonny, but it slipped past him.

"Yeah, I guess so." He nodded. "Well, I've got to go see my missus. Nice talking with you, Jackie-boy."

As he stood, Jack noticed a bit of brown leather peeking out from underneath the bottom of Sonny's Hawaiian shirt. A holster. "Are you wearing a gun?"

Lifting his shirttail, Sonny revealed a small semi-automatic pistol tucked inside a belt holster. "I just bought it last week. Figured my customers would feel safer knowing I was armed. Now, I'm not just a driver, but I'm also security."

Sonny owned a limo service and did most of his driving at night. His customers included celebrities, professional athletes, politicians, and business executives—the kind of people who probably needed a little extra security. Still, it troubled Jack that a man who continued to grieve over his wife's death would be walking around with a loaded gun on his hip.

"You got a license for that thing?"

"I got me a concealed weapons permit, and that's all I need in Florida."

Jack shook his head. "If you're offering your service as armed security, then you need a security license. You'll have to take a course to get a badge."

"I don't need a badge," Sonny argued. "Not if I'm carrying concealed."

"Yes, you do. You—" Jack's cell phone rang, interrupting him. He picked up the phone and glanced at the displayed number. The call was from Sarah; he breathed a sigh of relief, happy for the interruption. "Excuse me. I have to get this."

Sonny removed the pistol from its holster, looking at it. "This thing would make one hell of a hole."

Jack answered the phone. "What's up?"

Returning the pistol to its holster, Sonny let his shirttail fall back in place and walked out of the office. "Goodbye, Jackie-boy."

Jack nodded, then turned his attention fully to the phone call from his wife. Sarah was upset; something strange had happened at the funeral home.

"Who sat up?" he asked, wanting her to repeat what she had just said. "But that sometimes happens; the muscles contract. You know that … What do you mean, he spoke? How could he speak? I think you had better calm down and start again from the beginning."

He rolled his chair from behind his desk and kicked the door shut, not wanting to be disturbed. Through his window he could see Sonny slowly climbing the hill to his wife's grave … the big man pulling the pistol from its holster and putting the muzzle against his temple.

"Fuck!" Jack jumped up, the cell phone still pressed against his ear.

"That's what I thought," Sarah replied, thinking the comment had been directed at her.

"Fuck, fuck, fuck, fuck …" Jack ran to the window.

"Exactly …" she said.

He tried to open the window, but it wouldn't budge. Someone had caulked around its edge, sealing it closed.

"Goodbye, Jackie-boy," Sonny had said as he left the office. Not "See you later," as he always said, but something far more permanent. Goodbye. A final farewell.

Jack beat on the window, almost breaking the glass. "Sonny, no!"

"Jack, what's going on?" Sarah's voice buzzed in his ear, like the droning of a small bee. He turned from the window and ran across the room, finally pulling the cell phone from his ear as he jerked open the door, racing across the lobby and out the front door.

Sonny had gone over the hill and was no longer in sight. Jack charged up the path as fast as he could, already winded and breathing hard, wishing he had spent more time in the gym or playing tennis with his wife. But he was a forty-year-old man who spent way too much time sitting behind a desk, and whose hobbies included camping, fishing, and shooting black-powder guns—activities that did not require much physical strength and never involved running.

He topped the hill, gasping for air. Sonny sat on his wife's grave in the valley below, the automatic still pressed against his temple.

"Sonny, no!" Jack yelled. "Don't do it!"

"Jack, what's wrong? What's happening?" The voice came from far away. A tiny voice, like one of the Whos in Whoville. Little Wendy Who. He glanced down and saw the cell phone clutched tightly in his hand. Sarah was still on the line.

"Hang up and call 9-1-1," he yelled into the phone. "Send the cops to Greenwood. Sonny's going to kill himself."

"Oh, God," she said, hanging up.

Jack shoved the cell phone into his pants pocket. "Sonny, no. Don't!"

He raced down the hill, stopping a few feet from where the troubled man sat. "Sonny, stop. Think about what you're doing."

Sonny slowly turned to look at him, a smile unfolding on his face. "It's okay, Jackie-boy. Everything is going to be fine now. You'll see. We're going to be together again … in heaven. She said she was waiting for me … said it was my time to cross over."

"No. Don't. Think about your kids."

The smile faltered. Sonny's eyes watered. "I am thinking about them. They don't want me to come around anymore … don't want to hang out with their old dad. This will solve all our problems."

His finger tightened on the trigger.

"For God's sake, don't do it!" Jack yelled.

Sonny blinked back tears. "Sorry, Jackie-boy. I really am. Sorry I've gone and made such a mess of things. Sorry—"

The finger tightened on the trigger and the gun went off with a deafening roar, the side of Sonny's head exploding outward in a cloud of blood, brains, hair, and pieces of skull, peppering two granite headstones and Jack's clean white shirt with crimson drops and bits of gore.

Sonny sat staring at him, fountains of blood squirting from the entrance and exits wounds in his head, the pistol still clutched tightly in his hand. And then he toppled over onto his side.

"Fuck!" Jack said, finally finding his voice. He stared at the dead man in horror, then looked down at his shirt, now plastered wet against his chest. "Fuck!" he said once more before throwing up, covering his dress shoes with the scrambled eggs and sausage he had eaten for breakfast. They had tasted much better going down than they did coming back up.

Jack wiped his mouth with the back of his hand. He started to step forward, but stopped. Sonny Harris was quite dead, tendrils of white smoke drifting from the two holes in his head. Nothing he could do for him. The area was now a crime scene, and the police would not like him trampling all over it.

Hands trembling, he grabbed his cell phone and dialed 9-1-1. He heard the wail of police sirens approaching in the distance, and knew his wife had already made an emergency call. No need for them to hurry now. No reason to arouse the curiosity of those living in the neighborhoods surrounding the cemetery.

Jack spoke with the 9-1-1 dispatcher as he staggered toward the front gates. There were no other visitors in the cemetery, and he wanted to secure the perimeter before someone showed up to spend time with a departed loved one. It wouldn't go over so good if they were to stumble upon Sonny's lifeless body, his head still smoking.

He glanced down at his shirt and almost laughed. It also wouldn't be good for someone to see him before he had a chance to change and clean up. They would wonder what the hell was going on at Greenwood, a cemetery already with a reputation for being haunted.

Jack closed the entrance gates, but did not lock them. The police would be there any second and he needed to let them in. In the distance, the wail of a police siren suddenly fell silent. No doubt they had received a call from the dispatcher and now knew there was no longer any reason to make so much noise.

Glancing down at his cell phone, he took a deep breath and made a call to his supervisor at city hall to report the suicide.

It was going to be one hell of a day.

CHAPTER 4

In his dreams, Luther Watie soared over the countryside on the wings of an eagle. He could taste the cold, crisp air and feel the updrafts that lifted him to touch the setting sun. In his dreams, he danced in the powwow arena as a young man, adorned in feathers, beads, and buckskins, challenging the other dancers, turning to face the drum when an honoring beat sounded. And in his dreams, he felt the flesh of women he had known long ago ...

Luther slowly opened his eyes, the visions fading back into the dusty corridors of his mind. In his dreams, he was many things, but in reality he was nothing more than a forgotten old man waiting to die in a state-run nursing home in the small town of Talbot, North Carolina.

Outside his window, oak trees rustled in the gentle spring breeze, their branches reaching up to touch the warmth of the noonday sun. But the breeze and the sun's rays never entered Luther's room, the window always locked tight against the elements. And instead of fresh air and sunshine, his surroundings were constantly draped in heavy shadows and smelled of disinfectant, medicine, and sometimes death.

From the bed he had occupied for nearly five years, the victim of frequent ailments associated with old age, he could occasionally catch glimpses of the outside world, just enough to remind him that life did exist beyond the confines of the nursing home. But most of the time the heavy curtains covering his window were drawn tight, because Charlie Henry didn't like the glare.

Charlie was a skeleton-thin black man who had been moved into Luther's room nearly six months ago, just a few days after the last roommate checked out on a one-way ride to the spirit world. Old Charlie didn't say much. As a matter of fact, he had not spoken in over a year due to a stroke, so Luther wondered how he could complain about the glare coming in through the window.

Truth be known, it was probably Charlie's family who had complained about the curtains being open. Perhaps they thought the sunlight streaming into the room would bleach the old man's skin to a lighter shade of black. Or maybe they were concerned that someone might peek into the room and see him lying there in a less than dignified state.

The stroke that had stolen Charlie's voice also caused the muscles in his face to tighten dramatically, leaving his mouth permanently open and drooling, tongue hanging out to one side.

For fun, when Charlie was sleeping, Luther would take some of the frozen green peas they served at dinner and toss them at his roommate's open mouth. He usually missed, with most of the peas ending up on the floor or under the bed, but every once in a while he was able to make a free throw and score two points. On one particularly good night, he lobbed three peas into Charlie's open mouth, much to the horrors of the nursing home staff.

To punish him for his antics with the vegetables, one of the male orderlies had tied Luther to his bed and rubbed vinegar in his eyes. Nor had they untied him when he needed to pee, forcing him to wet himself and lie in a puddle of his own urine. But that hadn't stopped the late-night basketball games. He still used Charlie's mouth as a goal, only now he tossed pieces of crushed ice instead of peas, leaving no evidence for the orderlies to find in the mornings.

From the room across the hallway came a piercing scream, followed by the words "mother fucker." That would be Ethel Wilson, and it must be Thursday, bath day at the Willows Nursing Home.

Ethel was the old-fashioned sort, all prim and proper, and hated being undressed by the nurses and orderlies, especially the male ones. She was perfectly capable of undressing herself and taking her own shower, but the nursing home staff forbade such personal liberties for fear one of the patients might slip and fall on the tile floor.

Instead, the elderly residents were physically undressed by the staff, wrapped in disposable paper gowns, and escorted to the showers. At the showers they were again undressed, scrubbed, and dried by two waiting orderlies, and then wrapped again in paper and taken back to their rooms. Those who were bedridden and could not make it to the showers were given sponge baths.

Another scream came from across the hall, quickly cut short and muffled. A second cry sounded, deeper in tone and volume, apparently made by the male orderly foolish enough to clamp his hand over Ethel's mouth. She may be old, but she still had most of her teeth and knew how to use them.

A loud thud followed the orderly's cry of pain—flesh on flesh—and then an eerie silence.

Luther hurried to thumb the remote beside his pillow, raising the head of his bed. Staring out the open doorway of his room, he found himself holding his breath as he waited to see what would happen next.

A few moments later, two male orderlies walked past his doorway. They carried the limp, naked body of Ethel Wilson, not even bothering to drape her in the prescribed paper gown. On the right side of her ample stomach shone an angry-red mark the size of a man's fist. The elderly woman had obviously passed out from the pain of the blow, and was being taken without effort to the showers.

"You bastards," he hissed, careful not to say it too loudly for fear of invoking the wrath of the orderlies. Rumor was that they had pushed several people down the stairs over the years, and really troublesome patients sometimes died mysteriously during their sleep.

The unconscious woman and her escorts disappeared from view. A few moments later, another orderly passed by his door—a young man, tall and thin, with angular features and an uncombed mop of brown hair hanging down over his ears. He must be new to the staff, because Luther had never seen him before.

It wasn't the orderly's physical features that got Luther's attention, causing his heart to skip a beat, but the shadow he cast on the wall opposite the door. The shadow of an animal, with hairy haunches and a bushy tail, and a head equipped with pointy ears and a long muzzle. The shadow moved in perfect sync with the young man, matching his pace stride for stride.

He gasped, recognizing the shadow.

Born and raised on the reservation of the Eastern Cherokee, Luther had learned the ancient customs and beliefs of his people from an early age. His father had been a tribal healer and teacher, a man of wisdom and medicine, and a member of the Great Council. He had taught his son about the Little People and the Tall Men, and the ghosts that moved like fireflies in the night, preparing him for the day when he too would be called upon to make the journey through Galun'lati

Luther had also learned about the old ones who could wear their skins both ways and walk in two worlds. They had sat beside him at the Council, and visited his home on many occasions. Some had become his friends, while others were not to be trusted and even dangerous.

While the shape-shifters were able to wear their skins inside out to alter their appearance, they could not change their shadows. The shadow could not be hidden or disguised, and always revealed a person's inner truth. That was why the Great Council took place around a roaring fire inside Hollow Mountain, the flames casting shadows for all to see.

The orderly continued down the hall, taking the shadow of the beast with him. Luther started to breathe a sigh of relief, but then heard the footfalls go silent and knew the man had stopped just past his doorway.

Perhaps the shadow had been a trick of the hallway's florescent lighting, which often flickered, and the young man was nothing more than a normal orderly checking in on the patient next door. Perhaps, but he didn't think so. Every fiber in his body warned him that something was amiss. He also knew that the room next to his currently sat unoccupied, the sole resident undergoing shower time and a morning regiment of physical therapy. No reason for the orderly to stop next door, no cause for him to linger.

He cocked his head slightly, straining to listen for sounds from the next room. But Luther heard none of the familiar noises associated with a room being straightened, a bed being made, or a bedpan emptied. Nor did he hear any additional footfalls on the tile floor to announce that the orderly had moved on. The man had stopped just past the open doorway, and there he remained.

Luther coughed weakly and found his voice. "Hello? Is someone there?"

No reply, only silence.

"Hello?"

In the distance, he heard the screams of a woman. Ethel must have awakened in the shower and voiced her displeasure over being naked and scrubbed. The orderlies would soon be returning the portly woman to her room. He would be safe then with others in the area.

He heard a muffled sound of movement; a shadow fell across the threshold. The thin orderly with the scruffy hair appeared in his doorway.

"Coyote," Luther said, a shiver caressing his spine. The Trickster was a known troublemaker with a deep dislike for humans.

The orderly smiled, revealing teeth that looked much too sharp to be human. "Ah, you recognize me."

"I am not afraid of you, shape-shifter." He reached for the medicine pouch that used to hang in the center of his chest. But the pouch, along with the rest of his personal belongings, had been taken from him by the nursing home staff.

Coyote raised his head and sniffed. "Yes, you are. I can smell your fear. It is sharp and strong, like the death that waits for you in the night."

"What do you want from me? Why are you here?"

"Have you forgotten your duties, old man? Do you not know what season this is, what moon is coming?"

Luther fumbled for the remote to raise the head of his bed even higher. "The Council ..."

"Ah, you do remember. Good. Very good. Now I will not feel so bad killing you."

"Kill me? Why?" he asked, shocked. "It is forbidden for members of the Great Council to harm one another."

Coyote laughed, a sharp yipping sound. "It was forbidden, but the rules have changed. We are sick of your people, tired of what they have done to this world. Wars without reason. Murder for sport. Genocide and pollution. It is time to put a stop to the madness once and for all."

"Not all people are bad," Luther tried to argue.

Coyote nodded. "Not all, but enough. It is time for a change ... time to let those of fur and feather rule once again. Time to put things back to how they were in the old days."

The old man shook his head. "You know that is impossible. The old ways are nothing but faded dreams, forgotten legends of long ago and far away. There is no going back. What is done is done."

"We'll see."

"And who will rule, then? Your people?"

"Why not?" Coyote snapped. "They can do no worse than what mankind has done."

"Stupid, Coyote. You can disguise your body, but you cannot hide your greed. The others will see through your plan and they will stop you. If they cannot see, then I will warn them."

Coyote's hands opened and closed in fists of rage. "You will do nothing but die."

He started to step into the room, but a commotion coming down the hallway caught his attention. The other male orderlies were returning with Ethel, and she fought them every step of the way.

The shape-shifter smiled. "I must go now, but I will be back soon."

"I'll warn the staff about you. You'll never get back in."

"Go ahead and tell them, they will never believe you." Coyote's grin grew wider. "Maybe I will return tonight when it is dark and everyone is asleep. Maybe tomorrow. And when I do return, I will eat your liver." He slowly licked his lips for effect. "And then I will kill your offspring … your daughter."

The young man retreated from the room, the shadow of a coyote following him down the hallway.

Luther watched the shadow disappear, terror clutching his heart.

"My daughter."

CHAPTER 5

Sarah sat in the back of the chapel, paying little attention to the family members and friends in attendance for the viewing. Her attention was instead focused on the body of Ray Talmage on display in the front of the room, fearful he was going to sit up at any moment and say something.

But the late state senator had not spoken again, and now looked rather peaceful lying in his charcoal gray casket surrounded by ornate displays of red and yellow roses. Perhaps he had said all he wanted to say earlier in the day and now slept the eternal rest, or maybe he was already in Heaven and having a delightful conversation with JC and the boys.

Sarah hoped that the spirit of old Ray had gone on its merry way, departing the funeral home while she was upstairs baking cookies, showering, and getting dressed for the service. For even though she still felt the numbing effects of the two glasses of red wine she had downed before coming back downstairs, her nerves were a little frayed from her previous conversation with the deceased, and she might lose it if he suddenly decided to get chatty again.

She glanced at her watch. The service was almost over, but Ray wasn't scheduled to be buried until the following morning. That meant he would be her responsibility for another night. It also meant the talkative corpse would be sleeping downstairs while she and Jack resided one floor above.

Deciding that the viewing was running smoothly, she got up and slipped out of the room. Stopping by her office, she grabbed her cell phone and sent a quick text message to Jack.

How you doing?

Jack texted back a few seconds later, *Up to my neck in paperwork and cops. How about you?*

Fine so far, she wrote.

Good. See you tonight.

Sarah smiled and switched off the cell phone. She and Jack had only been married for a year, living together for three years before that. They were complete opposites in many ways—he the laid-back country boy, she the more sophisticated girl from Wisconsin—but they did have similar jobs and were very much in love.

Of course, Jack had played hard to get when they first met, forcing her to use feminine tricks to get his attention. Standing in the doorway of his office at Greenwood one fateful February afternoon, she had casually slipped an index finger beneath the waistband of her black slacks, pulling the strap of her thong into view. The trick had worked, and he had asked her out to dinner that same day. They had been a couple ever since.

Leaving the cell phone on her desk, she exited the office just as the viewing was drawing to a close. The gathering had been small and private, with only the immediate family and a few close friends allowed entrance. Those not on the guest list had been turned away, including the assistant mayor of Sanford and a reporter from the local paper.

Positioning herself by the front door, she bid farewell as the guests left the funeral home. Several people complimented her on the ceremony, and the fresh baked cookies, amazed she had gone to so much trouble.

Shutting the front door, she returned to the chapel. Only Ray's widow, his oldest son, and the minister remained in the room, and they had stayed behind to watch her close the casket.

Sarah double-checked to make sure no one had placed a gift with the departed, then lowered the lid and locked it with a casket key.

She had once buried a man who had been an avid golfer in life. One of his friends thought it would be a great idea to slip a golf ball into his pocket during the service, just in case there were a few fairways on the other side. It was a nice gesture, except the ball fell out of the dead man's pocket and slipped beneath the false bottom, rolling back and forth as the pallbearers carried the casket from the room and creating one hell of a racket.

She placed the casket key in a cardboard box and gave it to Ray's oldest son, assuring the family that no one would be able to disturb the body or steal Ray's jewelry before he was laid to rest the following day.

Of course, she had several such keys in her office and could easily open the casket again, but the last thing in the world she wanted was to take another look at Ray Talmage. The old man was quiet, and she didn't want to give him an opportunity to strike up another conversation.

As she saw them to the front door, Sarah quickly went over the schedule for Ray's funeral service the following day, followed by the burial at a local cemetery. In addition to the hearse and flower van, two limos had been ordered to carry immediate family members from the church to the cemetery. The tent, chairs, and casket-lowering device would be provided by the company doing the opening and closing.

Bidding the three of them a goodnight, she closed and locked the door, and turned off the lights in the entranceway. The funeral home was quiet and still, except for a soft tapping coming from the chapel.

Tap ... tap ... tap ... tap ...

Sarah froze in place, a tingle of fear walking down her spine on spider legs. There was no one in the chapel, only Mr. Talmage. So, what was making the noise?

Tap ... tap ... tap ...

She stood there in the shadows, her head cocked slightly to one side, listening to the sound coming from the other room.

Tap ... tap ... tap ... tap ...

Not a terribly loud noise, but noticeable nonetheless. Sharp, like fingernails striking wood. Like something tapping to get in ... or trying to get out.

Her mouth went dry. She suddenly recognized the noise and was terrified, for it was the sound of something gently striking the lid of a sixteen-gauge steel casket. And not just any old casket, but a beautiful charcoal gray container from the Batesville Casket Company.

Tap ... tap ... tap ...

Frightened, yet at the same time drawn by the noise, she quietly tiptoed back down the hallway to the tiny chapel. The strange tapping stopped as she reached the open doorway, and she found the sudden silence even more disturbing.

She looked around the room, but it was just the two of them: her and the deceased.

"Mr. Talmage, was that you?" Her voice sounded stained, even to her own ears.

Pull yourself together. He's dead ... embalmed. He is not tapping to get out. It's only your imagination.

She entered the room, slowly approaching the casket.

"Mr. Talmage, do you want out?" she asked timidly, hoping not to hear an answer to her question.

Sarah was still a few feet away from the casket when she spotted something on its lid, something that had not been there when she left the room. It was a black feather, about five inches long and a half-inch wide, resting on the casket lid above the dead man's chest.

Picking up the feather, she held it up to the light. It was inky black, with a faint bluish sheen to it. The feather of a crow, or perhaps a raven, a large bird with a sharp, pointy beak.

She looked down at the casket's lid, almost expecting it to be marred with small dents, but it was shiny new and unblemished.

… something gently rapping, tapping at my chamber door.

She hadn't read Edgar Allan Poe since high school, but his epic poem "The Raven" sprang eerily to mind. Sarah spun around, expecting to find a large black bird perched above the doorway. But there was nothing there but an unlit emergency exit sign.

"Enough of this." She placed the feather back on the casket. "I'm out of here."

She hurried from the room, not even bothering to turn off the lights, fleeing for the safety and comfort of her living quarters upstairs and the half-full bottle of wine that awaited her.

CHAPTER 6

Raven was tired and his wings hurt. He had flown for many miles, and still had a long way to go. The sun was already sinking in the western sky, casting long shadows over the mountainous countryside below. Soon the temperatures would be falling, the chill night air making his trip even more strenuous.

Deciding he needed to lose the feathers, and find himself a different mode of transportation, he dipped a wing and followed a narrow ribbon of blacktop through the Appalachian Mountains. The countryside below was rugged and sparsely inhabited, and had once been home to the Cherokee, Catawba, and several bands of the Little People. But the Indians had been removed from their native land years ago, forcibly marched to a new home in Oklahoma, and most of the Little People had turned their backs on the world of men and returned to their original home in Galun'lati.

The blacktop road he followed led to a nameless little town at the foot of the mountains. Soaring lower, he passed over empty streets and abandoned warehouses, searching for signs of life, and transportation. He was almost to the end of town when the sound of music drifted up from below and caught his attention.

He turned into the wind and circled back around, taking aim at the brick building below him. The rectangular sign mounted on the roof identified the dwelling as JIM'S PLACE, informing would-be patrons that it was the home of "good food and cold beer." The sound of music and loud voices spilled from an open doorway.

Raven alighted on the sign, turning to study the crowded parking lot in front of the bar. Having spent considerable time in the world of men, he was familiar with mechanical devices. They were a necessary evil, and even a blessing when the weather turned foul. Unfortunately, all the vehicles before him were the two-wheeled variety and would offer little warmth on the open road.

His only other option was to rest for the night and start again fresh in the morning, but he knew time was running out. Coyote and his followers were already on the move, setting into motion their evil plan.

Taking a moment to stretch after his long flight, he flew off the sign and landed beside a green trash Dumpster behind the building. Safely out of sight in the shadows, he used his sharp beak to tug at the feathers covering his chest. He pulled several loose, and then plunged his beak deep into the bare spot he had created, causing his flesh to magically separate and his cloak of black feathers to fall away like a discarded overcoat.

For a moment, he stood naked against the elements, a supernatural being whose body shimmered a glowing translucent silver. Picking up the discarded skin of feathers, he shook it and turned it inside out, quickly slipping it back on with the flesh side out and the feather side in.

A transformation took place as he turned his skin inside out and slipped it back on, his body growing in size and changing into that of a man. His bones popped and lengthened as they realigned themselves, the skin stretching tight and sealing itself over the new body.

Raven was one of the old ones, a shape-shifter, and could reverse his skin to walk in two very different worlds. In Galun'lati, he was a bird, but in the land of the Great Turtle he often wore the skin of an Indian man, his body thin and muscular, his long hair falling loose to his shoulders—hair the same color as the shiny black feathers he now wore on the inside.

Ignoring the itching in his skin, knowing the sensation would soon fade, he stood completely still as his new body made its final adjustments. He also ignored the bitter cold, a reminder that he was naked in a world that frowned upon public displays of nudity.

He looked down and smiled. How much easier things would be if his man skin came already dressed, but there was no way to turn into a raven while wearing clothing. He had tried once before, with nearly disastrous results.

Since he didn't have any clothing of his own, he must find something to attire himself. Looking around, he spotted a soiled white apron on the ground beside the Dumpster and hurried to put it on. The apron covered most of his front, but left his backside bare to the elements. He needed more garments.

Crouching in the shadows, he slipped around to the front of the building. The parking lot was still crowded with motorcycles. Several of the bikes were equipped with saddle bags and luggage carriers, and might contain raingear or something else he could wear. Thankful the bar was windowless, and the front door now closed, he hurried across the lot to one of the bikes.

Luck was on his side, for he soon found a rolled-up pair of blue jeans his size. He also found a black T-shirt that was a little snug, and a pair of steel-toed boots only a few sizes too big.

Grabbing the stolen items of clothing, he hurried around to the side of the building to put them on. The jeans fit perfectly, and he could lace the boots tight enough to keep them from falling off his feet.

On the front of the black T-shirt was the image of a gun, with the slogan: *That's why we call it tourist season.* The message was completely lost on him.

He had just donned the shirt when a large, two-door car pulled into the parking lot. The car was faded blue and rusting, adorned with patches of gray primer; a vehicle no one would go out of their way to look for if stolen.

Perfect.

Standing in the shadows, he watched as the car's owner, an elderly man, climbed out and entered the bar. The man hadn't even bothered to lock the driver's door, and it was extremely doubtful if the vehicle came equipped with an alarm system. Raven waited a few more minutes, then hurried across the parking lot.

Opening the driver's door, he quickly slipped behind the steering wheel. He was hoping the owner had left the keys in the ignition, but they weren't there. He looked above the visor and under the seat for a spare key, even checked the glove box, but didn't have any luck. Sadly, hot-wiring a car was one skill he had not mastered. Such knowledge usually wasn't needed for one who could change his skin and fly.

Climbing back out of the car, he ran his hand underneath the wheel wells in search of a magnetic box containing a spare key. He was searching along the passenger side when he heard someone call out, "Hey, Red. There's some guy out here wearing your shirt."

A second voice sounded, "What the hell? Hey you!"

He turned to see a tall, red-haired man crossing the parking lot. He was followed by a muscular bald man with too many tattoos. The red-haired man pointed at the shape-shifter.

"Hey, you. That's my shirt you got on. I just bought it."

Raven glanced down at the shirt, realizing his mistake. The design must be unusual, and the owner's friend had spotted it from a distance.

"You've got some explaining to do," Red said in a menacing voice.

"Yeah, some explaining to do," echoed his bald-headed companion.

Raven looked around for an escape route, but there wasn't one. He was on foot, and probably couldn't outrun the two men, especially since he now wore boots in danger of slipping off his feet. Nor would he be able to hide anywhere long enough to turn his skin around and slip back into bird form.

"Where did you get that shirt?" Red asked again.

Running his fingertips over the T-shirt, Raven replied, "I found it."

"Found it, huh?" asked the shirt's rightful owner. "Found it where?"

"Yeah, found it where?" echoed the other biker.

"I found it in your saddlebag, right after I stole these jeans." Raven threw a vicious right cross, hitting Red square in the jaw, and catching him by surprise. The man's knees buckled and he dropped like a rock. Pivoting, he threw another punch at the bald-headed biker but missed.

Baldy moved like a cat, his speed surprising for a man so big. He ducked Raven's fist and fired back with a powerful punch of his own, catching the shape-shifter in the solar plexus. Raven staggered backward into the car, the air knocked out of him.

Had the big man hit him again, Raven would probably have been knocked out and seriously injured. Instead, the biker stepped forward and grabbed him around the neck. Raven tucked his chin to protect his throat, countering with a vicious knee to the man's groin.

Baldy cried out in pain, doubling over and clutching his testicles. Raven grabbed the man's head with both hands and slammed another knee into his face, smashing the cartilage in his nose.

The biker hit the pavement with his arms spread wide, his eyes rolling back into his head.

"Hey!"

Raven turned to see half a dozen men racing out of the bar. Several of them carried wooden cue sticks, and seemed less than pleased about having two of their friends beaten up.

"Time to go," he whispered under his breath, again needing an escape route.

But luck was on his side. In addition to the angry bikers pouring out of the bar, he spotted the owner of the car he had been attempting to steal. The elderly man was halfway across the parking lot, well ahead of the others, carrying two Styrofoam boxes and the keys to the car. Apparently, he had been picking up an order of food.

Raven raced across the parking lot, desperate to reach the car owner before the bikers got to him. Before the old man could react, he snatched the car keys out of his hand.

"Sorry."

He also grabbed one of the Styrofoam boxes.

"Really, I am."

Turning, he sprinted to the car and jumped in the driver's side. He tossed the food on the seat and closed the door, jamming the key into the ignition. Starting the engine, he threw the car into gear and stomped on the gas.

The car lunged forward, nearly running over the men charging out of the bar. One of the bikers leaped onto the hood, but a sharp turn of the wheel sent him rolling across the pavement. Another biker swung a cue stick, but only dented a fender. Raven spun the steering wheel again and roared out of the parking lot onto the street. But he wasn't out of danger, for a quick glance in the rearview mirror showed several men hurrying to mount motorcycles and give chase.

Flooring the accelerator, he headed south out of town, residential areas giving way to country roads. The pursuing motorcycles closed rapidly on the slower, heavier car. They had almost caught up to him when Raven spotted a possible escape route.

Jerking the steering wheel, he turned onto a narrow gravel road. He slowed and waited for the bikers to turn after him, allowing them to almost overtake the car, before mashing the gas pedal to the floor. The sudden acceleration caused the vehicle to fishtail all over the road, spraying gravel everywhere.

The bikers suddenly found themselves under attack as the back tires of the car launched hundreds of stone projectiles. The rocks struck machine and men, leaving dents, scratches, and plenty of bruises. Several of the men lost control in the deadly cloud, skidding into the ditches that bordered the graveled road and crashing into each other. In a mere matter of moments, there was but a single biker left to give pursuit to the fleeing car, and he stopped his Harley for fear of ending up like the others.

Raven laughed out loud, watching the mayhem in his rearview mirror. He turned onto another gravel road, and then took a second road that connected back up to the main highway. Turning, he continued his journey to the south.

No longer being chased, he slowed the car to a safer speed and opened the Styrofoam box sitting beside him on the seat. It contained a cheeseburger and an order of French fries. Rolling down his window, he tossed the greasy meat patty into the night, content to eat just the bun. Cheeseburgers were not for him, for he was still a raven on the inside.

CHAPTER 7

Despite being already married, Wednesday night was still considered date night for Sarah and Jack, an opportunity for the two of them to enjoy a nice meal and a couple drinks in an atmosphere far more romantic than that offered living above a funeral home.

Date night also gave her a break from having to cook dinner, and for that she was extremely grateful. Not that she hated to cook; she actually enjoyed showing off her culinary skills for Jack and their friends. But on this particular evening, she wanted nothing to do with her kitchen, living quarters, or the temporary resident of the funeral home downstairs.

Sarah checked her watch again, frowning. Naturally, Jack would be late. Why should married life be any different than when they were single? Not that he was prone to tardiness; he was just often busy at the cemetery, and every time he tried to take off a little early something always seemed to come up, like Sonny shooting himself.

People are just dying to get into Greenwood.

Greenwood was the largest and oldest cemetery in Orlando, with gravesites occupied by founding fathers and local dignitaries. Everyone who was anyone wanted to be buried there.

To appease overcrowding at Greenwood, new sections had recently been opened on the west side of the cemetery, where the black community of Jonestown had once stood. But even the new sections were quickly filling up, and it wouldn't be long before the graveyard had no more burial spaces left to sell.

Sarah finished her margarita, and was looking over the menu, when Jack entered the restaurant. He didn't need to look around to find her; they were regulars and always sat in the back, well away from the bar and a piano player in need of singing lessons. As he approached the table, she set down the menu.

"About time you got here."

"Sorry, I got tied up with paperwork." He pulled out a chair and sat down on the opposite side of the table.

"So, Sonny finally did it? My god, how awful."

She and Jack had often talked about Sonny's daily visits to the cemetery, and his emotional state since losing his wife. They both worried it was only a matter of time until he did something drastic.

He nodded. "Right in front of me."

"Jesus."

"The city is having fits because I got his blood on me. They want me to get checked out, which means I'll probably be getting more shots."

"Better safe than sorry." She took a sip of water. "What did you do with your clothes?"

"I didn't think the blood stains would come out, so I threw them in the Dumpster. Lucky for me, I had a change of clothing in the truck. No way I could have gone home to change, not with a graveyard full of cops and crime scene investigators."

The waitress arrived to take their order. Jack didn't feel much like eating, electing instead to order a beer and a shot of bourbon. Sarah also skipped the heavier entrees offered on the main menu, instead ordering another margarita and a couple appetizers. They waited for the waitress to leave before continuing their conversation.

"What about you?" he asked. "What the hell happened at the funeral home?"

She quickly described all the strange things that had occurred earlier in the day, pausing only when the waitress returned with their drinks.

Jack listened quietly, downing his whiskey in one gulp and sipping his beer.

"I'm not sure how to explain it." She shrugged. "Maybe I'm starting to hallucinate. I'd blame it on the sixties, but I wasn't even born then."

"You're just a child." He grinned. He was eight years older than her. Theirs was a May-December wedding.

"Maybe I have a tumor … too many years sniffing formaldehyde. Or maybe it's God's way of showing me that I've been in the funeral business too long, and it's time for me to seek employment elsewhere."

He laughed. "You know you wouldn't be happy doing anything else."

"You're right, I wouldn't," she agreed. "But I'm telling you, what I saw was weird. Mr. Talmage sat up and spoke to me. Twice."

"Are you sure it wasn't just muscle spasm?"

"Positive. There wasn't any rigor in the body. And that wouldn't explain him talking …"

"Death rattle? Trapped air escaping the lungs?" he suggested.

"At first I thought that's what it was. But his lips moved, and he spit out the wax I used to firm up his upper lip."

"Was his jaw wired?"

She nodded. "I checked first thing this morning."

Jack clenched his teeth together and said her name, "Sarah … Sarah …" He unclenched his teeth, speaking normally again. "You're right. It's definitely hard to speak with your jaws wired shut, even for a live person."

"You're being sarcastic." Anger crept into her voice.

"No. I'm not. Honest." He held up his hands, defensively, not wanting to invoke his wife's wrath. "I'm just trying to figure out what the hell happened. We both know that dead people don't sit up and talk. There's no way in hell I'd be working at Greenwood if they did."

The waitress arrived with the appetizers: fried calamari, and stuffed mushrooms. Jack ordered another beer and Jim Beam. Sarah switched to ice tea.

"Careful with that stuff," she warned. "You know what bourbon does to you, especially on an empty stomach."

"I had some grits earlier. It's the only thing I could keep down." He always kept packets of instant grits in his office, for days when he didn't have time to take lunch. He usually made them extra runny, drinking them from a Styrofoam coffee cup.

"Okay. I just don't want to be carrying you out of here later."

"If you do, the body board is still in the back of my truck." Disinterments sometimes took place at Greenwood, so he always kept a plastic body board and two biohazard suits in the back of his truck in case they were needed.

"Like I was saying," she continued. "Mr. Talmage sat up and spoke to me, clear as a bell. He said 'Beware, Blue Sky Woman.'"

"Blue Sky Woman? What the hell is that supposed to mean?"

Sarah shrugged. "I haven't got a clue."

"It's got to mean something."

"Yeah, it means I have a freaking tumor."

"That, I doubt," he reassured her. "Sounds Native American. Maybe your father would know …"

Her eyes flashed fire, and Jack knew he had said the wrong thing. Sarah's biological father was indeed Native American, Cherokee, but she never spoke about him. The subject was taboo, and on the two

41

occasions he had made the mistake of bringing up his name she had burst into tears.

Something bad had happened during her childhood, something that resulted in her father being labeled crazy, even potentially dangerous, with Sarah taken from him and sent to live in an orphanage. She had spent two years in the home before being taken in and raised by a white foster family in a small Wisconsin town.

Whatever happened to Sarah as a child was bad enough for her to block the memory from her mind. He suspected she had been molested, or physically abused, but there was no way of ever knowing for sure. She refused to open the vault to her memory, and wanted nothing to do with her biological father.

"Sorry," he said, certain he was in for a long night of the silent treatment.

She stared at him for a few moments, then took a deep breath and slowly exhaled. Her features softened. "You're right. He might know what it means, but that's one road I don't want to go down."

"Well, we'll just have to figure it out another way. We've got so-called psychics and mediums all the time coming to Greenwood in search of ghosts. Maybe one of them could give us some advice."

"Maybe." She frowned. "But if word of this gets spread among the paranormal community, they'll be showing up at the funeral home in droves. I don't want to be part of any ghost tour."

"Neither do I," he agreed. "I'll be discreet if I talk to any of them. I won't give your name or the location."

"Okay."

"There's another option."

"What's that?" she asked.

"Why don't you just go ask Mr. Talmage what he meant?"

"You're funny. Real funny. The casket is already locked, and there's no way in hell I'm going to open it again."

"Chicken."

"Cluck-cluck." She set her fork down and wiped her mouth with a napkin. "You ready to get out of here, or do you want another beer first?"

"I'm ready." Jack caught the attention of their waitress, motioning for her to bring the check. "I want to go home and take a hot shower. I think I still have a little Sonny on me."

CHAPTER 8

In the beginning, all the people and animals lived and dwelled in a world above the sky, a magical place called Galun'lati. But as the years slowly passed, the sky world grew too crowded, causing much fighting and bickering among the different tribes. Knowing they could not live peacefully in such a cramped place, the tribal leaders turned their attention to the ocean world that existed below the sky.

They wondered if there might be land beneath the water, and sent Dayuni'si, the little Water-Beetle, down to investigate. The little beetle darted all over the surface of the water, but could not find a solid place to rest.

Determined not to fail, the little beetle dived deep beneath the water, to the bottom, and came up with soft mud. The mud quickly grew and spread, becoming the island we call the earth.

The animals and people were anxious to make their homes in this New World, and sent down different birds to see if the land was dry enough to live on. The birds flew all over the earth until they were very tired, and their wings hurt, but they could not find a place where they didn't sink deep in the wet mud.

The old ones were very frustrated, but they waited and the days passed slowly. At long last, the earth seemed dry enough, so they sent down Buzzard to have a look. Now this was no normal buzzard, but the grandfather of all buzzards with wings that spanned the sky.

The Great Buzzard flew low over the earth, but the ground proved too soft. By the time he reached Cherokee county, the Buzzard had tired and his wings began to flap and strike the ground. And in those places where his giant wings struck the earth, valleys were created, and when they turned up again mountains formed.

The animals watching above were terrified the New World would be nothing but mountains and valleys, so they called Buzzard back to Galun'lati. But to this day, the original home of the Cherokees remains full of mountains and valleys.

The earth finally dried, and the animals and people came down from the sky. At first, the New World was dark, so they got the sun and set it to pass over the land from east to west. But they set the sun too low, and Tsiska'gili, the little Crawfish, had his shell scorched a bright red.

Not wanting to be burned like the little Crawfish, the shamans of the different tribes used their medicine powers to raise the sun higher and higher, until it sat just under the sky arch. Every day the sun goes along this path, returning to its starting point at night.

In the early days of the New World, all the tribes of animals and people spoke the same language. But this common tongue was lost over the years as the tribes separated and spread out across the face of the earth. Only the members of the Great Council still have the ability to communicate with each other. But it is said that the gift of tongue returns to all of us when we leave this world and make our final journey back to Galun'lati.

Luther awoke with a start, his heart pounding. It was quiet in the nursing home. Too quiet.

He lay there in his bed and listened to the silence, his fear building. There were always sounds in the home: the quiet footfalls and whispered voices of orderlies and nurses making the rounds, the garbled drone of distant televisions and radios, the occasional ringing of a phone, wet, phlegmy coughing, moans of pains and discomfort, and the rattled breathing of those suffering from emphysema and other dreaded diseases of the lungs.

But there were none of those sounds now. Even the electrical devices used to monitor Charlie while he slept had stopped their constant humming.

He turned and looked at his roommate, listening carefully. There was no snoring, no labored breathing, and his chest did not rise and fall.

Luther knew old Charlie had finally found peace.

"Goodbye, old friend. No more basketball for us."

Luther pushed the button to raise the head of his bed, and when it didn't move he realized the power was out. That explained why the machines had stopped, and why the only light in the room was the glow of a distant streetlamp seeping in around the closed curtains.

But why hadn't one of the staff checked on Charlie when the power went out?

"Hey!" he yelled, trying to get someone's attention. "Hey, nurse ... Orderly ... Someone come here; there's a dead guy in my room."

His attention went to the window, a chill marching down his spine as he suddenly realized how late it was. Night had already settled over the land, and with the darkness would come the shape-shifter.

He had tried earlier to stay awake, only pretending to swallow the sleeping medicine the nurse had given him. He had also tried to warn the staff that Coyote was on the prowl, but they only laughed at him. The ranting of a senile old man, they had said, mocking him by making coyote ears on the sides of their heads with their fingers.

He had tried to stay awake, but he was an old man used to going to bed with the setting of the sun. He had slept deeply, even without the medication, dreaming of powwows and beautiful women and journeys through strange and magical lands. But now he was wide awake, his dreams fading away and the nightmare becoming real.

The door to his room stood open. The hallway beyond was dark, lit only by the dim red glow of an emergency exit sign at the far end. And in that dark hallway Luther thought he heard movement, the quiet, stealthy sound of death approaching on padded paws.

Throwing back the sheet that covered his bony legs, he released the catch holding the bed's side rail in place and slowly lowered it to keep it from making any noise. Easing his legs over the side of the bed, he stood and crossed the room in his bare feet to peer carefully out the doorway.

The hallway stood empty, but even in the dull light cast by the emergency exit sign he could see the blood. Splattered on the walls and smeared over the tile floor, it looked thick and black. And if it wasn't for the coppery smell that permeated his nostrils, he might have mistaken it for motor oil.

But there was no denying that it was blood, lots and lots of blood, gallons. And in that instant, Luther realized that Coyote had made good on his promise. He was perhaps the only person still alive in the nursing home.

But why hadn't Coyote taken his life while he slept? Luther considered the question for a moment, and thought he knew the answer. Coyote was the Trickster, and he had not taken the old man's life while he slept because there was no sport in that.

Backing away from the open doorway, he quickly crossed the room to a beat-up wooden dresser. Opening the top drawer, he removed a flannel shirt, jeans, socks, and a scuffed-up pair of cowboy boots, hurrying to put them on. The clothes were kept on-hand for when family members came to visit, or in case he were allowed outside to enjoy the weather—even though Luther had never been visited while in the home, nor had the staff ever allowed him outside.

He pulled on his boots and went to the window and tried to open it, but the latch was either frozen in place or he was too weak. His struggles were in vain. Reluctantly giving up on the window, he crept across the room and looked out the doorway. The hallway to his left passed four rooms on either side before ending at a metal door. The door was supposed to be an emergency exit, the dimly lighted sign above coming on whenever the power went out, yet Luther knew the staff ignored state laws and kept the door locked. They were more afraid of someone sneaking out in the middle of the night for a little fun than they were about the residents being trapped and perishing in a fire.

No escape that way, so he turned his attention to the opposite direction. The hallway running to the right passed six more rooms before coming to an intersecting hallway. Beyond that was the bathrooms, showers, and the day room.

A nurses' station sat where the two hallways crossed each other, more of a guard shack than anything else, a place for male orderlies to gather and socialize while keeping a watchful eye on the elderly residents. Luther knew from experience that it was impossible to make it to the restrooms or dayroom without being stopped and questioned by one of the orderlies on duty.

The nurses' station was always occupied, twenty-four hours a day, but it wasn't occupied now. The orderlies had left their post and had gone elsewhere, or something had removed them.

Taking a deep breath to steady his nerves, he quietly moved into the hallway. Eerie silence washed over him as he left his room, a deep stillness that made the hairs on the back of his neck stand straight up.

Crossing the hallway, he peered into the open doorway of the room belonging to Ethel Wilson. The room was layered in blackness, too dark to see the single metal frame bed or its occupant.

"Ethel, are you awake?" he whispered, afraid of raising his voice. He stood in the doorway listening, but did not hear a reply. Nor did he hear the woman's deep snoring, a familiar sound late at night.

Entering the room, he moved by feel until he reached the foot of her bed. He reaching out, touched the mattress, and then the body lying atop it. Ethel's chest did not rise and fall with the breath of life, and the thin sheet covering her felt wet and sticky.

He moved closer until he stood near the head of the bed. Bending down, he could just make out her face, her eyes open and staring, her lips drawn back in a silent scream of terror.

Luther reached out and gently touched her cheek. As he did, her head fell away from her body, tumbling off the bed with a dull thud and rolling away into the darkness.

He staggered back, horrified, staring at the body but not really seeing it. And though the room was nearly pitch black, Luther dared not look down, fearful that he would see Ethel's severed head staring up at him from under the bed.

Turning, he clamped a hand over his mouth and headed toward the doorway. He was afraid of gagging, but he was more fearful that a scream would finally escape his lips—a scream that would alert Ethel's murderer to his presence.

Luther wished he had a gun, or even a knife. He had such things in his youth, and had been well-versed in the use of both for hunting and self-defense, but they were not allowed at the rest home. Even pointed scissors and silverware were forbidden, forcing the residents to eat with plastic forks and spoons, and cut their paper dolls with the kind of rounded scissors used by school children. Perhaps the staff knew better than to allow the residents anything that might be used as a weapon, for one or two of them would surely have been stabbed.

He paused in the doorway, shivering, too afraid to step out into the bloody hallway, but way too terrified to remain in the dark room with Ethel's headless corpse. He wanted to go back into his room and close the door. It didn't lock, but maybe he could find some way to barricade it. The dresser was heavy; maybe he could slide it in front of the door to keep out the danger.

He shook his head. That was a foolish thought. The dresser might be heavy for him, but it wasn't big enough to keep out Coyote. All he would accomplish by hiding in his room was to trap himself. He would then be easy to find when the shape-shifter came calling.

His only chance of survival was to flee. He needed to get as far away as possible, but that might be what Coyote wanted. The Trickster might enjoy a chase. Luther didn't care. He refused to die in the nursing home, his blood mixing with that of Ethel and the night staff.

He turned his attention to the nurses' station and the darkness beyond, noticing for the first time a man's arm on the floor, attached to someone lying behind the wooden station. The arm obviously belonged to an orderly unlucky enough to be on duty when Coyote came to call. He hoped it was the same son of a bitch who had punched Ethel in the stomach, but that orderly had probably gone home hours earlier.

Knowing he was running out of time, Luther gathered his courage and hurried toward the nurses' station, his cowboy boots making way too much noise on the tile floor. He cursed under his breath, wishing he had elected to remain barefooted.

Stealth now out of the question, he tried to break into a run, but his elderly body wouldn't go any faster than a quick walk.

He reached the nurses' station, giving the orderly lying behind it little more than a passing glance. The man was definitely dead, half his face removed by sharp teeth or claws.

Luther hurried toward the front of the building, passing several administrative offices as he headed for the front lobby, not even bothering to check them for he knew the doors would be locked. Another door, marked Storage, stood partially ajar, but he didn't stop to see what might lay behind it. Dark places were best avoided, especially at a time like this.

Beyond the storage room was the front desk, now unoccupied, and beyond that were the two glass doors leading to the parking lot and freedom. One of the doors stood open to the night, making his escape even easier.

Between the doors and front desk were the bodies of three more staff members, two men and a woman. They had been butchered and stripped naked, carefully positioned on their backs, their arms and legs spread wide. It was Coyote's sick and twisted attempt at humor, making mockery of a species he despised. An unlit cigarette had even been placed between the lifeless lips of one man.

Luther moved past the bodies and headed for the open door, but stopped suddenly as doubt crossed his mind. So far, his panicked flight had been easy. Too easy. The open door beckoned to him, providing an escape route from the scene of carnage, or perhaps providing the opening to a well-placed trap. Did freedom and safety wait beyond, or did something evil lurk within the darkness?

"Are you out there, Coyote?" he asked aloud, his voice barely a whisper.

As if in answer to his question, a howl suddenly sounded from somewhere outside the building. Coyote was indeed waiting for him in the night.

But no sooner had the howl sounded from outside, when it was answered by a similar call from deep within the building.

Luther spun around, his heart pounding. There were two of them, one outside and one within. Of course, Coyote the Trickster was a coward and would never hunt alone, not when there were so many to kill. One or more of his kind hunted with him.

The old man looked around for another means of escape, or a weapon he could use. His gaze fell upon a Zippo lighter lying near the body of a naked male orderly. It wasn't much of a weapon, but fire did have its uses against the forces of darkness. Coyote and his minions were creatures of the night, and would avoid the flame.

Grabbing the lighter, Luther remembered the storage room he had passed—a room where the personal effects of the residents were stored. Somewhere in there, a cardboard box contained items of great importance to a man who once walked the medicine path and made the journey to the Great Council. Better yet, the door to that room had been unlocked and now stood open.

Checking to make sure the lighter still worked, he hurried back past the administrative offices to the open door marked Storage. He struck the lighter's tiny wheel, the flame pushing back the blackness as he entered the room. Closing the door behind him, he began examining the boxes and cases stacked ceiling-high on metal shelves.

But he was up against a nearly impossible task. There were dozens and dozens of identical boxes within the room, and the lighter's tiny flame made reading what was written on them extremely difficult. He was about to give up, when he found the box with his name on it.

Taking the cardboard container off the shelf, he hurried to open it. Inside he found his black leather wallet, minus the money it had contained upon his arrival, an old Camp King pocket knife with one of its blades broken off, a bear claw necklace with red and white glass beads, a plastic pocket comb, two tarnished silver rings, and a small dyed leather bag attached to a length of leather cord—his personal medicine pouch.

He removed the medicine pouch from the box, slipping the cord over his head so it hung over the center of his chest. He had worn the pouch for most of his life, and knew that the medicine it contained had not gone bad from spending time in a box. Holding the pouch, he said a quick prayer of thanks and asked the spirits for help.

Luther hurried to put on the silver rings and bear claw necklace, and then slipped the wallet, pocket knife, and plastic comb into his pants pockets.

He reached back into the box to remove the final item: a large leather bag containing a mixture of sage, tobacco, cedar, corn pollen, and gun powder—along with a two-inch piece of charcoal. He had just loosened the leather thong that tied the neck of the bag, when he heard movement outside.

Something sniffed at the base of the door, searching for him.

Luther froze, his mouth going dry with fear. The door was closed, but unlocked, and there was no way to lock it from the inside. Not without a key.

Opening his bag, he hurried to grab a handful of the powdered mixture. Crossing the room, he sprinkled a line of the herbs and gunpowder across the threshold, creating a barrier to keep out evil. He used the Zippo to light one end of the barrier, the gunpowder in the mixture igniting with a flash.

The door knob turned, and the door swung open.

Luther jumped back out of the way.

Standing in the doorway was the shape-shifter who had earlier visited his room, but he no longer wore the identity of a man. He had reversed his skin and now wore it fur side out, revealing that he was indeed Coyote. The Trickster had stopped his transformation mid-change, and towered in the doorway as half-man and half-beast. Standing upright on hind legs, he stood nearly seven feet tall, his fur mattered with blood and bits of gore from the victims he had murdered.

Behind Coyote were two more of his kind. Smaller and less ferocious, they stood on all fours for they did not have the power to turn their skins and walk upright.

Coyote looked down at the burning mixture barring his way, his lips pulling back in a snarl. "Stupid, old fool. Do you think your tricks can stop me?" The shape-shifter spoke in his native tongue, a series of growls and yips, but Luther understood him, for all members of the Great Council were given the gifts of animal and human speak.

"Stop you? No." Luther answered, knowing Coyote could also understand him. "Just delaying you long enough for what I need to do."

Turning his back on the Trickster, he crossed the room to the back wall. He removed the piece of charcoal from his leather bag and drew a large rectangle on the concrete blocks. Reaching back into the bag, he removed another small handful of the herbal mixture and sprinkled a line on the floor in front of the rectangle.

He whispered a few words of power, and then touched the lighter's flame to the powdered mixture on the floor. As before, the gunpowder ignited with a flash, causing the other ingredients to burn. Gray smoke drifted up and touched the wall, and the concrete blocks within the rectangle disappeared, creating a doorway

"You shall not get away!" Coyote howled.

Luther stepped through the opening, but he did not find himself outside the nursing home; instead, he entered a world few men had ever seen. But he had walked the shadowy land of Galun'lati many times on his journeys to the Great Council.

As the mixture barring entrance into the storage room finally burned out, Coyote charged into the room and chased after Luther, but as he raced toward the back wall, the magical doorway suddenly closed and the Trickster crashed headfirst into concrete blocks.

Coyote howled with pain and anger, while fading into the night could be heard the laughter of an old Indian man.

CHAPTER 9

Raven drove east, following the two-lane road through the mountains. He kept a watchful eye on the rearview mirror, but the bikers pursuing him had given up the chase long ago. He imagined they had much better things to do on a Saturday night then chase after a stolen junk car and used articles of clothing.

Still, he worried the owner of the car might have notified the police. He wasn't sure if local and county law enforcement agencies worked together in such matters, but there couldn't be too many vehicles on the road that looked like the one he drove.

His best bet would be to ditch the car and find himself another set of wheels, something a little less conspicuous, but he was pressed for time and his destination lay only a few miles ahead. He could always steal another ride later.

Reaching into the Styrofoam box on the seat beside him, he grabbed a soggy French fry and shoved it into his mouth. He wasn't hungry, but he needed something to take his mind off the nervousness building inside him.

His instincts warned him that danger drew near. Coyote and his minions were on the hunt; he could smell their stench in the night wind entering the car through the open windows, could feel the fear of the smaller creatures dwelling in the darkness. He needed to reach Luther Watie before it was too late.

Raven had befriended Luther many years ago at a previous Council meeting, thanking him for the kindness he had shown to the winged creatures of the forest. The elderly Cherokee made it a point to leave pieces of bread and other treats outside when the snow was thick and the ground frozen solid. He would often go hungry himself just so his feathered brothers would not starve. He was a good man, in a world where good men were becoming harder to find.

It had been a long time since Raven last saw him, not since Luther's body had grown old and frail and he had been sent to live in the home of the dying.

He had tried several times to visit Luther at the Willows, but the staff would not allow him to enter while in human form, citing that only close relatives could visit the patients. Nor had he been able to see him while wearing his feathers on the outside, for the thick

52

curtains covering the windows prevented him from peeking into Luther's room. Even tapping his beak against the glass had gone unanswered.

Raven started to take another French fry, but decided against it and tossed the rest of them out the open window. Some would call it littering, but he was actually offering the rest of his meal to his winged relations—those who didn't have the power to turn their skins.

Reaching the tiny town of Talbot, North Carolina, he slowed the car to the posted speed limit of thirty-five miles per hour. It was late and the town seemed to have already gone to bed for the night. None of the stores along Main Street were open; even the local tavern had turned out its drunks and closed. The only thing still open for business was a Shell gas station and it was probably open twenty-four hours a day.

He glanced down at his gas gauge and thought about pulling in to fill up, but then he remembered that he didn't have money. Luckily he still had almost a quarter tank, and his destination was less than a mile away. He would worry about gas later.

The downtown quickly gave way to a residential area. Scattered among the two- and three-bedroom homes was an occasional house converted into a real estate, a doctor's office, and a church. An industrial area followed, with a feed store, grain elevator, railroad depot, and a concrete plant.

Turning just past the concrete plant, he followed a narrow road through a wooded area until he reached the entrance to the Willows Nursing Home.

There were half a dozen vehicles in the parking lot, and Raven was pretty sure they belonged to the night staff. Parking in an empty space, he turned off the engine and headlights.

As he sat looking at the nursing home, wondering how he was going to get inside, he noticed one of the front doors stood ajar. Lights inside the building were also off, the entrance dark and foreboding.

A feeling of dread settled over him.

He sniffed the air, detecting a slightly musky scent.

"Coyote."

Raven slipped out of the car, quietly closing the door behind him. He kept to the shadows and quickly crossed the parking lot to the open doorway, peeking inside.

It was dark inside the nursing home, the only illumination coming from the emergency exit sign above the doors. But there was still enough light, his night vision good enough to see the three bodies lying in the center of the entrance lobby. Two men and a woman, nude and posed in vulgar positions. He wasn't sure if they had been posed for his benefit, or for the eyes of someone else, but the deep gashes upon the lifeless bodies were obviously made by an animal.

Coyote or one of his followers had been here ahead of him, for the three people just inside the doorway were killed by a shape-shifter. A normal person could not create such carnage, and an animal would have no interest in posing someone after making a kill.

Could Bear have been the killer? The Council leader had been swayed by Coyote's treacherous words, but would he risk his position in the circle by bloodying his own hands?

Entering the lobby, he circled around the three bodies. There was no need to check if they still lived. The massive claw and teeth wounds, and the blood pooled around them, told him that their spirits had already crossed over to another world.

"I am sorry, my friends," he whispered under his breath. "I promise you that Coyote will pay for this."

Crossing the lobby, he paused to listen, but there were no sounds other than his breathing and the beating of his heart. The silence was as complete as the darkness around him. And as he stood there, he knew the Willows was no longer a home for the old and sick. It had become a temple for the dead.

The smell of blood, urine, feces, and death lay thick upon the still air, lifeless bodies in pitch black rooms already beginning to fester and rot. Raven did not know how many lay dead inside the home, and dreaded the thought of venturing deeper inside the charnel house to find out, but he had to locate the room of Luther Watie, had to know if his old friend still lived.

And if his friend was among the dead. What then? Luther's place at the Council would automatically pass down to his offspring. He had a daughter who lived somewhere in the land of warm winters, a daughter who may not know of the danger she now faced. If the father no longer lived, then he must do everything within his power to protect the daughter.

But did Luther still live?

Raven took a deep breath to steady his nerves, cringing at the smell of death surrounding him. Fully aware that he was unarmed, and without benefit of flight or even a sharp beak and talons, he quietly crept past the reception desk and several administrative offices.

While most of the doors he passed were closed, one among them stood open—a door to a storage room. He had just stepped past the open doorway when a strange tingling shot up his arm and down his back.

Magic.

There could be no other reason for the sensation he felt. Someone had worked powerful medicine.

He stopped and sniffed, detecting a slight odor of herbs drifting out of the storage room: sage, cedar, tobacco, even corn pollen. Something else too, a catalyst to bond the other elements one that smelled like rotten eggs when burned … sulfur. Gunpowder.

Raven backed up, peering into the tiny storage room. Herbs had been placed on the floor, just inside the doorway, and burned, leaving behind a thin line of ash—a magical barrier to keep out darkness and evil.

He smiled. It was doubtful Coyote or his followers would have created such a barrier. The Trickster's magic was of a simpler nature, and far more cruel. He had no need of such tricks.

Entering the storage room, he found a second line of ash next to the back wall. On the wall itself someone had drawn a rectangle with a piece of charcoal, creating a doorway to another world. The doorway must not have stayed open long, however, for in the center of the rectangle several strands of brown hair and drops of blood adhered to one of the concrete blocks.

Raven covered his mouth to keep from laughing out loud. Luther must have made his escape through the now closed doorway, and Coyote or one of his followers had tried to give chase, only to run headfirst into the stone wall when the door closed.

It looked as if his old friend had gotten away from the Trickster and almost certain death. Still, he had to be certain.

Leaving the storage room, he made his way deeper into the bowels of the nursing home, searching the rooms lining each side of three different hallways. Inside those silent rooms elderly residents had been murdered and mutilated in an orgy of violence, many dying in their sleep.

In one room he found the body of an old black man, the left side of his face strangely twisted, his tongue protruding from an open mouth.

The second bed in the room was empty, but draped in soiled linen and a threadbare blanket. It also contained the scent of Luther Watie.

He could tell a lot about a person from their smell, and the scents lingering on the empty bed told Raven that Luther was not a well man. The musty odor clinging to the wrinkled sheets and soiled mattress spoke of old age, sickness, and the encroaching end of life. There was also the smell of fear and misery mixed in with the sour odor.

Scents of fear and misery clung to the other bodies he examined, which surprised him, for most had died during their sleep and not seen their attacker. That could only mean their lives in the nursing home prior to death had been wrought with suffering and despair. Such misery was common in the world of men, for humans had a nasty habit of casting away the things that no longer interested them, or no longer proved useful, including their own family members.

Leaving Luther's room, he followed the hallway in the opposite direction, checking the other rooms as he went. Raven was so intent on inspecting that he didn't notice he was no longer alone in the hallway, and knew not of Coyote's presence until a furred body slammed into him from behind.

He hit the wall hard and bounced off, pain exploding white hot behind his eyes. Raven landed on his back in the middle of the hallway, his head spinning and his vision blurred. He rolled over and got to his knees, trying to get back on his feet, but a furry foot lashed out and caught him in the chest, knocking the air from his lungs.

A second powerful kick followed the first. Raven grunted in pain. Another kick followed, and then his attacker grabbed him by the throat and pulled him to his feet.

Raven found himself nose to nose with a murderous creature of fur and fang, standing nearly seven feet tall in a hallway that suddenly seemed very small. Coyote's dark eyes studied him, his lips pulling back in an evil snarl.

"Who are you?" Coyote snarled, speaking in his own tongue. The Trickster turned his head and looked at the wall, but Raven did not cast a shadow in the darkness.

Coyote pulled him closer, sniffing. His lips pulled back in a toothy grin. "Ahh … my dear, Raven. It is you." There was no warmth in the Trickster's voice. "What are you doing here, my old friend?"

"I know what you and Bear are planning," he replied, coughing. "I came to stop you."

Coyote's grip tightened. "What do you know? Who sent you?"

"No one sent me. I overheard the two of you talking."

"And you decided to interfere with our plans?" Coyote threw his head back and laughed.

"What you are doing is wrong."

Coyote's laughter turned into a growl of anger. "Why should you care what happens to these Man-things? They have been nothing but trouble since the day they set foot in this world. Have they not hunted your people for sport as they have hunted mine?"

Raven tried to nod, but Coyote held him too tight. "Yes."

"Then why help them?"

"Because not all of them are bad, and they must be represented in the Council. That is the rule."

Coyote laughed and yipped. "Rules … rules … rules. Rules are made to be broken."

"The Great Council must be complete, each tribe represented," Raven argued. "That is why I came to stop you."

Coyote's grip tightened. He lifted Raven off the floor and shook him like a rag doll.

"You are in no position to do anything!" Coyote roared, his anger boiling over. "Do not think that I won't take your life, as I have taken the lives of the others in this place. Do not interfere in my plans, winged one, for I will have no mercy upon you. My people have eaten many of your kind, so I know you will make a fine meal."

The Trickster shook him once more, then stopped. An evil grin unfolded upon his furry face. "Very well. If you love these humans so much, I will see that you remain in their company."

Coyote dragged Raven through the drying pools of blood next to the three naked bodies in the lobby. He laughed as he carried him to the front desk. Lifting the telephone's receiver, Coyote used a clawed finger to dial 9-1-1. He waited until an emergency dispatcher answered the call, then set the receiver down beside the phone.

The Trickster had spent enough time in the world of men to know that it wasn't necessary to speak to an operator to summon the police. Phone calls made to 9-1-1 could be easily traced, and just dialing the number was enough to get a patrol car sent to your front door.

"Soon you will have plenty of Man-things to play with." Coyote howled with mirth. "You wanted to help these puny humans; you can start by explaining what happened here tonight. But I doubt if you will be believed, especially with the blood of the dead upon you."

Turning quickly, he threw Raven against the closest wall.

Raven tried to tuck his body and brace for the impact, but there wasn't time. He hit the wall hard, his back and head slamming against the concrete blocks.

Everything went black.

CHAPTER 10

It was a little after 10:30 p.m. when Sarah and Jack walked out of the restaurant. Even though it was still fairly early for a Friday night, most of the businesses in Sanford's historic district had already closed for the evening. Only a few cars remained parked along Main Street, and most of those probably belonged to food service employees.

Sarah's Honda occupied a space directly in front of the restaurant, while Jack's black Ford F-250 pickup was parked at the curb half a block away.

He waited until she got into her car and drove off before walking to his truck and climbing behind the wheel.

The city of Sanford had done a lot to improve and revitalize the historic district in the last few years, turning a row of rundown and deserted buildings into a charming shopping district, building an attractive river walk along the west bank of the St. Johns River, and converting nearly twelve blocks of rundown tenements into an upscale neighborhood of old Victorian and historic register homes.

But even with all the improvements, Sanford's historic distinct could still be an unsafe place to walk after dark, for mixed in among the stately Victorian homes were crack houses and dwellings occupied by less than desirable characters.

Satisfied that Sarah was safely on her way home, he started the truck and backed out of the parking space. He took a right on the first cross street and traveled five blocks to their house, pulling into the driveway just as Sarah was climbing out of her car.

Reaching the front door ahead of her husband, Sarah stepped aside and waited for him to unlock the door and go in first. She was still a little shaken from the day's weird events and in no hurry to enter the funeral home.

Jack stopped just inside and turned on the lights. "You wait here while I have a quick look around."

She also stepped inside, closing and locking the door behind her. "No way. I'm going with you. If our house guest is still in a talkative mood, then I want to hear what he has to say."

He studied her face for a moment, but couldn't tell if she was teasing or being serious. He shrugged. "Suit yourself."

They walked down the short hallway to the chapel, the wooden floorboards creaking softly under their feet. Sarah entered the chapel and turned on the lights, but remained standing by the doorway. The charcoal gray casket at the other end of the room looked exactly as she had left it: surrounded by colorful floral arrangements, with the black feather laying on top of it.

Jack approached the casket to get a closer look. He picked up the feather, holding it up to the light. "You're right. Too big for a black bird. I'd say a raven for sure." He set the feather back on the casket. "Kind of creepy."

"In an Edgar Allan Poe sort of way," she added.

He turned to her, noticing she had not ventured beyond the doorway. "If you want, I'll get a casket key and open it up … see if old Ray has anything else to say."

"Not necessary. He's locked in and that's the way I want to keep him. Come ten o'clock in the morning, Senator Talmage becomes somebody else's problem. And maybe you're right, maybe it was nothing more than muscle contraction and escaping air. I've been doing this job for too long to start believing that the dead can sit up and talk."

"Good girl." Jack grinned. "See how reasonable you get after a few drinks?"

She faked a frown. "I'll have you know, I'm quite reasonable when I'm sober too."

He crossed the room and gave her a hug. "Of course, you are, darling. How silly of me to ever doubt you."

She stepped back, smiling. "At least muscle contraction is a better explanation than a brain tumor."

"And far less painful in the long run."

Turning off the lights, they proceeded up the stairs to their second-floor residence. Entering the living room, he tossed his keys on the coffee table and checked the answering machine for messages. Sarah plopped down on the sofa.

"Dibs on the shower," he said, finding no messages on the machine.

"Okay, go ahead. Just don't use up all the hot water. I want to take a shower too."

"We can save hot water by taking a shower together," he suggested, grinning.

"No way. I know where that will lead." She laughed.

Jack crossed the living room to the bedroom, grabbing a change of underwear from the bottom drawer of the dresser. He then proceeded to the bathroom and started the shower.

Sarah grabbed the remote and turned on the television. From the bathroom came the sounds of the shower running, and Jack singing off-key. She smiled.

She had just switched to a local news channel when the phone rang. Sarah glanced at her watch, wondering who could be calling her so late.

Scooting down to the other end of the sofa, she picked up the phone. "Hello?"

No one answered.

"Hello ... can you hear me?"

Again, no answer, but the line was open and she knew someone was listening. And then she heard breathing, a heavy raspy sound. It sent shivers up and down her spine.

"Hello ... I can hear you. If this is some kind of joke, I'm not amused."

The breathing continued, deep and gravely. More animal than human. Probably an obscene phone call.

"Listen up, dumbass. I have caller ID. I've got your number. When I hang up, I'm calling the cops to report you."

She grabbed the phone's base and spun it around to read the caller ID screen. She expected the information to be blocked and the screen blank, and was quite surprised to see a number, which had a North Carolina area code. She only knew one person in North Carolina.

"Father?"

Sarah hadn't spoken to her father since she was a little girl, not since the state of North Carolina took her away from him.

She heard the raspy breathing again.

"Luther, is that you? Luther Watie? ... father?"

The breathing stopped suddenly, replaced by the sound of saliva being sucked from lips. A voice finally came on the line, every bit as gravely as the breathing moments before.

"Sarah ..."

The skin at her temples pulled tight. "Luther, is that you?" She asked the question, but somehow knew it was not her father. Her instincts told her the voice on the other end of the line belonged to someone dark and dangerous, not to an old Cherokee Indian.

"No ... not Luther."

She wanted to hang up, wanted to pull her hand away from the receiver for fear of being contaminated by something evil, but she was caught in the middle of some kind of weird drama and had to see it play out to the end.

"Who is this?"

She turned and looked toward the bathroom, suddenly afraid to be alone. Jack was still taking a shower. She could hear the water running, and his singing. He seemed a million miles away. In the bathroom there would be warmth and light, while where she sat seemed to grow cold and dark from the voice on the phone.

"Not Luther," the voice repeated.

For some strange reason, she felt as if the unknown caller was speaking to her in a language other than English, perhaps not even human. Behind the voice, she could almost detect a series of yips, grunts, and growling sounds. She tried to tune in on those sounds, only to have them fade farther into the background.

"Not your father, Blue Sky Woman. Not your friend."

Sarah's mouth went dry.

For the second time that day someone had called her Blue Sky Woman.

Not your friend. There was something about the phrase that filled her with dread, causing tears to leak from the corners of her eyes. The person on the other end was dangerous, a threat.

"Who is this?" she repeated, swallowing and finding her voice. "Who are you? What have you done to my father?"

"Nothing *yet*. But we will do something soon."

We? The voice on the phone had an accomplice, or accomplices.

"And then we will be coming for you."

The line suddenly went dead. The person at the other end hadn't hung up, but the connection had been broken.

"Hello ... hello ..." She hit the disconnect button, then tried dialing the number on the caller I.D. But the phone at the other end of the line did not ring, nor was there a busy tone. There was only silence, an empty quiet that spoke volumes.

She hung up and sat staring at the phone. Perhaps the gravelly voice on the line was only someone playing a practical joke.

He called me Blue Sky Woman.

It must have been her father. She hadn't spoken to him in over twenty years; it could have been his voice on the phone. Maybe he was senile, deranged, and got his kicks tormenting a child who had been taken away from him long ago.

But her instincts told her it wasn't her father. It was someone far more dangerous, someone coming for her.

Jumping off the sofa, she hurried into the bedroom. She was afraid to stay in the living room alone, and felt a need to arm herself. Jack kept several rifles under the bed, but they were obsolete military firearms he had bought at gun shows and would probably blow-up if fired.

He also had a pistol, a reproduction of an 1861 Colt single-action revolver modified to shoot .45 cartridges. It wasn't an antique, so she didn't have to worry about it exploding in her face, and it fired a big enough round to have some serious stopping power.

Sarah opened the drawer of the nightstand on Jack's side of the bed and removed the pistol, checking to make sure it was loaded. Five rounds were in the cylinder.

She sat on the foot of the bed, trying to calm her racing heart, facing out the doorway toward the living room and kitchen. She almost expected the front door to burst open and a man with a raspy voice to charge up the stairs. And she almost screamed when the bathroom door suddenly opened and Jack stepped out wearing nothing but a towel.

He saw her sitting there and removed the towel with a quick flick of his wrist, standing naked and grinning. "It's playtime—"

But his grin quickly disappeared when he spotted the revolver clutched tightly in her trembling hands.

"Honey, what is it? What's wrong?"

CHAPTER 11

He couldn't have been unconscious for very long, only a few minutes at the most. It was the lights that woke him: the flashing blue lights of the patrol cars pulling into the parking lot, and the sweeping flashlight of a police officer—sent to investigate a 9-1-1 call—who had found the entrance door standing open and the naked bodies in the lobby, and now waited in the doorway as backup arrived.

Raven awoke to find himself on the floor behind the reception desk, which was why he hadn't been spotted by the young officer. The beam of his flashlight passed over the desk, but it did not fall upon him.

That was a good thing, for Raven found that while he was unconscious someone had placed a box-cutter in his right hand. The box-cutter's razor was sticky with blood, as was the palm of his hand. And as the fog of unconsciousness slowly lifted from his mind, he knew he had been set up.

Coyote.

The Trickster had called the police, and then placed the bloody box-cutter in his hand, hoping to pin the nursing home murders on him. He had promised that Raven would soon have lots of human company, but had neglected to say the companionship would be police officers and the fellow inmates of a federal prison.

Several car doors slammed, getting his attention. The police had arrived in force and were rallying outside. He tossed aside the razor knife, instantly regretting his action for the metal box-cutter clattered quite loudly as it hit the tile floor.

The beam of white light shining from the doorway turned his way, seeking him out.

"Who's there?"

He shifted to his knees and slowly rose to peek over the desk. The officer was looking his way, but the flashlight was aimed at the three naked bodies on the floor. The name "Michael Blackwing" had been carved into the chest of the dead man closest to Raven, probably with the box-cutter. Names had also been carved into the other two bodies, but he could not read them from where he crouched.

Coyote was once again having fun and games at the expense of others. The Trickster knew what name Raven often used when walking in the world of men, and was trying to pin the murders on him by carving it into the body of the dead man.

I've got to get out of here.

As he crouched, looking at the name carved in the man's body, he allowed too much of himself to rise above the wooden desk. The flashlight's beam suddenly shifted away from the bodies and hit him full in the face.

"You there. Freeze!" yelled the officer in the doorway, pointing his pistol.

Panic flashed through the shape-shifter. He could not allow himself to be captured, or shot. Luther Watie and his daughter were still in danger, and Coyote was on the loose.

"I said freeze," yelled the officer. "Show me your hands. Now!"

Raven raised his hands in the air and slowly stood, his mind desperately trying to come up with a plan for escape. But as he rose, he knew he had again made a mistake. The flashlight's beam was bright, and the police officer holding it could clearly see Raven's shirt and hands covered with blood.

Raven glanced at his palm. "Damn it."

"On the ground!" yelled the officer.

Of course, he couldn't obey. If he got on the ground, they would handcuff him and take him to jail. They would also find the box-cutter with the victim's blood and his fingerprints on it, and whatever else Coyote might have done to set him up.

"I'll get you for this, Trickster," he muttered. Footfalls approached from outside as others raced toward the front doors, beams of light from flashlights dancing, and the distant wail of sirens. In a few seconds, the nursing home would be swarming with armed police officers.

"I said get down!" the officer in the doorway screamed, the fear sounding in his voice.

"I'm afraid I can't do that." Raven spun around, racing deeper into the nursing home. Shots rang out behind him, hurting his ears. The bullets barely missed, passing close enough that he could feel their heat.

Turning, he raced down the hallway to Luther's room. He wasn't sure why he chose that particular room, maybe it was because the dead black man hadn't been mutilated and torn apart like the others.

There was no stench of blood or raw flesh, only the aura of great sadness.

Entering the room, he closed the door and attempted to lock it. But there was no lock on the inside of the door. Panicked, he grabbed Luther's empty bed and dragged it against the door. The bed would not keep out the police, but it might slow them down.

Raven could hear the officers coming down the hallway as he hurried to remove his clothes.

"Down here," someone yelled. "He came this way."

"There. There. He went in there," someone else added.

"Are you sure?"

He tossed the stolen black T-shirt on the bed, wishing he could return it to its rightful owner. The boots and pants quickly followed.

Police officers banded together just outside the door. They would be coming through any moment. They would not take him into custody, would not risk the chance of getting hurt. They would enter the room with guns blazing, shooting him down like a mad dog in the street.

Taking a deep breath, he thrust the fingertips of both hands into the center of his solar plexus. He pushed hard, the nails of his fingers piercing the flesh and drawing blood.

In the movies, shape-shifting was always such an easy thing to do. One second you're Lon Chaney Jr., and the next you're the Wolfman. But in real life, shape-shifting was very painful, which is why those with the ability to change their forms did not go from one to the other often. They stayed in one shape rather than going through the agonies of transformation.

"Great Spirit, give me strength," Raven said aloud as he plunged his fingers even deeper into his midsection. Rivulets of blood cascaded over his fingers and ran down his stomach and legs. And only when his fingers were imbedded past the first knuckle did he pull his hands away from each other, widening the rip he had created in his flesh, removing his skin as if it was a zip-up jacket.

"Aaaaayyyyyaaaa …" The pain forced a scream from his lips as he completely removed his skin, hurrying to turn it inside out.

He turned his skin feather side out and slipped back into it, his body shrinking and changing shape from a human into bird. The transformation happened almost instantly, and he found himself smoothing wrinkles and adjusting feathers with a sharp beak rather than hands.

Something hit the door from the other side, knocking the bed away from it. The door opened a few inches, wide enough to allow a bang grenade to be tossed into the room.

Raven used his beak to close the tear in his chest, sealing his skin back into one piece. He turned and flew to the window just as the grenade exploded, the concussion of the blast hitting him with enough force to nearly knock him through the glass.

As the grenade exploded, the door slammed open and half a dozen officers entered with weapons drawn. Flashlights mounted on assault rifles and shotguns swept the room, searching for the Indian man with blood on his hands, but Michael Blackwing no longer existed and was now nothing more than a name carved into the chest of a dead man.

"Where did he go?" one of the officers yelled, searching for the suspect.

"He's not here. The room's empty."

"He's got to be here. What about the other bed?"

"Not here either. It's just a dead guy."

"Check the window. Maybe he got away."

Bright beams of light swept toward the window. As they did, Raven launched himself off the sill and took flight, soaring toward the officers. Several ducked as he flew over their heads and out into the hallway.

"What the hell was that?" one of them yelled.

"A bird, I think."

"It was a fucking bat. A big one."

"Shoot it."

"Never mind the freaking bat. Check the damn window."

Raven sailed down the hallway and was at full speed when he reached the lobby. Flying out the open doorway, he soared up into the night sky, grateful to be free of the nursing home and its suffocating stench of death.

He circled the building, searching for Coyote, but there was no sign of the Trickster. But that didn't matter. He knew which way Coyote would be going. They would meet again soon.

CHAPTER 12

Special Agent Eric Kelly had been with the FBI for over ten years, had even served as an Army captain during Desert Storm, but he had never seen anything like the sight that greeted him as he entered the Willows Nursing Home.

The FBI office in Asheville, North Carolina had received a call from the Talbot Police Department around 11:00 p.m. requesting assistance with a crime scene at the home. His office had been informed that there were several homicide victims, mostly elderly, but the police had neglected to mention exactly how many bodies. The count currently stood at eleven, but there might be more.

With so hideous a crime, the FBI would step in and assume complete jurisdiction of the case. Their agency had more field investigators and better crime labs at their disposal than the local or even state police. Eric had already made a number of phone calls after his arrival and preliminary inspection, and over a dozen agents and specialists were on their way to the Willows. Most would be flying in via helicopter within the hour. The mobile laboratories were also in route, but probably wouldn't get there before morning.

In the meantime, Eric would utilize the local police to seal off the area in an attempt to keep it from becoming any more contaminated. The Talbot Swat Team had already made a thorough sweep of the building to make sure a killer—or killers—wasn't hiding inside, and paramedic units had searched for survivors among the dead.

There were no survivors.

He had expected the local chief of police to argue about having his case taken away, knowing there was going to be lots of publicity in the coming days and weeks, but Chief Dawson was more than happy to hand off the investigation to the FBI, promising the full support of his department.

The chief had obviously been shaken by what he had seen inside the nursing home, and had spent the past hour puking and chain-smoking cigarettes in the parking lot.

Eric, on the other hand, was starting to get used to the stench of blood and death that filled the building, and had even enjoyed a black coffee and jelly doughnut while standing in the middle of the lobby making phone calls to his superiors in Washington.

As he entered the nursing home for the fourth time that night, he stopped to examine the three nude bodies just inside the doorway. Someone had taken a piece of chalk and traced an outline around them. It was an unnecessary thing to do, because knowing the position of the bodies would not aid in the investigation.

The agent thought about covering the corpses with a sheet, but he was fearful of ruining trace evidence and left the bodies exactly as they had been found.

Bending down, he examined the names carved into the chests of the two male victims: Michael Blackwing and Luther Watie. The name Sarah was sliced into the stomach of the female victim. The names were clues, but he wasn't sure if they were those of the victims or those who had committed the crime. Would the killers be so bold as to sign their work? He didn't think that was likely, not unless the perps wanted to be caught, or were stoned out of their minds.

"Excuse me, Agent Kelly?"

He looked up from the bodies. Police Sergeant Tom Martin entered the building, carrying a medical folder in his hand.

"Sorry to disturb you, sir." Sergeant Martin held out the folder. "One of my men found this in the parking lot, and I thought it might be important." He nodded toward one of the nude male victims. "The name on the folder matches the one carved in that guy's chest."

Eric quickly glanced through the medical records of Luther Watie, a patient with the Willows Nursing Home for the past five years. According to the records, Luther had been assigned to bed number one, in room seven.

"Sergeant, have one of your men take a look in room seven, see if the first bed is occupied.

"We already did, sir. It's empty."

"You already looked?" The agent looked up from the folder.

"Yes, sir. Seven is the room my men chased a suspect into earlier, and bed number one is what he used to barricade the door."

"The suspect that got away …"

The sergeant's face blushed red. "Yes, sir."

"… even though your men had the room covered and the only window was sealed shut?"

Sergeant Martin nodded. "I can't explain it. There's no way he could have gotten past—"

"But he did."

"Yes, sir."

Eric turned his attention back to the folder, leaving the sergeant to stand in uncomfortable silence. Maybe Luther Watie had checked out for the weekend, gone home to visit relatives. Eric read the next page and scratched that idea. Mr. Watie had been in his room at 7:00 p.m. that evening when the night nurse had given him his medication: a pill for pain, and another to help him sleep.

He read the names of the medicine and whistled. "Jesus, if he was taking both of these in combination, he should have been out like a light."

"That's what I was thinking," replied the sergeant, obviously having read the records before handing them over. "But he's not in his room."

"What about the bathroom, or the showers? Or maybe one of the other rooms? Any extra bodies unaccounted for?"

"No, sir. The patients all died in their beds, and the nursing home staff were wearing name tags." He pointed at the bodies in the lobby. "Except for those three, and we've already located their uniforms and tags. The only one who seems to be missing is Mr. Watie."

The FBI agent scratched his chin in thought. "Well, I'm sure he'll turn up somewhere. Maybe he was lucky enough to get away from the killer, and he's hiding out in the woods somewhere. He might have Alzheimer's, or maybe he's in shock."

He turned to Officer Martin. "Grab a couple of men and search the woods behind this place, see if you can locate him. If he's alive, then he's a witness, and I want him."

"Yes, sir." The sergeant hurried out the front door to begin the search.

Eric looked back down at the folder. At the bottom of the first page was the name of Luther Watie's closest living relative, and a contact number. It was the same name carved into the stomach of the dead woman at his feet.

"Sarah."

The name and phone number were circled in blood.

CHAPTER 13

Coyote sat in the darkness at the edge of the parking lot, watching the activity taking place at the Willows Nursing Home. He had changed fully into his animal form, and would probably be mistaken for a dog in the darkness.

He had seen Raven fly out through the open doorway, and knew his opponent had somehow managed to avoid being arrested by the police. No doubt he was flying off in search of Luther Watie, hoping to reach the old man first.

The Trickster smiled and scratched himself behind the ear. Luther had gone into the original world, leaving behind a trail that would be easy to follow. The old man was also feeble and weak, and wouldn't be much of a challenge when it came time to kill him.

It was Luther's daughter he was worried about. At first, he didn't know where she was hiding, but then he had found the old man's medical records and her phone number. She was called Sarah in this world, but Coyote knew it was Blue Sky Woman when she answered his long-distance phone call.

And though they had only spoken for a moment, their minds had touched and he had learned everything he needed to know about her: her desires, fears, strengths, and weaknesses, even the name of the place she called home.

Blue Sky Woman was young and strong, but she had never walked the medicine path and was untrained in the ways of her people. In time, and with the proper training, she might be a dangerous opponent, even to him, but now she was little more than a baby wrapped in a blanket. That was why he needed to reach her first, before her father could pass on his mantle, and before Raven or any of the other Council members could interfere with his plans.

But he could only move so fast, in this world or in Galun'lati, and there were many miles between Talbot, North Carolina, and the Florida home of Sarah Reynolds. He needed to enlist the aid of his brothers and sisters of the night, those who would also benefit once mankind had been eliminated from the Great Council, and the New World was again ruled by creatures of fur and feather.

Throwing back his head, he called out to those who prowled the darkness on silent paws, or glided upon whispered wings, children of the shrinking forests and fields of Turtle Island.

He summoned them from the darkness, his haunting cry carried upon the night wind. And from that darkness they came, crawling through the underbrush, and landing in the branches of the surrounding trees, coming to listen to what he had to say and offering allegiance to his cause.

Coyote gave them instructions, telling the creatures gathered around him what needed to be done. Those who could travel the fastest would be his eyes and ears, seeking out the home of Blue Sky Woman and making sure that she could not hide from him or escape his wrath.

Only brother Mouse did not offer his allegiance, for he knew Coyote was not one to be trusted. Nor would he ever join company with those who had dined upon his family, as Coyote and his relatives had often done. Mouse was also rather fond of people, despite the deadly traps they set, for their houses offered warmth and shelter during the cold winter months and their kitchen cabinets provided fine meals.

So as Coyote and the others made their secret plans, swearing blood oaths to one another, Mouse slipped away in the darkness and headed south.

CHAPTER 14

Luther laughed as the magical door he had opened between the two worlds quickly faded and closed, leaving a very frustrated Coyote on the other side.

As the doorway faded from view, so too did the storage room, and the Willows Nursing Home, and the old man found himself standing in the middle of a strange and wonderful forest. The forest was crowded with massive trees that towered upward into the sky, their branches disappearing into the thick grayish mist that hung over the area like wet gauze. Beads of moisture gathered on the leaves and fell in heavy drops to the forest floor, striking fallen vegetation with a steady tap-tap and releasing earthy odors into the air.

Luther took a deep breath, inhaling the rich aromas of the primeval forest surrounding him. It was a forest he had been in many times before, and though it too had its mysteries and perils, it was a far safer world than the one he had just left behind.

He looked around in an attempt to get his bearing, but he saw no recognizable landmark. Apparently, he was far off the familiar paths he often walked, in a section of Galun'lati he had never traveled before.

"This isn't good. Not good at all."

Time and distance differed in Galun'lati, and Luther could make far greater speed with less effort than he could in the New World. But in order to make such haste, he needed to know where he was and which way to go.

But he would have to worry about direction later; right now he needed to put distance between himself and the doorway that closed, before Coyote figured a way to open it again.

Using only instinct and blind luck to guide him, Luther started walking between the trees, hoping to spot a well-worn path or trail marker. But he now moved in the world of spirits and the old ones, and knew that signs and markers did not exist, and well-worn paths were few and far between.

But luck was on his side, and it wasn't long before he came upon a trail running through the forest, one that shimmered with the glow of spiritual energy left behind by those who had passed before him. Of course, he had no way of telling who had made the trail, or where it led, but walking along it was far easier than pushing his way through the thick underbrush of a mighty forest.

Luther paused and whispered a short prayer, asking the spirits for their help and guidance. When there was no reply, he spit into the palm of his left hand and slapped the tiny puddle with the first two fingers of his right hand. Most of the spit flew to his left, so that was the way he turned upon the trail. He could have just as easily flipped a coin to choose his direction, had he a coin in his pocket, or even played "Eenie, meenie, miney, mo."

Tucking his leather bag under his belt, he shuffled along the trail, feeling truly alive for the first time in years. With each step he took, he felt his long-lost youth slowly seep back into his ancient body, such was the magic of Galun'lati. It was a place of renewal and healing. Even the pain of an arthritic hip, his constant companion for so many years, seemed to magically fade away.

"This place is good medicine." He smiled. But his smile quickly disappeared as doubt crossed his mind. Maybe there was another reason he no longer felt any pain.

The old man stopped, suddenly wondering if he was still alive, or if he had died in the nursing home and now made his way down the path to the eternal resting place. Maybe he only thought he had gotten away from Coyote. Worried, he slipped his hand beneath the fabric of his shirt, breathing a sigh of relief when he felt the faint beating of his heart.

"Whew ... Thank you, Grandfather."

He did indeed still live, and he was feeling better because of the journey he now took and not because he had finally cast off his frail body. Perhaps purpose and grand adventures were the keys to good health and vitality, not the medications prescribed to him in the nursing home. Had he known, he would have returned to the original world years ago. Instead, he had allowed his mind to be dulled by the white man's tiny pills, his will to live almost destroyed by those who constantly reminded him that he was old and useless, and better off dead.

With a new spring in his step, Luther continued his journey along the trail. His mind clearer, he focused on the threats made by Coyote, and the dangers now facing his daughter, paying little attention to his surroundings. He didn't wonder why the misty forest was so eerily quiet, or notice the frightened eyes watching him from the shadows of the underbrush. And it wasn't until he had traveled over a mile that he noticed the sounds of something following him.

A chill danced up and down Luther's spine. He stopped and turned, looking back down the trail, listening to the snapping of small twigs and the occasional dull thud of something solid impacting the ground. It didn't sound like footsteps, but something indeed followed him. The noise grew louder, more threatening.

"What the hell?" Luther fingered the bag hanging on his belt, wondering if it might be wise to create another doorway and make a hasty retreat back into the New World. But he was hesitant to do so for fear that the Trickster might be waiting for him on the other side.

Instead of removing the bag, he reached inside the right front pocket of his jeans and withdrew his pocket knife, quickly opening the blade. The tiny knife wasn't much of a weapon, but he felt much better now that he was armed.

The sounds of something coming down the trail grew even louder.

Snap, crackle, thud. Snap, crackle, thud.

It was now fight or flight. Even though he was experiencing a renewed vigor in Galun'lati, he knew his days of a quick retreat, or an even faster escape, were far behind him. Nor could he hope to outrun Coyote or one of his followers. Therefore, Luther chose to stand his ground and face whatever manner of beastie now approached. Perhaps it was only a fellow traveler looking for companionship, or maybe even one of the other members of the Council making their way toward Hollow Mountain. But he knew the Council members usually followed familiar paths, and the trail Luther stood upon was narrow and seldom used.

Perhaps it was a wayward spirit that now approached, even though he had never known a spirit or ghost to make such a racket. What followed him had to be a creature of flesh and bone, something of substance.

Did Coyote's henchmen now follow him down the trail, intent on doing to Luther what they had previously done to the others?

Luther glanced down at the knife. The tiny blade would be a poor defense against beasts of fur and fangs.

Again, he considered opening a doorway back into the New World. But if it was Coyote or his people who followed, the use of magic would be like a beacon to them. They would see the brilliance of the burning powders, know he was opening another door, and make great haste to reach him before he could escape again.

He had gotten away earlier only because he had caught Coyote off guard, the Trickster not expecting such magic. Coyote was not stupid, and would not fall for the same trick twice.

Luther was still considering trying to escape when something suddenly appeared back down the trail. It rolled out into the open with a crashing of twigs and a dull thud, coming to a spinning stop in the middle of the path. At first he thought it was a boulder, but then he noticed a pair of large eyes, a flattened nose, a mouth, and long black hair.

"What the—" Luther said aloud, not believing what he was seeing.

Sitting in the middle of the trail was an enormous head, easily measuring three feet in diameter. It sat right side up, looking at him, eyes open and blinking, heavy lips pulling back to reveal rows of pointy teeth.

"Foom, foom, foom … I see you." the head cried out, its voice sounding like thunder. "Zoom, zoom, zoom … here I come to eat you."

The head rolled forward, moving toward him like a giant bowling ball. It quickly picked up speed, its long black hair whipping around wildly.

"Shit!" Luther turned and fled, moving as fast as an old man with a bad hip could, and from behind him came the crashing sounds of the giant head as it rapidly gained on him.

"Foom, foom, foom … Give me some room," cried the giant head. "Foom, foom, foam … I will eat all your bones."

Luther didn't doubt the giant head's threats, and he was desperately trying to come up with a plan to keep his bones safely inside his skin. He would stand and fight, but knew the head would knock him down as easily as a professional bowler picking up a spare pin. His only option was to run, but the head was far faster.

As the giant head rapidly gained on him, Luther decided on a plan of action. It was almost upon him, when he suddenly turned and plunged into the dense thicket of the forest. The head was bigger and faster, but he was thin and easily slipped between trees and tight areas.

But the head wasn't fooled by Luther's sudden change in direction, and crashed into the underbrush after him, knocking over the smaller trees that got in its way.

The tops of saplings slapped the old man's back as they were flattened. Luther yelled in fear and changed directions again, squeezing between the trunks of two stout trees that grew only a foot apart. He emerged on the other side, barely in the lead as the head circled the two trees and continued the chase.

"Can't we talk about this?" he yelled, frustrated he was unable to give the head the slip. "I'm a Council member."

"Foom, foom, foom," the giant head replied.

Luther stumbled upon a smaller trail leading through a section of the forest where the trees grew closer together, one wide enough for a thin old Indian, but far too narrow for a giant rolling head. Without hesitation, he turned and changed paths. But the trees were small and thin and the head was able to easily topple them in its pursuit.

Luther felt his heart pounding, and knew he would have to stop and rest soon. He was already exhausted, his breath burning the back of his throat.

And just when he could not possibly take another step, the trail opened upon a clearing, putting him in even more danger. Luther no longer had the protection of the trees and brush, and the head would be able to run him down and feed upon his bones.

He spun around, the tiny pocket knife clutched tightly in his hand. But nothing exploded from the forest behind him; instead, the head stopped at the edge of the clearing, glaring in anger.

"Come and get me," Luther Watie yelled, knowing he was about to die. But the head didn't move. It looked past him instead, and he saw fear in its eyes.

Luther felt the skin at his temples pull tight. Slowly, he turned to see what terrified the head. He expected a towering monster to be standing behind him, and instead found himself facing a dozen wooden scaffolds. Made of poles lashed together with vines, each stood about ten feet off the ground. They were old and rotted, and looked in danger of falling down. Some had already fallen, for numerous poles lay scattered on the ground in a jumbled collection.

Luther couldn't see what was on the scaffolds, but he suspected they held the bodies of the dead, for mixed in with the poles on the ground were bones of various size, shape, and description.

"A burial ground," he whispered, realizing why the head had stopped its chase. Such places were taboo, and likely filled with ghosts. Few in Galun'lati would dare venture into a burial ground.

He turned to look behind him, but the giant head was nowhere to be seen. For a moment he thought it had given up the chase, and had withdrawn deeper into the forest, but then he spotted it peeking out from behind the trunk of a tree.

"You can't fool me," he called out. "I see you."

"Foom, foom, foom …" replied the head, withdrawing into the shadows.

Luther could not go back, for the giant head was obviously waiting for him. That meant he would have to take his chances and cross the burial ground, hoping to pick up the trail on the other side. But he would rather take his chances with angry ghosts than have to face the rolling head again.

Folding his knife and putting it away, he squared his shoulders and continued his journey through the original world.

CHAPTER 15

Jack had been hoping for a little fun and games in the bedroom, something to take his mind off of the day's earlier events, but such hope and expectations vanished when he saw Sarah sitting on the bed holding his revolver. And as the bathroom light spilled out into the bedroom, he saw such a look of fear in her eyes that it left him cold, despite the hot shower he had just taken.

He sat beside her, trying to assure her that the scary voice on the phone was nothing more than a practical joke from an obscene caller. Of course, that didn't explain why the man with the sinister voice had called her Blue Sky Woman, the same exact phrase said to her earlier by the corpse of Ray Talmage.

Not that he really believed a corpse had sat up and spoken to her. It was probably just a mild hallucination brought on by stress and working too many hours. She just needed a rest; they could both use a vacation. Maybe they could take another cruise to the Bahamas, or spend a few days in the Keys fishing and taking in the sights. She would like that.

It took nearly an hour for him to convince Sarah that the voice on the phone was only a prank call, and not some demonic serial killer out to get her. She had still been upset over the day's earlier events, and her mind had probably tossed a few words into the conversation that wasn't said by either of them.

It had taken an additional thirty minutes of comforting before she relinquished the revolver. He thought about unloading it, to be on the safe side, but really didn't think she was a danger to herself or to him. Past girlfriends might have been tempted to put a bullet or two in him, but Sarah was a sweetheart and wouldn't hurt a fly.

After putting the revolver away, he made the two of them hot cocoa. The caffeine in the chocolate might have added to her nervousness, but he had ground up a Valium and slipped it into her drink. Jack's father was a retired pharmacist, and the bottle of "mother's little helpers" had been given to him earlier in the year.

His wife now slept soundly on her side of the bed, thoughts of evil voices and talking corpses pushed aside for a nocturnal trip through la-la land. Jack should have probably taken a Valium himself, but he didn't like how the tiny yellow pills made him feel in the morning.

Being groggy was never a good thing, especially when he had a nine o'clock appointment with the mayor to explain why Sonny Harris had committed suicide at Greenwood Cemetery.

So instead of a good night's sleep aided by medication, he found himself at three in the morning staring up at the bedroom ceiling. He wanted desperately to sleep, but every time he closed his eyes he saw Sonny, still wearing his brightly colored Hawaiian shirt, the back of his head blown clean off.

How's you's doing, Jackie-boy?

Punching his pillow for the umpteenth time, Jack rolled over on his side and tried to go to sleep. But he instead studied the illuminated dials of his alarm clock, watching as the few remaining hours until morning slowly ticked past. And as it always seemed to happen when sleep was an impossibility, the steady *tick, tick, tick* of the clock seemed to grow in volume until it was a nearly unbearable tempo beating on the inside of his head.

Tick ... tick ... tick ... Tick ... TICK ... TICK ...

As he lay there listening to the clock, he became aware of another noise coming from downstairs, a peculiar scratching, as if the tiny clawed feet of some nocturnal animal moved and danced across the wood floor.

A mouse.

That was the first thought that popped into his mind, even though they had never had a mouse problem before. But he had seen on the local news that there had been an outbreak of mice infestations in the town of Apopka, just twenty miles up the road. Maybe the little varmints had migrated south, following the toll roads and interstate to Sanford. Perhaps they had hitched a ride heading up the St. Johns River, stopping off at the town once known as Mellonville.

A single mouse wouldn't be much of a problem, but a whole nest of mice would be something altogether different. Once the varmints set up housekeeping in the old Victorian house, it would be nearly impossible to get rid of them.

He heard the noise again, a little louder this time. Maybe it wasn't a mouse, but a rat. Florida had lots of rats, but they were mostly citrus rats and usually stayed outdoors, rarely venturing inside dwellings in search of food or shelter. They weren't like the sewer rats that infested major metropolitan areas, like New York and Chicago. Those rats were bigger, meaner, and much nastier.

Still, it would not do to have a rat, or even a mouse, inside their home and place of business. But maybe it was something a little less furry that had invaded their private domain. Perhaps a lizard or a large palmetto bug had found its way inside and now scratched at a downstairs window to get out.

Jack tossed aside his covers and climbed out of bed, slipping on his pants and shoes. He might have some serious rat kicking or cockroach stomping to do, and didn't want to attempt it in his bare feet and underwear. Leaving the bedroom, he crossed the living room and entered the kitchen. He turned on the florescent lights, but there were no nocturnal creepy crawlers to be seen, with either four legs or six

Crossing the kitchen, he headed for the back stairs and descended to the first floor. He searched through the dressing room, the prep room, and the office, even looked in the chapel where the body of Ray Talmage rested peacefully in its casket, but could not find the source of the noise.

He was about to call it quits and go back upstairs, when he again heard the strange scratching, this time from the front door. Something was on the outside, scratching at the wood.

"What the hell?"

Jack slowly approached. There was a small, diamond-shaped window set high in the door that allowed a clear view of the sidewalk and the funeral home's tiny front porch. He was halfway to the door when the scratching stopped, and the door knob jiggled back and forth.

He froze. A scratching might have been produced by a rat, mouse, lizard, or even an oversized cockroach, but there was no way in hell any of those creatures could jiggle a doorknob. Someone was on the other side of the door, turning the knob to see if it was locked. Someone was trying to get in.

Standing motionless a few feet from the door, he watched as the knob moved, unsure of what action to take. He wanted to rush to the door and peer through the tiny window to see who was there, but at the same time he was afraid to look.

Childhood fears suddenly washed over him in waves, fears of the dark and the unknown, stories of the bogeyman and things that go bump in the night, nocturnal terrors that still caused him to sleep with one leg safely tucked under the covers. His skin went damp and cold under a thin sheen of sweat, and he became aware of the fact that he was unarmed.

The jiggling of the knob lasted a few more seconds, then stopped. A tense silence fell over the front of the funeral home, and for some strange reason he knew something still crouched and waited on the other side of the door, something that knew he was standing there.

Taking a deep breath to steady his nerves, Jack slowly approached the door. He had to raise on his tiptoes to look out the tiny glass window, and when he did there was nothing to be seen. The tiny porch was empty, as was the street that ran past the funeral home.

Jack started to unlock the deadbolt and open the door, but a shadow moved past the window. He stopped, holding his breath to listen. Something was back on the front porch.

A burglar. Or maybe a crack-head. Someone seeking to rob them in the night.

Fear again washed over him as the door handle jiggled. Had he unlocked the deadbolt, they would have gotten inside.

He thought about retreating into the office to call the police, but he needed to get a look at the would-be burglar so he could give a description in case they left before the authorities arrived. Rising once more on his tiptoes, he again looked out the window, but didn't see anyone. The handle continued rattling, however.

And then he saw not a person but a dog walking away from the door and moving out into the street, long-legged and gray, like a small German Sheppard but with eyes that shone yellow in the glow of the streetlight. It reached the middle of the street and stopped, staring back at him.

That's impossible. How can a dog turn a door handle? There must be someone else, the dog's owner perhaps.

But there was no one there. The tiny porch was empty.

Ridiculous. Dogs cannot turn doorknobs, and they sure as hell don't try to break into buildings at night.

Curiosity overcoming his fear, Jack unlocked the deadbolt and opened the door. He had a clearer view of the animal now as it stood there watching him. It was thin, with a bushy tail and hunched shoulders, its head lowered and ears turned forward. It was an evil looking beast, more feral than domesticated breed, something found where people feared to tread—a wolf-dog hybrid perhaps, or maybe a coyote.

He started to step farther onto the porch, when the coyote suddenly lunged forward and charged straight at him. It came at an alarming rate of speed, head lowered and teeth bared, and he barely had time to retreat back into the house and slam the door.

The coyote hit the door at a full charge, crashing against it and causing the wood to shutter. Jack jumped back, startled, then threw himself against the door and engaged the dead bolt. The frenzied animal on the other side snarled and growled, frantically scratching to get in, causing him to wonder if the door would hold.

The commotion lasted for almost a full minute before the sounds died out and he heard the beast trotting off.

He waited a few more minutes, then peeked out the window.

The porch and the street beyond were empty.

"What the hell was that all about?"

Things were getting stranger by the minute: suicides, talking corpses, obscene phone calls, and now a pissed-off coyote. Maybe the animal was rabid. But that wouldn't explain why it was trying to get inside the funeral home, or how it knew to turn a door knob, but that could be the reason why it tried to attack him. One thing for sure, it was dangerous and shouldn't be walking the streets.

Double-checking to make sure the door was securely locked, Jack hurried into the office to call animal control.

CHAPTER 16

There was no opportunity for Raven to change his skin to human form, or reclaim the car he had stolen, for the parking lot of the Willows Nursing Home was swarming with police officers. If he was foolish enough to try it, he might be arrested or even shot. And though he was a shape-shifter, and a person who walked in two very different worlds, he was not bulletproof.

So instead of a comfortable warm ride, he was forced to continue his trip the old-fashioned way, on feathered wings.

Had he a bag of magic tricks, he would be able to open a doorway into Galun'lati and make far greater time in his travels, but he had no such bag, and the existing doorways from one world into the next were few and far between. Those doorways were not listed on any map, but could easily be detected by the shape-shifter for they were places of great power where energy radiated from the old world into the new.

To the north, one such doorway still existed atop a bald mountain where the Little People once danced and held their ceremonies. But to use that doorway meant backtracking and losing valuable time. It also meant risking another encounter with Coyote, for he too would know of that particular doorway and probably use it in an attempt to catch up with Luther.

Another doorway existed due west, guarded in ancient times by a thirty-foot statue of a giant sitting wolf. But the statue of Nee Yah Kah Tah Kee had been destroyed when the white man built his railroad through the mountains, making the doorway to Galun'lati all the more difficult to find.

There were other doorways far to the south, in black hammock forests where crystal clear water bubbled out of the cavernous ground. Once thought to be sources of eternal youth, those doorways were now guarded by the medicine men of the Seminole and Miccosukee tribes, used only by those who knew how to safely pass through them.

As Raven circled the area one final time before starting south, he noticed a disturbance in the forest below him. Numerous animals moved through the underbrush, radiating out from a central point. Something odd must have transpired for so many different species of feather and fur to come together. Curious, he flew lower and glided, trying to pick up bits of animal speak carried on the wind.

So intent on finding out what was happening below, Raven didn't know he was being stalked until something hit him hard from behind.

The blow caught him between the wings, sharp talons parting feathers and cutting through flesh, causing blood to flow. Luckily, it was only a glancing blow. Had he not been descending, the attack would have landed solidly, sending him tumbling helplessly to the ground.

Raven tucked both wings and dove headfirst toward the safety of the forest. As he descended, he saw the attacker out of the corner of his eye: Owl.

The other bird circled around to strike again, his silent wings glowing like new fallen snow in the moonlight. He pivoted his head as he made the turn, his two large eyes tracking his prey like twin gun sights.

Raven was still fifty feet above the treetops when Owl pulled his wings in close to his body and dove at him like a missile. There was no sound, not even a rustling on the wind, and Raven held his breath as he tried to outrun certain death.

Under ordinary circumstances, he would have tried to reason with the nocturnal raptor, for it was forbidden to kill or eat a member of the Great Council, but this was no time to be diplomatic. He was in grave danger, and only the laws of nature and the speed of his two smaller wings were going to save him.

And though he couldn't see behind him, his sixth sense told him that Owl was about to strike again. Raven waited until the last possible moment and then darted to the right, causing the big bird of prey to soar past him, his deadly talons missing by mere inches.

But he wouldn't have a third chance to deliver a killing blow, because Raven was among the treetops of the forest, twisting his body one way and then the next to pass safely between the branches. Fearful that Owl would come after him, he didn't land until he was safely on the ground and hiding among the underbrush.

Standing motionless in the darkness, his heart pounding from fear and adrenaline, he watched Owl circle the area twice and then fly off in search of an easier meal to catch.

"That was a close one."

The voice startled Raven, nearly causing him to cry out. Turning, he saw a pair of eyes watching him from the darkness beneath the same bush in which he had chosen to hide.

"Who said that?"

Raven stepped back, fearful it was a snake who spoke to him. He didn't want to escape a winged predator only to end up in the belly of a reptile.

"Come out where I can see you."

It wasn't a snake, but Mouse who moved out into the moonlight. Raven breathed a sigh of relief.

"Brother Mouse, what are you doing here?"

"The same thing as you, hiding from Owl."

"It is not a safe night for anyone when Owl is hunting," Raven replied. "But why would he attack a Council member? Does he not know he will be punished for his actions?"

The little Mouse moved closer. "I'm afraid it is all Coyote's fault."

"Coyote?"

Mouse nodded. "He sang his night song, calling the others to him. He told them of his plan to rid the world of people, and many have joined his cause."

"Coyote's songs are filled with treachery and lies. They must be told the truth. What he is doing is wrong, and in violation of the Great Council's laws."

"It is too late to talk to the others. They swore allegiance and gave blood oaths."

"Including Owl?"

"He was the first to give his oath. Coyote told him about you too, said that you were against his plan."

Raven stretched his neck and ruffled his feathers. Pain flashed white hot up his back.

"And what of you, my little friend? Where do you stand?"

"I am against Coyote, and all that he stands for. Long before people came into this world, Coyote and his family hunted and killed my relatives. When he couldn't catch us with speed and cunning, he used trickery and deception to lure us out of our comfortable homes. We have often offered him the hand of friendship, only to have that hand bitten off at the wrist."

"It is good to know that I have at least one ally." He again ruffled his feathers, flinching in pain.

"You are hurt, Mouse said, concerned."

"It is nothing. Just a scratch."

"Here, let me have a look." Mouse circled around behind him. Standing up on his back legs, stretching his neck to make himself even taller, he studied the gash running down the center of Raven's back.

"Tsk ... tsk ... tsk ..." Mouse said, shaking his head. "It is a nasty cut. You are very lucky to be alive."

"It is nothing. I will heal."

"You should clean it. And you must rest until the bleeding stops."

"There is no time to rest. I must continue my journey."

"You cannot fly far like that. You will tire easily, and the smell of blood will attract other predators."

"I do not have a choice. I must continue my journey south. I have to protect Blue Sky Woman from Coyote. It is a promise I made to her father long ago."

"South, you say?" Mouse hurried around to stand in front of Raven, rising up on his back legs and twitching his nose in excitement. "How far south are you going?"

"As far south as possible, to the very tip of Turtle Island."

"Ah, to the place where there are no winters. But that is a very long journey ..."

"Yes, it is."

"And very hard for someone who is injured."

"Yes ..."

"That is why I am going with you."

Raven was shocked. "What? You? Impossible. I cannot wait for you to walk all the way to Florida; it will take too much time."

"But I will not walk. I will fly ... You will carry me."

"Why would I want to carry you? It will slow me down."

"I will not slow you down much. I am very light." To illustrate his point, Mouse jumped up and down. "See, light as a feather. I hardly weigh anything. You will not even know I'm there."

"Impossible ..."

"You are injured, in need of medicine. Take me with you and I will lick your wound until it heals. My tongue is soft and warm, and very long." Mouse stuck out his tongue and wiggled it. "See? You cannot fight Coyote if you are hurt."

"But I am a shape-shifter," Raven argued. "Before I fight Coyote, I will turn my skin around."

Mouse shook his head. "It does not matter. The injury you have will be on both sides of your skin. It cannot heal itself."

Raven thought about it for a moment, then nodded. "You are right. A warrior cannot afford to be injured when going into battle. Brother Mouse, I accept your kind offer. You can go with me."

"Yippee!" Mouse exclaimed, doing a backflip. "We're flying south. No more cold winters for me."

Raven allowed the little Mouse to do two more backflips before trying to calm him down. "We must go; time is wasting. Climb up this tree to the tallest limb. I will meet you there."

Mouse scurried up the tree to the tallest limb. Raven waited for him to get there, then flew up and landed beside him.

"Now climb on my back, but be careful not to step on my cut."

"I will be careful."

Mouse climbed onto Raven's back, taking care where he placed his feet. He stopped in the center of his back, between his wings, holding onto his shoulders. And as promised, Mouse immediately started licking Raven's wound to clean it.

"Hold on tight, and don't let go." Raven launched himself from the branch, flapping his wings hard to climb higher into the night sky.

Mouse held tight onto Raven's feathers, hunkering low.

"Wheeee …"

CHAPTER 17

Morning seemed to come far too early the following day, and Sarah found herself awaking to an empty bed. She sat up, ran her fingers through her hair, and turned the alarm clock around to read the time. It was nearly 8:00 a.m.

"Crap." She climbed out of bed and staggered into the bathroom, quickly wiping her face with a washcloth and brushing her teeth. She paused to study her reflection in the mirror, noticing the dark shadows under her eyes. She had slept poorly and it showed, her dreams troubled with talking corpses and strange phone calls. Turning off the water, she left the bathroom in search of her missing husband.

She found Jack sitting at their dinette table, reading the newspaper and drinking coffee.

"Good morning." She made straight for the coffee maker on the counter, grabbing a clean cup from the drain rack.

"Hello, sleepyhead." Jack set down the paper. "That's last night's coffee. We still had half a pot and I didn't want to throw it out."

"It will do." She added cream and sugar to the cup of coffee and took a sip, frowning at the bitter taste. "Why didn't you wake me?"

"I figured you could use the extra sleep, especially after yesterday."

She crossed the room to the table, kissed him on top of his head, and took a seat. "That's really sweet of you, but Mr. Talmage has a ten o'clock church service, which means the hearse will be by early to pick him up and I have to be ready for them."

"Ten o'clock? Why didn't you say something last night? I would have gotten you up."

"I did say something about it, but you must have forgot."

He frowned. "I did have a lot on my mind."

"What time did you get up?"

"Real early. I heard a noise downstairs and went to investigate. Thought we had burglars, especially when the doorknob jiggled."

"Someone was trying to get in?"

"That's what I thought at first, but when I looked out there was no one there. Just a dog."

"What kind of dog?"

"I'm not sure. Might even have been a coyote."

Sarah put down her coffee cup and gave him a funny look. "A coyote?"

"It looked like one, but then again, I've never seen one in real life. Only in pictures ..."

"And in cartoons."

He smiled. "And in cartoons, but this didn't look like Wile E. Coyote. It was dirty and rabid-looking."

"Poor thing. It was probably lost and hungry, looking for something to eat. I didn't know we had coyotes in this area."

"I didn't either, but I guess we do. Mean son of a bitch ..."

She smiled. "How do you know it was mean?"

"Because it tried to attack me."

Her smile faded. "I think you'd better start at the beginning."

He told her everything that had happened downstairs in the early hours of the morning. She listened without interrupting, quietly sipping her coffee.

"I figured it was rabid, so I called animal control. If it's still in the area, they should have no trouble catching it."

"We're only a few blocks from Lake Monroe, so it might have gone back into the woods."

"Or back to its owner, because I don't think a wild coyote would know how to turn a door knob. It had to be trained."

"If it actually did turn the knob."

"There wasn't anyone else."

"You didn't see anyone, but that doesn't mean they weren't there. It was probably a homeless person, or a crack-head trying to get in ... maybe someone looking for drugs. Some people use embalming fluid to increase the potency of marijuana."

"Yeah, idiots who want to get lung cancer."

"Serves them right. But whoever it was, they must have been frightened off by the coyote, especially if it's as vicious as you say it was."

"Believe me, it was definitely vicious. Damn thing scared the hell out of me. You should have seen its eyes, and the way it stood there looking at the house."

Sarah finished her coffee and carried the empty cup to the sink. "Well, I'm sure it's long gone."

"Maybe, but I won't be taking any late-night strolls around the neighborhood."

"Not that you ever did before."

"I was thinking about it." He patted his stomach. "I could use the exercise."

She turned around, and smiled at him mischievously. "You can get plenty of exercise, with me. Besides, I like your love handles; they give me something to hold."

"You'd like me even better if I slimmed down." He slid his chair back and stood.

"Are you going into work today?" she asked.

"I had planned on it, why?"

"Nothing. Just asking."

"Are you worried about being here alone?"

She shook her head. "No. Nothing like that. I just figured they would give you a day off after what happened at the cemetery yesterday."

"No chance of that. I have a stack of paperwork that needs to be filled out, and the city wants to send me for bloodwork this morning." He studied her for a moment. "You sure you'll be okay by yourself?"

"I'll be fine," she assured him. "Ray Talmage will be out of here this morning, and things will be back to normal. You'll see."

It was a little after 9:30 a.m. when Jack arrived at Greenwood Cemetery. He parked his truck behind the office. The building sat in the shade of a towering oak tree where, according to legend, a Seminole Indian was once hanged by white settlers.

Climbing out of the truck and walking around to the front of the building, he took a moment to look out over the grounds. The cemetery had been his sanctuary for almost ten years; a peaceful oasis of rolling hills and live oak trees, dotted with thousands of headstones.

As it was with most days, there seemed to be an invisible blanket of serenity hanging over the area, muffling the sounds associated with the nearby toll roads and surrounding city. Perhaps the sensation was due in part to the residents of Greenwood, who no longer had to participate in the rat race of modern man. After all, the dead did not worry about paying bills, fighting rush-hour traffic, or striking it rich on the New York Stock Exchange. Such ambitions and annoyances were a thing of the past for them. They were quite content to lie in their graves and quietly rot, perhaps watching as the world around them slowly changed.

Jack caught movement out of the corner of his eye, turning in time to see one of the cemetery's resident bald eagles fly past, probably heading off to a nearby lake in search of fish for breakfast.

As his gaze followed the eagle's path, he spotted the bright yellow barrier tape sealing off the area where Sonny Harris had committed suicide the previous day. Instantly his tranquil state of mind was pushed aside and reality came crashing back down on him.

He sighed and turned his back on the cemetery, entering the building. As he stepped through the front door, he heard the voices of two women talking.

One voice belonged to the office secretary, Anna Santos; the other was that of Alice Montgomery, the City Clerk, who was also Jack's boss.

Jack crossed the lobby and entered the main office, setting his laptop computer on the round wooden table in the center of the room. Alice sat in one of the four chairs circling the table, her back to the doorway. She was being entertained by Anna, who sat behind the large wooden desk at the opposite end of the room. Both women stopped talking and turned to look at him when he entered the room.

"Good morning, Jack," Anna said, her thick Hispanic accent always making his name sound longer than just four letters. "I heard about what happened yesterday. That's horrible."

Anna was fortunate enough to have taken the previous day off, missing out on the bloody spectacle of Sonny killing himself. Good thing too, for she had a reputation for passing out at the sight of blood. She also had a reputation for freaking out over snakes, lizards, cockroaches, and other creepy crawlers, often to the delight of the caretakers who would occasionally put something in her desk drawer.

"Yes, it was horrible." Jack nodded, trying not to conjure up mental images.

He turned his attention to Alice, who hadn't said anything to him yet. "I guess you're waiting to see me? We can go into my office. It's quieter there."

Alice followed Jack into his office, taking a seat in one of the two chairs facing his desk.

Walking around behind the desk, he plopped down on the leather executive chair.

"I would have been here sooner, but traffic was heavy today."

She smiled. "I'm surprised you came in at all. I would have taken the day off."

"I thought about it, but figured somebody had to be here in case the press showed up."

"You won't have to worry about the news media. My office already gave them a statement. We also told them there would be funerals taking place today, so they promised not to send anyone out to take pictures."

"Good. That's one less thing I have to deal with."

Alice set her briefcase on his desk and opened it, removing a thick manila folder. "Now comes the fun part. Paperwork. I'm going to need a complete report about yesterday's incident."

"I already turned in a report," he protested.

She nodded. "That was a police report. Now you get to write another one for the mayor's office. Take your time and don't leave anything out; the city of Orlando wants to cover its ass on this one. We don't want any of Sonny's family members coming after us saying we could have prevented his suicide." She looked at him for a moment, as if trying to read his face. "We couldn't have prevented it, could we?"

He shook his head. "His actions came as a complete surprise."

Jack hadn't told anyone, not even his wife, that Sonny had shown him a pistol a few minutes before putting a bullet through his head. Had he been a little more observant, paid more attention to what was being said, he might have realized what Sonny was about to do.

His mind had been preoccupied with what Sarah had told him on the phone, with images of Ray Talmage's corpse sitting up and speaking. He barely heard what Sonny was saying, hadn't noticed any telltale signs that might have indicated the man was about to commit suicide.

Alice stared at him for a moment longer, then nodded. "Okay. Good." She slid the stack of paperwork in front of him. "Then start writing. After you're done, we'll talk about sending you down to have bloodwork."

Jack groaned, but knew it wouldn't do any good to protest. He removed a ball-point pen from his shirt pocket and started filling out the first form.

He had a good case of writer's cramp by the time he finished with all the forms, giving a detailed description of what had happened. Alice read through his report, nodding her approval.

"Good, good. This ought to please Mayor Davis. Definitely doesn't read like you're making it up."

"Why would I make it up?" he asked. "That's what happened."

"Oh, I believe you. So does the mayor. It's just that everyone downtown is worried about getting hit with another lawsuit."

"They can't sue us if we didn't do anything wrong."

She looked at him and laughed. "That's what I love about you, Jack. You're so trusting. But we're living in a world where a person's actions are never their fault. Take the guy who bought a cup of coffee in the drive-through of a fast food restaurant. He puts the cup between his legs and drives off, spilling hot coffee all over his crotch. Burns the hell out of his penis then sues the restaurant for making their coffee too hot, even though it's his own fault for not putting the cup in the holder beside his seat."

"Worried someone might hold the cemetery to blame for Sonny's death?"

"Exactly. And not just the cemetery; they might hold you to blame."

"Me?"

"You said you spoke to him right before he killed himself. Some smart lawyer might try to say it's your fault for not noticing his depressed condition."

"But I'm not a psychiatrist."

"I know it, and you know it, but some of the dummies they put on juries might not know it. And you said Sonny stopped by on a regular basis, sometimes five or six times a week? They might say that was a warning sign, and you should have notified someone."

"It's not against the law to visit a loved one's grave on a regular basis. If it was, then half the people who visit the cemetery would be guilty of that. Sonny was no different than many of the others; he lost someone he loved very dearly and was having a hard time dealing with it."

"Had he been drinking?"

Jack shook his head. "A couple of the times he came here he had been drinking, I could smell it on his breath, but he was sober yesterday."

Alice thought about it for a moment, then nodded. She took the papers from him and put them back in her briefcase, closing it. "I really think we're okay with this. As long as you didn't know about the gun, then there is nothing you could have said or done to prevent his suicide."

Jack could no longer keep his silence. He had to tell her the truth.

"I knew about the gun."

"What?" She looked stunned.

"Sonny showed it to me yesterday."

"And you didn't think that was odd? Warning bells didn't go off in your head?"

"No. Not really. This is Florida; a lot of people carry guns. It's fairly easy to get a concealed weapons permit. Sonny owns a limo service, and was providing security for his customers. When he showed me the pistol, I had no idea he was going to use it on himself."

"And you left this out of your original report because …"

He shifted uncomfortably under her gaze. "I left it out of the report because I didn't want some lawyer trying to make a name for himself by picking it out as the reason for Sonny's demise. I figured if it was in print, it might be a problem, which is why I waited to tell you."

"And you weren't sure you were going to tell me until a few moments ago?"

He nodded. "I know I can trust you. It's the rest of the world I don't trust."

She smiled. "Don't worry, I've got your back on this. Just don't wait so long next time to give me all the details."

"I promise."

"Good. Now, let's get out of here and get some lunch. I'm buying. But before we go, have one of the caretakers take down the barrier ribbon around Mrs. Harris's grave. It's no longer a crime scene. And have them turn on the sprinklers. We want to wash away the blood before anyone else sees it."

"Consider it done." He stood up and followed his boss out of the office.

Outside the sun was shining brightly. It was going to be another beautiful day at Greenwood.

CHAPTER 18

The ancient burial ground seemed to go on forever, the soil littered with the skeletons of people, animals, and those who had turned their backs on the New World and returned to their original home in Galun'lati. Some of the bones were bleached white as new fallen snow, others stained and yellowed, bits of dried flesh still clinging to them like pieces of old parchment paper.

Several skeletons still resided on scaffolds raised high above the ground on wooden poles. Draped in heavy layers of mist, they looked like offerings to an unseen sun. Others lay in jumbled heaps at his feet, a mismatch assortment of bones and the tattered remains of tribal garments. Mixed in with the pieces of colored cloth and moldy leather were tarnished armbands and jewelry, mostly copper and silver, and brightly colored glass beads, the strings and sinew once holding them together long gone.

Luther paused to rest and get his bearing. A few feet from where he stood, an enormous human-like skull watched him with empty eye sockets. The skull was three times the size of a man's and had once belonged to a member of a race of giants known to Indian people as the Tall Men. It was big enough that Luther could have worn it as a helmet, had he the desire to wear such a thing on his head. In addition to its impressive size, the skull possessed a double row of teeth, top and bottom, with each molar and incisor stained black as ebony.

He wondered what the Tall Men chewed to get their teeth so shiny black, and made a mental note to ask the question should his path ever cross with a member of that tribe. The Tall Men used to sit at the Great Council, but that was before Luther's time and no one he knew had seen one of the giant people in recent years.

A few feet farther away lay a tiny skull no bigger than his fist. He thought at first it was the cranium of a child, but then noticed the pronounced ridge of bone above the eye sockets.

"Little People." Luther said and smiled.

He had met many of the Little People during his travels through Galun'lati. They were a friendly folk, but loved a good joke and could be mischievous at times—especially to those who doubted their existence. While most of the Little People had long ago returned to their original home in Galun'lati, there were still a few tribes scattered throughout the New World. One of the tribes resided in the mountains of North Carolina, and had been living there long before the Cherokee called that area home. They lived in tiny caves, and kept to the shadows, so they were rarely seen by outsiders. But every year in the fall the Little People could be heard as they held their dances and secret ceremonies upon the tops of bald mountains.

Moving cautiously among the dead, he came upon a narrow, well-worn path branching off from the overgrown trail he traveled. It might have been nothing more than a game trail leading to the den of some furry forest dweller, but he was willing to take that chance. As a Council member, he could understand animal speak and even a four-legged brother might be able to give him directions.

Luther looked up at the sky, but the mist clinging to the treetops prevented him from seeing the sun. He could not tell what time of day it was, nor which way he traveled. Better to ask directions from a creature of fur than risk wandering around in circles, especially with Coyote still sniffing at his heals.

Although the smaller trail veered away from his original path, it did not lead him out of the burial ground. If anything, it seemed to continue deeper into the heart of the eternal resting place, for the bones of the dead became even more numerous, jumbled assortments of skulls, femurs, rib bones, fingers, and toes, lying half-buried in the leaf-covered ground.

While the bones became more numerous, the wooden scaffolds soon became nonexistent, causing Luther to suspect this part of the burial ground was far older than the section traveled. He had been following the path for a good thirty minutes, or so he guessed, when he came upon a small clearing.

In the center of the clearing was a tiny cabin, with walls made of upright saplings and a bark-shingle roof. It stood only about five feet in height, reminding him of the tree forts he built as a child.

Surrounding the cabin, and making the clearing in the forest seem even smaller, were stacks and stacks of bones. Piled higher than the cabin's roof, they had been carefully divided by type, size, and apparently species.

To the left of the cabin were the skeletal remains of humans, arm and leg bones making up the base of one pile, followed by row after row of skulls—all facing outward from the center of the stack—with smaller bones stacked carefully on top of them.

To the right of that pile Luther spotted a stack of bones belonging to the beaver people, their prominent curved front teeth sharp yellow against glistening white skulls. Like the humans, the beaver people's bones had been carefully arranged in a stack that towered a good twelve feet above the ground. And beyond the stack belonging to the beaver people was a pile of carefully stacked bones dedicated to the elk tribe.

Someone had gone to a great deal of trouble to carefully stack so many piles of bones. It must have taken years to accomplish such a feat, for there were at least a hundred stacks in the tiny clearing, many rising a good twenty or thirty feet in height, leaving only narrow spaces between them to walk.

But not all the bones had been so diligently stacked, for there were numerous piles thrown together with absolutely no sense of order. Many of those stacks looked in danger of falling down, or collapsing upon themselves, and some had apparently already done so, making a portion of the clearing to the right of the cabin look like a junkyard of the dead.

Luther was still standing there, looking at the hundreds of bone piles, truly amazed by what he saw, when the cabin's tiny wooden door suddenly opened.

A little man walked out. He was terribly thin and very old, and probably stood no more than three feet tall, and with a slight stoop that made him seem even shorter. He was almost bald, the top of his leathery brown head circled by a fringe of very long white hair that cascaded down to his shoulders. He wore but a simple leather breechcloth and a strand of teeth for a necklace. His fingernails were almost as long as the fingers themselves, and stained black with dirt and grime; they were also wickedly sharp looking, like those of a cat or a bird of prey.

The tiny man with the terribly long fingernails was a member of the Little People, even though he was far more ancient than any Luther had ever seen before. He didn't notice that he had a visitor—or intruder, for the Little People relished their privacy and sometimes didn't take kindly to strangers, especially those who dropped by unannounced.

As Luther watched, the tiny man clambered spider-like up one of the messier piles of bones. He moved quickly for someone of his age, and with a grace that bespoke he had done such climbing many times before. Reaching the top of the pile, he stood and started examining the bones lying at his feet, tossing aside those that did not meet his approval.

"No. Not this one, too much work. Not this one either, too clean … This one will do nicely … And this one."

Selecting several bones to his liking, the little old man climbed down the pile. He started to go back into his cabin, but stopped and turned to stare at Luther.

"Go away. They're mine. You cannot have them back.

Luther was caught off guard by the remark. "Excuse me?"

"The bones. They belong to me now. If you've come here looking to get yours back, you cannot have them. Now go away."

"I didn't come here for bones," Luther said.

The little man cocked his head to the side and looked at him, puzzled. "You didn't?"

Luther shook his head. "No."

"You are not a spirit on the journey?"

"I'm not a spirit."

"A ghost then come to haunt me?"

"I'm not a ghost, either. I'm alive."

He looked surprised. "Alive? You cannot be alive. This is the land of shadows … the land of the dead."

"But I am alive. I am Luther Watie, member of the Great Council."

"A member of the Great Council, you say?" laughed the tiny man. "Well, Luther Watie, you are obviously lost and followed the wrong road. Now go away and leave me alone, I have work to do." With that, he took his bones and entered the cabin, slamming the door behind him.

Luther stood there, somewhat dumbfounded. This was not the kind of greeting he had expected to receive, especially in Galun'lati. But then again, it had been several years since he last visited the original world. Perhaps people here were getting just as rude as those living in the New World. He hoped not.

He turned and looked back down the path, wondering if he should turn around and go the way he came. But he knew that the giant rolling head still waited for him, and then there was also Coyote to think about. No. Going back was definitely out of the question. He needed to continue onward, but that was also a poor choice when he didn't know where onward led. He still needed directions.

Determined, Luther squared his shoulders and marched across the clearing, navigating between the towering stacks of bones until he reached the front door of the tiny cabin.

He knocked on the door.

"Go away, I said," cried the voice from inside.

Luther pushed on the little door, and it opened easily.

The inside of the cabin was just as small as its exterior. And it too was crowded with bones. Though there was nowhere near as many bones on the inside as there were on the outside, there were numerous stacks of skeletal remains scattered around the single-room dwelling.

There were bones stacked along the walls, and piled high on a wooden table. Skulls were stacked in all four corners, and circled the fire pit in the center of the dirt floor, while femurs hung from the rafters like morbid wind chimes.

The terribly small man sat hunched on a three-legged stool behind the table. He held an arm bone in his left hand, and used the long fingernails of his right hand to carefully remove dried pieces of flesh still clinging to it. He had apparently been doing so with other bones, for there was a pile of dried flesh in the center of the table.

"I said go away," the man said, annoyed at being interrupted.

"I cannot do so," Luther said, frustrated, "when I do not know which way *away* is. I am terribly sorry for bothering you, but I have not been to this part of Galun'lati before, and do not know how to get to where I need to go. Nor can I stay here, for Coyote is chasing me."

The little man paused his work, eyeing Luther suspiciously. "Coyote is chasing you?"

Luther nodded.

"Then why didn't you say so in the first place?" He jumped off his stool and hurried around from behind the table, ushering Luther into the cabin. "That miserable Trickster, he and his followers have stolen some of my finest bones. No respect for the dead."

Luther entered, careful not to hit his head on the ceiling. He was not a particularly tall man, but he had to stoop in order to stand inside the cabin.

The little man closed the door and motioned for Luther to take a seat at the table, even though there was but one chair.

Not wanting to take advantage of his host, Luther decided to sit cross-legged on the floor. He watched as the tiny man scampered around the room, grabbing a gourd filled with water and two drinking cups. He also produced a chunk of pemmican, made from dried pieces of meat mixed with berries and fat.

"You must be parched. I have water from the spring out back. And hungry too. I have pemmican, made it myself from only the tastiest pieces of meat. Eat. Drink. And then you will tell me your story. Any enemy of Coyote is a friend of mine. That beast. What has he done now? No respect for the dead, I tell you. Stole some of my finest bones."

Luther gladly accepted the cup of water, even though it had a peculiar taste, causing him to wonder how many bones might line the nearby spring. But he refused to eat any of the pemmican, claiming he was full, fearful that the tastiest pieces of meat from which it was made might in fact be pieces of dried flesh pulled from the bones of the dead.

"I am Bonepicker," said the tiny man, taking a seat on the floor beside his guest.

"That is an unusual name," Luther replied.

"It is not a name," he corrected. "That is what I do. I prepare the bones of the dead by peeling the dried flesh from them, with these." Bonepicker held up his hand, displaying his long, blackened fingernails.

Luther was glad he hadn't accepted any of the pemmican, for there were tiny pieces of dried flesh clinging to the underside of the little man's fingernails. Dried pieces of the dead.

Bonepicker clicked his fingernails together, smiling, obviously proud of his occupation. "Now, tell me. Why is Coyote chasing you?"

Luther told him about Coyote's evil plan, and what had happened to the helpless patients at the Willows Nursing Home. Bonepicker listened carefully, nodding occasionally, and throwing in a thoughtful grunt when needed. The little man became very agitated when Luther told him about his daughter.

"Your daughter prepares the dead for burial?"

Luther nodded.

"Then she too is a Bonepicker."

"Well, not exactly."

"Then I will help you," Bonepicker said, getting to his feet. He moved around the cabin, talking in an excited voice and making gestures at the air. "We must stop Coyote ... must protect your daughter. I will show you the quickest path through the forest ... tell you the location of a portal back to the New World. It will take you very close to where you want to go … very close."

Before sending him on his way, Bonepicker gave Luther a small leather bag containing pieces of dried flesh picked from various bones.

"What is this for?"

"There are many dangers along the path you must travel. And many hungry ghosts. Better they eat the flesh of the dead than the flesh of the living."

CHAPTER 19

Sarah breathed a sigh of relief as she watched the black Cadillac hearse slowly drive away with the casket containing the body of Ray Talmage.

"Thank God."

She had been on edge all morning, despite her assurance to Jack that everything was fine and the events of the previous day and evening nothing more than a fading memory, and probably nothing more to begin with than an overactive imagination.

But her memory wasn't fading, the events of the previous day still vivid in her mind. Even the Valium Jack had slipped her hadn't helped to quell her anxiety, but it had left her a little groggy around the edges that morning and with a serious case of dry mouth.

She stood in the doorway and watched the hearse until it turned the corner at the end of the street, disappearing from view.

Stepping back into the funeral home, she closed the door behind her. She stood there for a moment, her back to the door, listening to the silence around her. The only sound came from the waiting room, the gentle tick-tick of an antique brass clock perched above a rarely used fireplace.

Sarah was alone in the house for the first time in days, no grieving families waiting to fill out the forms and documents necessary to lay a loved one to rest, no one interested in buying caskets or crematory urns, no bodies needing to be drained of fluids in the embalming room, or waiting to be dressed and put on display.

Empty. All Alone.

For some reason, the thought of being alone made her nervous and a little fearful. She had never been afraid of being alone before, not even as a little girl when she would take long walks through the forest by herself, accompanied only by companions of her own imagination: knights in shining armor, wizards and witches, furious beasts, and even ghost children. Lots of ghost children.

Her fascination with the dead had started early in life, after finding a small forgotten cemetery deep in the woods. It was a single-family plot, eight simple markers enclosed by a wrought iron fence. Three of the headstones identified the graves of children, two girls and a boy, with the old-fashioned names of Abigale, Beula, and Thaddeus.

Often, she had climbed the wrought iron fence to sit at the foot of those three graves, wondering about the children buried beneath the black soil. All three were young, ranging in age from four to seven; members of the same family, whose lives had been cut short by sickness and disease. Abigale and Beula had both died of yellow fever, according to the inscriptions on their stones, while Thaddeus—the youngest of the trio—had succumbed to the dreaded measles.

Sarah spent so much time in the tiny cemetery that soon the children were real to her. She could see them clearly in her mind's eye, youngsters of flesh and blood, with wiry limbs and smiling faces. She would carry on one-sided conversations with them, telling stories, and sharing her hopes and dreams. They became her best friends, much more so than the other children at the orphanage where she lived after being taken away from her father.

The kids at the orphanage were mean, and used to tease her relentlessly. They knew what her father had done to her—at least they thought they knew—and would constantly repeat those stories in vivid detail, or make up new ones.

Because of the endless teasing, Sarah retreated into a shell, spending more time playing with the dead than with the living, wanting little to do with the other children. Her actions caused her to be labeled odd, making her a less than desirable choice for adoption. It wasn't until she was nearly eleven that a family had taken her into a real home.

And when she was finally adopted, driving away from the orphanage with her new family, she saw Abigale, Beula, and Thaddeus for one final time. They stood at the edge of the forest, waving goodbye to her. There were tears of sadness in the eyes of the three imaginary ghost children; there were also tears in Sarah's eyes, for she knew that she would never again visit her special friends deep within the forest. But she never forgot them, even when she grew too old for imaginary playmates, and it was those special memories that eventually steered her toward a job as a funeral home director, allowing her to again spend time with the dead.

And for the most part, her time with the dead had always been pleasant and rewarding—or at least had been, up until the previous day when Ray Talmage sat up and spoke to her.

The shrill ring of the office telephone sounded, startling Sarah and pushing her childhood memories back into her subconscious where they belonged.

She hurried down the hallway and into the office, grabbing the phone before its fourth ring. "William Powell Funeral Home, Sarah speaking."

"Hello. Is this Sarah Reynolds?" It was a man's voice, rich and deep, and very business sounding.

"Yes, it is," she replied, taking a seat in the leather chair behind the desk.

"Miss Reynolds. My name is Eric Kelly. I'm a special agent with the Federal Bureau of Investigation."

FBI? What could the Feds want with me? I paid my taxes.

"Yes, sir," she said, clearing her throat and sitting up straighter in her chair. It wasn't everyday that the Federal Bureau of Investigation called her. As a matter of fact, she couldn't remember ever speaking with an FBI agent before.

"Miss Reynolds ..."

"It's missus."

"My apology, Mrs. Reynolds. I'm calling to inquire if you are the daughter of one Luther Watie."

Luther?

It was the second time in less that twenty-four hours that a caller had mentioned her father's name. A chill walked slowly down her back as she thought of the mysterious call the previous evening, a phone call made by someone with a voice dipped in evil.

"Yes, sir. That's my father's name. But I haven't seen or spoken to him in years, not since I was a child. How did you get my number?"

Agent Kelly hesitated before speaking, and she could hear the sound of papers being leafed through. He was obviously looking at notes or printed pages as he spoke. "I got your name and phone number from your father's medical folder; I have it here before me. He was a patient at the Willows Nursing Home, here in North Carolina. You're listed as next of kin."

"Next of kin? Why? Has something happened?" she asked.

"Yes, ma'am. I can't go into details at the moment, but there was a homicide at the nursing home last night. Several people were killed."

"Oh, God. That's terrible."

"Yes, it is. Your father was not one of the victims, but he is a person of interest."

"You think he had something to do with the murders?"

"No. Not really. But he is missing, and we think he may have been a witness to the crimes."

"Missing?"

"We haven't been able to locate him yet, and wonder if you might be able to help. Does your father have any friends in the area, someone he might turn to in times of crisis?"

Sarah laughed.

"Something funny?" Agent Kelly asked, not sharing her humor.

"No. No. Nothing funny." She coughed. "Sorry. I shouldn't have laughed, but you're asking the wrong person. Like I said, I haven't seen or spoken to Luther Watie since I was a kid. I really don't know anything about him, or where he might be."

"Yes, ma'am. I understand. Like I said, your name was listed in his records …" The agent paused, perhaps for dramatic effect. "… and carved into the body of one of the victims."

"Someone carved my name into a body?" she asked, shocked.

"Yes, ma'am. Your name, and your father's. That's why we're looking for him, hoping he can shed some light on this situation."

"And you think he did it?"

"We're not sure, but we don't think so. Your father was an elderly man in a nursing home. Whoever did this had to be quite strong, because some of the victims are young adult males. I doubt a man in his seventies could have murdered them, not without a gun, and they weren't killed by a firearm. They died violently."

"Jesus." Sarah's thoughts were spinning, causing her head to pound. "Listen, I don't think I can help you."

"Do you know a Michael Blackwing?" Agent Kelly interrupted.

"Who?"

"Michael Blackwing? Do you know anybody by that name?"

She thought for a moment. "No. I don't think … As a matter of fact, I'm sure I don't know anyone by that name. I have a pretty good memory for names; it's a necessary part of my job, and a name like Blackwing would be hard to forget. Was his name also carved into a body?"

"Yes, Mrs. Reynolds. It was."

"Jesus. Sorry. I didn't mean to sound flippant, it's just that—"

"I understand, Ma'am. Listen, I won't take up any more of your time. You've really been a big help. I'd like to give you my name and personal cell phone number. Your father may be running scared. Can't blame him after what he's seen. He may try to get in touch with you—"

"Crap." Sarah said, interrupting the agent.

"You remember something?"

"Yes, sir," she replied. "I probably should have said this sooner, but your call caught me off guard. It's been crazy around here the last couple of days. I got a phone call late last night. The caller I.D. said it came from North Carolina."

"Was it your father?" Agent Kelly asked, very interested.

"No. I don't think so, but I can't be sure. He said he wasn't my father."

"The caller was a man?"

She nodded, then realized her gesture could not be seen over the phone. "Yes, sir. It was a man. But he didn't sound elderly, not what I'd expect my father to sound like."

"But you can't be sure."

"No. But I remember my father speaking with a strong accent. He's Cherokee Indian, born and raised on the reservation in North Carolina. Sometimes people had a hard time understanding him, especially white people. The man who called me last night didn't have an accent, he just sounded ..."

Sarah paused, remembering the voice of the caller from the previous evening.

"He just sounded evil."

"Evil?"

"It's hard to explain. His voice was spooky smooth, and as cold as ice. It's what I would expect the devil to sound like."

"Or a killer."

"Or a killer," she agreed, swallowing hard. "He said he was coming for me. No. No. Not he. The man on the phone said *we* will be coming for you."

"Then there may be more than one," Agent Kelly said, more to himself than to her.

She looked around. It was early in the day, but the west side of the house was still draped in heavy shadows. As she spoke, the shadows seemed to grow darker, reaching out for her from the corners of the room.

"Am I in danger?" Sarah wanted to flee the shadows and rush out into the bright light of day. She felt chilled, a cold that came from deep inside her, and wanted to warm herself in the Florida sun.

The FBI agent did not respond, and Sarah felt the skin at her temples pull tight in fear.

"Agent Kelly, am I in danger?" she asked again.

"We're not sure, Mrs. Reynolds. If you want, I can arrange for you to be placed in protective custody."

"What about my husband? I won't go without him."

"Your husband too, if necessary."

Sarah thought about it a moment, but decided against the idea. She did not want to be placed in protective custody, nor did she want to continue her conversation with the FBI agent. What she wanted was her husband. She was suddenly very much afraid, and wanted to call Jack.

"That's okay," she said, quickly composing her thoughts. "I appreciate your offer, Agent Kelly, but I don't think our being placed in protective custody will be necessary. Besides, I have a business to run and just can't go into hiding. Florida is a long way from North Carolina; I'm sure we'll be safe enough."

"If you change your mind—"

"No. No. It won't be necessary." She wanted to end the call and hang up. "Listen, I wish I could be of more help, but I've told you everything I know. You have my number, so you know how to reach me if you have any more questions."

"Please, let me give you my number," said the agent. "That way you can call me if you think of anything else."

Sarah waited while Agent Kelly gave her his phone number. "Okay. Got it. I'll call you if I think of anything."

"Or if you get another phone call from North Carolina."

"That too."

"Thank you, Mrs. Reynolds, for your time."

"You're quite welcome, Agent Kelly. You have a nice day now. Goodbye."

She didn't wait for the agent to say goodbye before hanging up. She waited a moment, then lifted the receiver and started to call Jack. But she stopped, deciding it would be better to talk with her husband in person. Getting up, she grabbed her car keys and headed for the front door. Next stop: Greenwood Cemetery.

CHAPTER 20

Though it seemed endless, the burial ground finally came to an end. There was no fence or dividing marker, nothing to identify the boundary of the ancient graveyard, but Luther finally realized he was no longer stepping on or over bones and broken pieces of scaffolding.

He turned and looked behind him, grateful to no longer be in the land of the dead, but concerned what other perils might lay before him. And as he stood there, he suddenly remembered the giant head that had earlier pursued him, fearful it had circled the burial ground and now waited for him somewhere along the trail.

Luther swallowed nervously. The head had threatened to eat him. Not that he would make much of a meal, being elderly and thin, but even a skinny Indian didn't want to end up as part of the food chain.

Gazing hard into the shadowy underbrush along the trail, he searched for the boulder-sized head. But there was no sign of the monstrous creature, and he suspected it had given up the chase—or still waited where he had left it—hoping to pounce upon him on his return trip through the forest.

"But there will be no return trip," he said aloud, appreciating the sound of his own voice. The woods around him were eerily quiet, making him uneasy. Where had all the forest dwellers gone? Where were the creatures of fur and feathers who had always delighted and entertained him on his previous journeys through the old world? It was as if they had all taken the day off. Maybe this part of Galun'lati was only for the dead, which would make his passage even more unwelcome.

The elderly Cherokee had journeyed through Galun'lati many times during his life, but his trips had always been in areas well-traveled by others.

But the region he now walked was the land of the dead, a place for spirits, ghosts, and creatures long forgotten by the members of the Great Council and other residents of Galun'lati. It was a place of strong medicine and magic, but that medicine was not always the good kind. Things of darkness traveled this land: original beings who had chosen to shun the light, spirits cursed for stepping off the path before reaching the other side, witches and some of the most dangerous skin-walkers.

When the original people and animals left Galun'lati and went into the New World, creatures and things of darkness moved into the lands they vacated. And when some of the tribes gave up on the New World and returned to Galun'lati, there had been a fight for territory, a virtual battle between good and evil, with the creatures of darkness pushed into the land of the dead.

Bonepicker's warning had not fallen on deaf ears. Luther had heard the stories about the dark places in Galun'lati and the creatures who inhabited them. Those stories had been taught to him by his grandfather, and often retold by the storytellers of various tribes before the roaring fire of the Great Council. Always before the warmth and comfort of the fire, for to tell such tales in the darkness would bring a shiver of fear to even the bravest of heart.

Satisfied that nothing waited to pounce upon him, giant rolling head or otherwise, Luther squared his shoulders and continued his journey through the original world, anxious to leave the land of the dead as quickly as possible and get back to more familiar trails.

He was thinking deep thoughts about his plight, and what he would say to his daughter when they met, when from somewhere off to his left came the haunting cry of a woodpecker. Luther slowed his pace, listening carefully.

The cry was answered a few moments later by a second woodpecker, calling out from somewhere farther down the trail. Luther had the gift of animal speak, yet he could not understand what was being said by the two woodpeckers, so he knew the calls were not made by real birds. On the contrary, they were instead made by someone, or something, doing a really bad imitation of a woodpecker.

A tingle of fear marched down his back. He reached into his front pants pocket, his fingers tightening around the pitifully small pocketknife that was his only means of protection. He longed for some kind of firearm, the bigger the better, or a good old-fashioned bow and arrow, even though he hadn't much experience with a bow and probably couldn't hit the broad side of a barn. Despite Hollywood's depiction of the noble savage, not all Indians could shoot a bow, ride a horse, or throw a tomahawk.

Continuing cautiously down the trail, he kept a sharp watch on both sides of the path. He heard no more woodpecker calls, real or otherwise, and was just beginning to breathe a little easier when the animated skeletons of two men suddenly emerged from the forest.

At least he assumed they were the skeletons of men, for both were very tall and dressed in breechcloths, moccasins, and necklaces of glass beads. And they wore flint knives that hung in sheaths at their belts, and carried painted war clubs of wood.

He was surprised by the sudden appearance of the living, animated skeletons, but he wasn't horrified. Nor was he completely shocked, for he had seen many strange things during his previous travels through Galun'lati: talking animals, Little People, ancient beings, and even ghosts. What were a couple of living skeletons in the midst of such strangeness? Why, they might even be expected, especially when traveling through the land of the dead.

The skeletons stepped fully upon the trail, completely blocking his path. Luther cast a quick glance back down the trail, and thought about turning and making a run for it. But he doubted if he would be able to outrun the bony warriors. Instead, he continued walking, only stopping when he reached the two skeletons blocking his path.

"I am He Who Kills," proclaimed the taller of the two skeletons, clacking his bony jaw and waving his wooden war club proudly in the air.

"And I am his brother, Makes Them Cry," said the second skeleton, curling his fingers into fists and putting them on his hips in bony defiance.

"I am Luther Watie, a member of the Great Council," he replied. "I come in peace, and ask that I be allowed to continue on my way."

"A member of the Great Council, you say?" laughed Makes Them Cry. "The Council does not meet for another moon. Why do you travel through the land of the dead?"

Luther thought quickly, choosing his words carefully. He did not want the warriors to know he was on the run from Coyote, for the Trickster had many friends in dark places. Instead, he dropped a name that carried great weight throughout all of Galun'lati. "I carry an important message for Bear, chief of the Great Council."

"A message for Bear," challenged He Who Kills, sticking out his hand. "Give it to me. I will see that it is delivered."

"I cannot do that," replied Luther, "for the message I am to deliver is in my head."

"Then Bear can fish the message from your skull when we deliver your head to him." He Who Kills took a threatening step forward, raising his war club. But Makes Them Cry placed a hand on his shoulder, stopping him.

Makes Him Cry whispered to his brother, pointing at the small leather bag hanging from Luther's Belt.

"That bag belongs to Bonepicker," He Who Kills said, pointing. "I recognize the design."

Luther touched the bag. "Yes. The bag is Bonepicker's. He gave it to me."

"What does it contain?" asked Makes Them Cry.

"Sweet treats perhaps?" added He Who Kills.

"Perhaps," nodded Luther.

Again, the skeletons whispered to each other, pointing and gesturing toward the bag of Bonepicker. Luther tried to hear what they were saying, but they spoke in low voices and he could not make out their words.

"It is not safe for a member of the Great Council to be walking through this forest alone," said He Who Kills, his voice suddenly as smooth as honey.

"No. No. Not safe at all," added Makes Them Cry, nodding in agreement with his brother.

"So, we have decided to offer you our protection, and accompany you on your journey," continued He Who Kills.

"Offer our protection," chimed his brother.

Luther took a step back, shocked. "No. No. Thank you, but that won't be necessary. I wouldn't want to trouble you, or take you out of your way."

"No trouble," said He Who Kills. "We insist."

"Insist," added Makes Them Cry.

Luther was in a real predicament, but he knew not what to do. The two living skeletons were not going to let him continue on his way alone, and he doubted if they would allow him to turn around and go back the way he came. They were dangerous, most likely cannibals. If he did not allow them to accompany him, they would probably kill him and eat his flesh.

Not wanting to end up as a midday meal, and having no means of escape at his disposal, he decided to accept their offer and play along with their game. Hopefully, they were more interested in the contents of Bonepicker's bag than they were in him.

"Well, if you insist." Luther cleared his throat. "Then we will make the journey together."

He Who Kills and Makes Them Cry stepped aside, allowing him to pass between them. They quickly fell in behind him, flanking Luther and making any chance of escape impossible. As they walked, he tried to engage the skeletons in conversation, hoping to learn their plans for him, but neither seemed willing to communicate and limited dialogue to an occasional grunt.

They had been walking for several hours, when He Who Kills and Makes Them Cry began to grow tired of the friendly charade, exchanging sneaky glances. Luther pretended not to notice, but knew the bony duo were up to no good.

"We have walked far enough." Makes Them Cry yawned. "I am tired and need to rest."

"I too am tired," Luther replied, playing along. "And I am very thirsty. We need to find someplace where I can drink."

"There is a small stream up ahead," He Who Kills said, annoyed. "We can rest there."

About half a mile farther along the trail, they came to a place where a small stream crossed the path.

"There, old man. Drink," He Who Kills ordered. "We will rest here."

Luther approached the tiny stream, kneeling down beside it. He cupped his right hand and dipped it into the water, shaking his head. "This is no good. The stream is too shallow. The water is muddy."

"It will not kill you," said Makes Them Cry.

"I cannot drink this," argued Luther. "I am an old man; I will choke. We must find deeper water."

"Where?" asked He Who Kills.

"There." Luther pointed. "Deeper in the forest." Before either of the skeleton warriors could protest, he got to his feet and left the trail to follow the stream.

"Wait!" shouted Makes Them Cry, but Luther did not wait. He plunged deeper into the woods, following the tiny stream, the wheels in his mind turning as he desperately tried to come up with a plan to rid himself of his unwanted traveling companions.

About two hundred yards from the trail, the ground suddenly slopped downward for a few feet and then leveled out again. Here the tiny stream widened and formed a deep pool. The pool was surrounded by a tiny clearing, perhaps made by animals coming to drink over the years. Next to the pool stood a large oak tree, one of its lower branches stretching out over the water.

"Perfect," Luther said aloud, not realizing his unwanted companions were behind him.

"What was that?" asked Makes Them Cry. "What did you say?"

"I said this is perfect," Luther answered, thinking quickly.

He Who Kills looked around. "Then we will rest here. Drink, old man."

Luther did not have to be told twice. He really was very thirsty. Kneeling down beside the water, he drank from the pool until he had his fill. Having neither a thirst, nor any reason to drink water, the two skeleton brothers took a seat on the ground a few yards back from the pool and watched while the old man drank.

"Mmmm ... that was good." Luther wiped a hand across his mouth. "So clear, so cold." He walked over to where the skeletons sat, taking a seat before them. "Now, if we only had something to eat ..."

He Who Kills and Makes Them Cry leaned forward in eager anticipation, looking at the bag hanging from Luther's belt. Had they lips, they probably would have licked them. Or perhaps drooled over them.

Snapping his fingers, Luther said. "I know what we can eat. I completely forgot all about it. Foolish me."

Deliberately taking his time, and making a show out of it, Luther slowly removed Bonepicker's bag from his belt. Opening the bag, he shook out some of the dried pieces of flesh into his hand and offered them to He Who Kills and his brother. He didn't take any for himself, despite being a little hungry. There were just some things he was not willing to eat, even in Galun'lati.

"So good ... so very good." He Who Kills tossed the tiny pieces of flesh into his mouth and chewed. Luther expected to see the pieces fall from behind his jaw bone, for the skeleton did not have a mouth or throat, not even a stomach, but they did not fall to the ground, seeming to vanish as he chewed.

"Mmmm ... such flavor," Makes Them Cry added, delighted with the tasty treat.

As the skeletons enjoyed their lunch, Luther stood and stretched and then casually walked over to the pool of water. He cast a glance behind him, making sure the two warriors were not watching him, then climbed the oak tree and shimmed out onto the limb hanging over the water.

He tied the cord of Bonepicker's bag to a small branch protruding from the underside of the limb. The pouch hung several feet below the limb, and only a few feet above the surface of the water. Double-checking to make sure it was securely tied, Luther crawled back along the limb and climbed down.

Hurrying back to where the skeletons sat, Luther again took a seat on the ground. Neither of them had noticed him get up, so thoroughly were they enjoying the flesh of the dead.

"More," Makes Them Cry said, holding his empty hand out for Luther to refill.

"Yes. More," added He Who Kills, not wanting to miss out on seconds.

"We will eat more later." Luther yawned, pretending to be sleepy. "We will rest first."

He Who Kills started to argue, then noticed that Luther no longer wore Bonepicker's leather bag.

"What have you done with it?" he asked, obviously upset.

"What have I done with what?" Luther faked another yawn.

"What have you done with the bag of Bonepicker?" asked Makes Them Cry, also noticing the bag was missing.

"Oh, that." Luther acted indifferent. "I hung it where it will be safe." He casually pointed a thumb over his shoulder at the tree beside the pool.

The two brothers were very upset when they spotted the bag containing the tasty meat hanging over the water, and clacked their teeth in anger. Luther ignored their protests and clacking, laying down on the ground.

"Now. If you will excuse me, I want to take a nap. We will eat more later. I've saved the tastiest pieces of meat for our next meal."

Stretching out on the ground, Luther closed his eyes and pretended to take a nap. But he watched his companions through slitted eyelids, amused at their anger.

"Look what he has done," hissed Makes Them Cry, keeping his voice low.

"It is a dirty trick," whispered his brother.

"Yes. A dirty trick."

"But he will not get away with it." He Who Kills turned to look at

Luther, studying the gentle rise and fall of the old man's chest. "Look. He already sleeps."

"Yes. He sleeps." Makes Them Cry pulled the flint knife from his belt. "Let us kill him and eat his flesh."

He Who Kills laid a bony hand on his brother's wrist, stopping him. "Wait, brother. There will be plenty of time for that later. Let us first steal the bag of Bonepicker, and the tasty treats it must contain."

Makes Them Cry put away his knife, nodding. "Bonepicker's tasty treats.

The skeletons slowly crept away from the clearing, careful not to wake Luther. Reaching the oak tree, they carefully climbed up and shimmied out onto the big limb hanging over the water. Makes Them Cry went first, with his brother following close behind.

Reaching the end of the limb, Makes Them Cry reached out for the leather bag tied to the little branch protruding from the underside of the limb. As he did, He Who Kills happened to look down and see the reflection in the water.

There in the reflection were two skeleton warriors, and one of them was reaching out to steal the bag of Bonepicker.

"Brother, look there!" shouted He Who Kills. "Two warriors are trying to steal our bag."

"I see them!" Makes Them Cry yelled. "Don't let them get it."

"I won't." He Who Kills pulled the war club from his belt. "Go away, thieves. The bag is ours."

Makes Them Cry also pulled his club. "Stay back or die."

Both skeletons yelled war cries and swung their clubs, not realizing they were seeing their own reflections. The limb to which they clung shook violently, causing them to lose their grip and fall.

He Who Kills and Makes Them Cry were still yelling and swinging their clubs when they splashed into the pool, quickly disappearing beneath the surface of the water.

Hearing the yelling, and the splash, Luther jumped up and hurried to the pool. He watched the two brothers disappear beneath the water, waiting for them to reappear. A few minutes passed, but the surface of the water remained calm. He Who Kills and Makes Them Cry were nowhere to be seen. Being skeletons, they obviously couldn't swim and had sunk to the very bottom of the pool.

Luther smiled. "Foolish warriors, did you think I was too old to have any tricks of my own?" He thought about climbing the tree and retrieving the leather bag of Bonepicker, but decided to leave it where it hung.

Turning his back, Luther continued his journey through Galun'lati

CHAPTER 21

They had flown through the night, the sun already high in the sky as they passed over Fort Bragg, North Carolina. Below them, men and women in military uniforms went about their daily routine, many training or performing duties that would keep the country safe during times of war. Home of the 82nd Airborne, the families living on the base knew what it was like to send loved ones off to the most dangerous parts of the world.

"Can't we stop to rest?" Mouse complained, wiggling around on Raven's back. "I'm tired."

Throughout the trip Mouse had complained about being tired, even though it was Raven who did all the flying.

"We will rest soon enough," Raven replied, turning his head slightly so his furry traveling partner could hear him. "Now stop wiggling around before you fall."

Raven flapped his wings with a steady rhythm, trying to ignore the pain that settled between his shoulders. Little Mouse had kept his word, and during their flight he had used his long soft tongue to clean the wound inflicted by Owl.

The wound no longer bled, and was already beginning to heal, but the rodent's tongue did absolutely nothing for the pain. Nor did it do anything to alleviate the weakness Raven felt from the blood loss. He would need to rest, and soon, but each and every minute was vital, and he could not afford to pause when Luther and his daughter were in danger.

"I'm hungry too," Mouse chided, filling Raven's ear with his annoying squeaking.

"You are already overweight," Raven replied. "It will do you good to skip a meal or two."

"Hmmmp," Mouse said, indignant. "I am not overweight. I am storing fat for the winter."

Raven laughed. "Storing fat for the winter? It is the middle of March. Winter is many months away."

"It is never too soon to prepare," replied Mouse. "It would not do you any harm to store some fat. You are too skinny, nothing but feathers and bones, a most uncomfortable ride. You need a good layer of fat beneath your skin, then you will be as comfortable as a bed in a human house. Ah, talk about something easy on the backside. So soft, so very warm. I once spent a winter sleeping in such a bed. The owners were away, perhaps visiting relatives. And their pantry ... such food. So many tasty treats. Cookies and crackers, and potato chips. I do love potato chips ..."

Raven listened to Mouse's endless banter, amused. While the little rodent couldn't help with the flying, he did keep him entertained with a humorous monologue—when he wasn't complaining. In human form, Raven might have been wearing headphones, listening to music stored on an iPod or MP3 player. But in bird form, all he had was Mouse.

As his traveling companion talked, never getting tired of his own voice, Raven studied the scenery below. Three C-130 cargo planes sat on the main runway of Pope Air Force Base, located adjacent to Fort Bragg, their turbo-prop engines running. A brigade of men stood near the planes, awaiting orders. They wore camouflage uniforms, helmets, and parachute backpacks.

"Must be jump day," Raven said, interrupting Mouse's banter about food and comfortable beds.

"Jump day?"

"There. Below." Raven pointed with his beak. "See the men lined up? They are going to go up real high in those airplanes and jump out."

"Jump out?" Mouse squeaked, unbelieving. "Why on earth would they want to do that?"

"It is what they do."

Mouse wiggled his whiskers, peeking over Raven's shoulder to get a better look at what was going on below. "I swear, I will never understand humans. They do the dumbest things."

Raven laughed. "But look at you, my furry little friend. You are riding on the back of a bird, a wounded bird at that. Some would say that is also quite foolish."

"But I am riding, not jumping. I am very safe."

"Oh? But what if I were to tire, or change directions suddenly. You might fall off. Like this—"

Raven dipped his right wing a little, causing Mouse to slip. The little rodent squeaked in terror, his tiny feet digging deeper into black feathers. A twinge of pain shot through Raven's back as one of Mouse's toe nails scrapped across the open wound.

"Don't do that!" Mouse shouted, angry. "I almost fell off."

"See. Humans are no more foolish than you," Raven chuckled. "Whoever heard of a mouse flying on a raven? Now, if you're done talking about what you ate last winter, my wound needs cleaning again."

Mouse started to protest, but decided against it and began cleaning Raven's wound. His tongue was warm and wet, like a rodent version of a sponge bath. Below them, the bases gave way to the town of Fayetteville, which would probably not exist were it not for the military.

Raven had been to Fayetteville many times before, in both human and bird form, and knew that Interstate 95 passed just east of the city. He wasn't planning on stealing another car, not when transforming back into human form would leave him naked in the middle of the day. But he was hoping that he could hitch a ride with someone.

Reaching Interstate 95, he turned and headed south. A few minutes later, Raven spotted a Department of Transportation weigh station. Two semi-trucks were lined up, and another was pulling off the highway to join the party, but all three trucks pulled boxcar type trailers, which did him absolutely no good. He could not ride on top of the trailers, not when the trucks would be traveling an average speed of seventy miles an hour. The wind would beat him half to death, or tear out more feathers than he could afford to lose. No. Those trucks were out of the question. He would have to find something else.

Just then, he noticed a truck leaving the weigh station, trying to pick up speed in order to merge back into the highway traffic. The big semi was pulling a flat-bed trailer loaded with 55-gallon barrels.

"Perfect," Raven said aloud, flapping his wings as hard as he could, desperately trying to catch up to the truck before it picked up more speed.

He called over his shoulder to Mouse, "Hold on."

Mouse dug his toes deeper into Raven's feathers, clutching at his skin. He hunkered lower, squinting his eyes, making himself less wind resistant.

Raven flapped harder, catching up with the truck and landing on one of the barrels. Soon as he landed, Mouse jumped off his back and scurried down the barrel, disappearing from view.

The wind increased as the semi gained speed and reentered the highway, so Raven also left the barrel and flew down to the floor of the trailer. He looked around, but did not see his furry traveling companion.

"Mouse, where did you go?" he called out, but received no answer. A few minutes later, Mouse reappeared from between two barrels carrying a half-eaten Snickers he had found.

"Mmmm ... peanuts." Mouse twitched his ears in delight, tearing the paper from the candy bar. "Nougat ... chewy center ... chocolate ..."

"Hey, save some for me," Raven cried. "I too am hungry."

CHAPTER 22

Bonepicker sat cross-legged on the dirt floor in the center of his cabin. In his left hand he carefully and lovingly cradled the femur of a long dead woman, tiny strips of dried flesh and little hairs still clinging to the bone.

With the long, blackened nails of an index finger and thumb, he carefully picked at the pieces, tearing them off the bone as one would gently remove a Band-Aid from a painful wound. He placed the pieces in the clay jar beside his feet, occasionally picking up the jar and shaking it to even out the growing pile of dead flesh.

He cheerfully hummed as he worked, a little ditty he had learned far back in the days of his youth, a treasured sonnet taught to him by his dear mother. Bonepicker's mother often sang to him when he was young, and the tune he now hummed had been one of her favorites. He felt it was only fitting he should bring forth that melody now as he worked, for it was his mother's femur that he held lovingly in his hand, and her dried flesh he peeled, carefully collecting each piece in the jar at his feet.

His mother had died in the early days of summer, her frail body no longer able to fend off a sickness carried to her on the wings of a mosquito. Bonepicker paused his song, carefully studying the bone he held, a slight frown tugging at the corners of his mouth. The tiny woman who had given him life had always seemed so strong; it was almost unthinkable that she had succumbed to one of the Creator's smallest creatures. But even the smallest of the forest dwellers could be deadly, especially in the hot summer months when water stood in stagnant pools.

The sickness that finally took her soul had laid upon her for weeks, stealing the beauty from her face and the color from her hair. While not a young woman, especially by the standards of Little People, she still had the black of night in her hair up until illness fell upon her.

The elders of his village had brought her to him early one morning, her body wrapped in buckskin the color of ripened wheat. They had laid her body at his feet, making the solemn journey back to their mountain home. Bonepicker had waited until he was alone, then he had wept openly, and sliced his chest in mourning with a flint knife. And when the blood had stopped flowing, the wound scabbing over, he had cut a dozen narrow saplings, building a scaffold to place her body upon.

His mother's body had laid atop the wooden platform for months and months, fully exposed to the elements. She had been cleansed by the falling rain, warmed by the sun, and kissed by the wind. Birds had fed upon her flesh, and tiny insects had made their homes beneath her clothing, seeking out hidden cavities and orifices.

And when the scaffold finally weathered, collapsing to the ground during a particularly windy day, he had sorted bones from weathered wood, carefully gathering together the remains of his beloved mother and placing her in a wicker basket. The basket had sat beside the fire pit in this cabin, awaiting the day when he could fully devote his attention to preparing her bones for a proper burial.

Bonepicker peeled off another strip of flesh from the femur and brought it to his nose, inhaling its aroma. It smelled of sunshine and green forests, reminding him of quiet paths where lovers might walk. He thought about tasting the tiny piece, but resisted the urge. It would be wrong for him to do so, no matter how tasty his mother might be.

Dropping the dried piece of flesh into the jar, he went back to humming happily. He only had a few more pieces to clean, then he would arrange the bones carefully in a basket and return them to his mother's village. There her remains would be buried, with much ceremony and celebration. He thought about burying them near his cabin, but was afraid they would become lost among all the other bones surrounding his humble abode.

He set aside the now clean femur, and started to reach for another bone, when he heard movement outside his cabin. Bonepicker paused and listened carefully, hearing the sound of something sniffing around the door.

The sniffing continued for a few more moments, then the wooden door slowly swung inward. Standing in the doorway was Coyote.

Bonepicker smiled. "Ah, Trickster. I thought that might be you."

Coyote gave a wicked grin and entered the cabin. His gaze darted quickly around the cluttered room, falling back upon the little man seated on the floor.

"My dear, Bonepicker. How very good it is to see you again. It has been much too long since our last visit." Again Coyote glanced around the room. "I am searching for someone …"

Bonepicker made the motion of looking about the room. "As you can see, my old friend, there is no one here but me."

Coyote nodded, the wicked grin staying etched upon his lips. He sniffed. "The one I seek was here earlier. I can smell him. His stench lingers on the air."

"There are a lot of smells here." Bonepicker shrugged indifferently. "Perhaps it is an old girlfriend that you smell, or maybe a family member."

Coyote's grin faded. He lunged forward, his hackles raised in anger. He towered over Bonepicker, his lips pulled back to reveal deadly fangs. "Do not toy with me, little man. I have no patience for such games. Which way did the old man go? Where does he travel? Tell me what I want to know or—"

"Or what? You'll kill me?" Bonepicker laughed. "Your threats do not scare me, Trickster. Can't you tell that the dead already know my name?"

Bonepicker grabbed a handful of dirt off the floor and threw it in the Trickster's face. Coyote roared in rage, his eyes filled with dirt and unable to see. He lunged forward and snapped blindly, but the little man jumped out of the way and raced for the open door.

Grabbing his tiny spear from where it hung on the wall, he fled from the cabin and raced down the same path Luther Watie had traveled.

Behind him, Coyote howled in anger and snapped at empty air.

CHAPTER 23

Sarah drove through the entrance gates of Greenwood Cemetery a little after 4:00 p.m. that Friday afternoon, pulling into an empty parking space in front of the office building.

Turning off the ignition, she lowered the visor and studied her reflection in a tiny lighted mirror. She had applied makeup while driving, a bad habit she picked up during her college days, but she was unable to hide the shadows under her eyes. The last couple of days had been rough and it showed. She needed a rest. Hell, she needed a vacation. Maybe she and Jack could go on a cruise to Mexico. She envisioned herself sitting on a sandy beach sipping a Corona beer, just like in all those commercials they showed on primetime television.

"You can't afford a vacation," she said aloud, flipping the visor back up. It wasn't the money. She and Jack both made good money at their jobs, and had been able to stash away a nice little nest egg. It was the inability to take off from work at that time of year. Not having a full-time staff at the funeral home, she couldn't just close up shop any time she wanted to get out of town. And Jack worked for the city, in the records section of City Hall in the morning and at the cemetery during the afternoon, so it was nearly impossible for him to get away without giving at least three weeks' notice.

"So much for Mexico." She pulled the keys from the ignition and stepped out of the car, closing and locking the driver's door. After entering the office building, she paused to allow her eyes to adjust to the sudden change in lighting.

The lobby could pass for a waiting room in any doctor's or dentist's office, decorated with two matching sofas and a pair of end tables. A couple of art prints hung on the wall, along with several framed newspaper articles about Greenwood, featuring photos of Jack in various poses.

Sarah smiled. Her husband was something of a camera whore, especially when it came to the press. It was something she had gotten used to over the years.

The wall running along the left side of the room featured a mural of the front gates of Greenwood, painted by a local artist years earlier. It was a beautiful mural, but rarely noticed by the grieving families that came to the cemetery.

Straight ahead of her was a sliding glass window that looked in on Jack's office. The window was closed and the room lights turned off, which meant he was probably out on property somewhere.

To her immediate left was another sliding glass window, this one open. Through it she could see Anna Santos seated behind her desk, talking with a customer on the telephone. Anna flashed Sarah a big smile, motioning for her to come into the office.

Anna was born and raised in Argentina, but had been living in the United States for the past twenty years. The attractive brunette served as secretary, receptionist, salesman, complaint department, and on many occasions a grief counselor. She handled all of the Spanish-speaking families that came to Greenwood, and in recent years that demography was growing ever larger. She also handled many of the English-speaking families, especially since Jack usually didn't arrive at the graveyard until after lunch.

Crossing the lobby, Sarah entered the main office just as Anna hung up the telephone.

"How you doing?" Anna came around the desk to give her a big hug. She smelled slightly of orange blossoms.

"Good. Good." Sarah returned the hug, and then stepped back. "How are you doing? I heard what happened."

Anna shook her head, her smile slipping off her face. "So sad. Poor Sonny. He was still very young. It's been very crazy here today. A reporter from the Orlando Sentinel keeps calling, wanting to talk with Jack."

"I guess that's one news story he doesn't want to frame and put on the wall," Sarah commented. "Definitely bad for business."

"I don't know. We've been busy today. Maybe they heard about the suicide and want to come here now." Anna shrugged. "Who knows? People are crazy. You want some coffee? My daughter brought it back from Argentina last week."

Sarah shook her head. "No. Thank you. I've been jittery enough lately. The last thing I need is a cup of strong coffee."

"It's not strong."

"Not strong for you," she said, laughing, "but you were raised on the stuff. Half a cup of your coffee and I'll be up all night. And believe me, I've been up enough lately."

She knew Anna was busy, and didn't want to take up too much of her time. "Is Jack around, or did he go back to City Hall? I didn't see his truck parked out back."

"He's still here." Anna nodded. "He's out in Unit 8, talking with Miss Grady."

"Oh, God. What is that woman complaining about now?"

Miss Grady was one of those people who had nothing nice to say to anyone. She owned four spaces in one of the newer sections of the cemetery, her mother and father already buried there. Not a week went by that she didn't find something to bitch about.

She usually fussed about the irrigation system, claiming the sprinklers didn't hit her spaces. Jack had already personally demonstrated on several occasions that the sprinklers did indeed hit her property, but that wasn't good enough. To win the argument, she took a screwdriver and broke the head off one of the pop-up sprinklers when nobody was looking.

Miss Grady was a mean woman, pure evil, which made it hard to believe that she taught fourth grade at an elementary school in Orlando. Sarah hoped the woman was much nicer to the children than she was to Jack and Anna, but she imagined Miss Grady was just as nasty to kids.

"Miss Grady is fussing about the grass again," Anna said, shaking her head. "The caretakers replanted fresh sod on her spaces, but she doesn't think it's growing fast enough."

"Tell her if she doesn't like it, go hire someone to replace it."

"Not that easy. She's threatening to go to City Hall again."

At that moment, the side door opened and Jack entered, striding angrily toward the main office, his cowboy boots echoing off the tile floor. He spotted Sarah with Anna, but the frown did not leave his face.

"That woman is crazy," he said aloud, making sure the lobby and office was devoid of customers or grieving families before speaking out. "Anna, call the sod company and have them deliver another pallet this week."

Anna touched Sarah lightly on the shoulder, then walked back behind her desk and took a seat. She picked up the telephone. "The sod company won't deliver less than two pallets."

"Then make it two."

"The caretakers won't be happy. They just threw two pallets."

"I don't care. That woman is driving me nuts. Her grass is a little brown, and if we don't replace it she's going to call the commissioner."

"Tell her to go to hell." Sarah grinned. "I would."

"You're not government. We have to play by different rules."

He strode across the room to the coffeemaker and filled an empty Styrofoam cup with cold coffee, took a sip, grimaced at the bitter taste, then turned his attention to his wife.

"So. What brings you to Greenwood?" he asked, the anger in his voice already fading. "Another body sit up and talk?"

Sarah flashed a quick glance at Anna, not knowing what Jack had already said and reluctant to talk in front of her. But Anna was busy speaking to someone at the sod company, and wasn't paying attention to their conversation.

"No. But I did receive a rather troubling phone call."

"Oh? From who?"

She again threw a glance in Anna's direction, then turned her attention back to Jack. "I was hoping you could take off early so we could talk about it. Maybe grab an early dinner somewhere."

Jack shook his head. "No can do. I've got a history tour tonight. Remember?"

"Oh. That's right. The tour." She had completely forgotten about it. Once a month, on the Friday closest to the full moon, Jack gave a two-hour walking tour through the historic sections of the cemetery, pointing out the final resting places of Orlando's founding fathers, mayors, and various city leaders. Greenwood was a who's who of the dead, with many of the permanent residents having city streets, schools and even entire neighborhoods named after them. The tours were very popular with the locals, especially those with a fondness for history. For others, it was a chance to take pictures in a spooky graveyard at night, hoping to catch a ghostly apparition—or even just an orb—on film.

"There's no way I can take off early," he said. "I've still got a few things to finish up before tonight."

"Did a lot of people sign up for the tour?"

"Almost eighty, so I'm expecting at least sixty people tonight."

"That's a lot—"

An ear-splitting scream suddenly split the room, causing Sarah and Jack to jump. Anna stood behind her desk, telephone still clutched in her hand, pointing in terror at a dead lizard on top of her desk. Someone—no doubt, one of the caretakers—had hidden the little brown anole beneath an interment order, and she had just moved the paper and discovered the surprise.

"Jesus, Anna," he said. "You scared the hell out of me."

Sarah just laughed.

Anna pointed at the lizard, horrified. "Jack ... take it away."

Despite living in Florida for over twenty years, a state with millions and millions of anoles running freely, she was still terrified of the tiny lizards. Her fear was a great source of amusement for the caretakers, and about once every other month a dead or sometimes alive lizard would find its way into the office.

"Jack ..."

He shrugged. "Sorry, Anna. It's not my lizard. I didn't put it there, so I'm not going to remove it. Call the caretakers."

Telling her to "call" the caretakers reminded Anna that she had been on the phone when she screamed. She quickly put the receiver to her ear, explaining to the person on the other end of the line what had happened and apologizing for the ear-splitting shriek. "I'm so sorry ..."

"Let's go into my office," Jack said to Sarah and smiled. "It will be quieter there."

Sarah nodded, following him out of the room. "Bye, Anna."

Jack unlocked the door and entered his office, flipping on the lights. He waited for Sarah to enter, then closed the door behind her so they would not be disturbed. She grabbed the seat closest to the door as he crossed the room and sat in the leather executive chair.

"So, what's up?" he asked, giving his wife his full attention. "You said something about a phone call?"

Sarah told him about the call she had received from FBI Agent Eric Kelly, being careful not to leave out any details. Jack was shocked, and sat shaking his head in disbelief.

"All of the nursing home residents were murdered?" he asked, horrified.

"That's what he said." She nodded. "I'm not sure how many there were. Did you see anything about it on the news?"

"No. I haven't had a chance to turn on the TV today. I glanced at the *Orlando Sentinel's* web page this morning, but didn't see anything about it."

"Maybe they're not releasing any information until family members are notified."

"Maybe," he agreed. "Dear God ..." Jack was visibly upset. "Those poor people, murdered in their sleep. And they think your father had something to do with it?"

"They're not sure. He's missing, so he might be a witness ... or another victim. Agent Kelly thinks he may have been the one who called me last night. It was either my father, or the killer."

"But why would the killer call you?"

"There's no reason, at least none that I can think of. My father and I aren't even close. I mean, I didn't even know he was in a nursing home until the FBI called."

Jack rubbed his chin in thought, a habit he always did when seeking the right words. "Sweetheart, you've always been reluctant to talk about your childhood, and I've never pried."

"No, you haven't."

"I know your mother died shortly after you were born, but you've said very little about your father. What did he do to lose custody of you?"

Sarah's eyes began to water, and Jack knew he had hit on a painful nerve.

"Did he molest you?"

She shook her head. "No. I don't think so, but I'm really not sure. Everything is a blank. I know something terrible happened, but I don't know what it was. All I remember is that he took me in the woods one night, said he was going to show me something ... something I had to see. Whatever it was, whatever happened that night, it scared the hell out of me. I freaked and took off running. They found me naked and hiding in a culvert three days later. I was out of my head, and in therapy for months. The authorities figured my father must have molested me, and I didn't say otherwise. I couldn't, because I didn't remember what happened. Hell, maybe he did molest me. There wasn't enough evidence to send him to prison, but they could legally remove me from the home on suspicion. He never fought it, and many thought that was an admission of guilt."

"But why would your father call you last night after all these years?"

She shrugged. "Maybe he was next on the killer's list, and wanted to put things right between us before he died. Maybe he was involved with the crime, and wanted to contact me before the cops nabbed him. I'm not sure. All I know is, whoever called, they gave me a warning and I don't think they were joking."

"A warning, or a threat?"

Sarah was quiet for a moment, replaying the phone call in her head. "It was a threat."

"Then we take appropriate action and treat it like one."

Jack wanted to cancel the history tour, but Sarah convinced him that she would be safer around a crowd than sitting at home alone.

"Do your tour," she said. "I think we'll be okay tonight. I'm quite sure the police and FBI will find my father and those responsible for the murders."

CHAPTER 24

The dense forest ended abruptly and Luther found himself standing on the edge of a vast plain, tall grasses stretching endlessly toward the horizon. According to the directions Bonepicker gave him, this was the location of Ataga'hi, the magic lake, except there was no lake.

Perhaps I am looking in the wrong direction.

Luther shielded his eyes and looked slowly from left to right, but could see no sign of any lake, magic or otherwise. But maybe his eyesight was failing him, and the lake was there but he couldn't see it from where he stood. He decided to continue onward, hoping to come upon the fabled waters.

He searched for another twenty minutes, stopping every so often to look around, but could find no sign of any lake. Pity, because searching an endless field of weeds and tall grasses was thirsty work, and he could use a cool drink of water.

"Or maybe a beer," he said aloud, smiling at his own humor.

A cold draft beer would really hit the spot. It had been a long time since he last enjoyed a beer. Alcohol was forbidden at the Willows Nursing Home. Beer, wine and mixed drinks were considered bad things, far too harmful for the elderly residents, but an endless supply of pain pills, tranquilizers, and other prescribed medicine was quite okay and even encouraged.

Of course, a cold beer was out of the question in Galun'lati; not a single bar or liquor store existed in the original world, not even a convenience store. But he could still have a refreshing drink of water, provided he could find Ataga'hi.

"Damn it. Where is that lake?" He licked his parched lips. Even fishy tasting water would be pretty damn sweet right about then.

He searched for another ten minutes, and was about to turn around and start looking in another direction, when he stumbled upon a wooden canoe hidden in the weeds.

"Hello. What's this?"

The canoe was about ten feet long and carved from the trunk of a tree, its inside hollowed out and blackened by fire. In the bottom of the canoe was a leaf-shape paddle, also carved from wood. Luther bent over and ran his hand along the outside of it, admiring the skill required to create such a vessel. Obviously, many hours of work had gone into making the canoe, so he wondered why the owner would go off and leave it in the middle of a field.

He straightened back up and looked around, searching for the owner, but there was no one in the field but him. The canoe had been abandoned.

"But why would they just leave it?"

There were no holes in the canoe, no damage, no reason to discard it. Not unless the owner had been in a hurry, and the weight of the canoe had slowed him down. Perhaps the owner had been fleeing from someone, or something.

A knot formed in Luther's throat. He remembered his encounter with the giant rolling head, and the two skeletons, and wondered if the vessel's owner had a similar encounter. If so, then that would explain why the canoe had been left behind.

But then again, maybe the owner had also been searching for the magical waters of Ataga'hi, and he had tossed the canoe aside when giving up the search.

Reaching down, he touched the canoe again. Pity he couldn't take it with him when he crossed back into the New World, for a hand-carved canoe would probably fetch a pretty price from collectors. He could give the money to his daughter.

A feeling of hopelessness came over the old man as he thought of Sarah. She was in trouble and needed his help, and here he was wasting time looking for a lake that did not exist. Bonepicker's directions were obviously wrong. The tiny man had told Luther about a little used passageway from Galun'lati to the New World, but that passageway apparently did not exist.

Frustrated, and in need of rest, Luther sat down beside the dugout canoe. He watched as the sun slowly sank in the western sky, thinking about a daughter he did not know, and all the previous journeys he had made through the magical land of Galun'lati.

As he sat there, lost in thought, he gradually became aware of the cries of waterfowl and the flapping of wings. Luther blinked and shook his head, listening carefully. No mistake, he heard birds: gulls, herons, even ducks. The ruckus seemed to come from all around him, but there was not a single waterfowl to be seen.

The bird noises grew steadily louder. Thinking they were perhaps hiding in the tall grass, he stood and started to flush a few of them out. But as he took a step forward, he heard a distinct splashing sound.

Looking down, he was shocked to see that he now stood in water.

Several inches of water covered the ground, spreading out in all directions. Furthermore, it was getting deeper, quickly rising over the toes of his boots and up past his ankles. With the water came a thick white mist, like a heavy fog, boiling out of the ground and swirling around him, covering the prairie like a blanket of cotton.

"I have found Ataga'hi!" he shouted, jumping for joy and splashing heavily. "It does exist."

The water rose above his calves and poured down into his cowboy boots. The sudden cold shocked and alarmed him. Luther turned around, horrified to see that he was standing in the middle of a vast lake. Worse yet, the dugout canoe was floating on top of the water and drifting away from him.

"Hey!" He tried to race after the canoe, but his boots were now full of water and weighed him down. He thought about stopping to pull them off, but was afraid the canoe would drift out of reach. Instead, he struggled forward, splashing and sloshing, the water now up to his knees.

A scream tore from his lips as he threw himself forward, arms outstretched, one hand grabbing onto the canoe. Heart pounding in his chest, he dragged the canoe against his body and pulled himself up and over the side. He landed in the bottom of the canoe, staring up at the sky, too exhausted to move.

Several minutes passed before he found the strength to roll over. He pushed himself up onto his knees and grabbed the wooden paddle. Around him, hundreds of waterfowl could be seen: ducks, swans, geese, herons, egrets, and other birds. They glided across the water, and even dove beneath it, moving alone and in pairs, even in groups, but all moving in one direction, as if they shared the same purpose.

Not sure which way to go now that he had found Ataga'hi, Luther decided to follow his feathered brothers. Dipping the blade of the paddle into the water, he guided the shallow canoe across the great lake.

So numerous were the birds covering Ataga'hi that he had to concentrate on his steering to avoid hitting any of them. Several times he shouted warnings for them to keep back or to get out of the way, but the birds seemed oblivious to the old man, and he had to paddle hard to avoid running over them.

One particularly large heron nearly crashed into the side of the canoe, and Luther reached out to push it away for fear of the vessel capsizing. But as he reached for the heron, his fingers passed completely through it.

Luther stopped paddling, shocked. What manner of bird could be heard and seen, but not touched? He tried touching another waterfowl, a duck, but his hand also passed through it. The birds seemed real enough, but his old eyes must be deceiving him.

He was still wondering if the birds surrounding him were real, when a gentle splashing sounded from behind him. Turning, he saw another canoe emerge from the mist about a hundred yards away. It was a dugout similar to the one he rode, paddled by a young Indian man with long black braids. Seated before him was a beautiful young woman dressed in a buckskin dress. She held an infant baby wrapped in a blanket.

"Hey there," Luther called, smiling and waving. "Hey."

He started to call out again, but as the other canoe drew nearer he realized he could see right through it. He could also see through the people.

"Spirits," Luther whispered, spellbound.

The ghostly canoe passed by on his right, no more than twenty feet away, not even making a ripple in the water. He didn't know if they saw him, because neither the man nor the woman acknowledged his presence. They sat facing forward, their gazes focused on some point in the distance.

As they passed by him, and faded into the mist, Luther again heard a gentle splash behind him. Turning, he saw another canoe emerge from the mist, and another, and another …

A flotilla of the dead crossed the sacred waters of Ataga'hi, spirits on a final journey to the hereafter. Men, women and children; they were semitransparent yet clearly visible as they floated past. Some made the journey alone, others traveled as families. They spoke not a word as they passed on either side of his canoe. The only sound was the gentle splashing of their paddles.

Luther waited for the last of the ghostly canoes to glide by, then fell in behind the parade, paddling at a slow but steady pace. This was the advice Bonepicker had given him: once he found the magic waters of Ataga'hi, he should follow the spirits, for they would guide him safely to the other side.

Following the other canoes, he studied the ghostly occupants. The spirits were both young and old, some dressed in traditional outfits, others adorned in modern garb. Their travels in the physical world were over, but their journeys in the spirit world had just begun.

His gaze focused on his eerie traveling companions, Luther didn't realize they had crossed the lake and were nearing the shore until the canoes in front of him began to fade from sight and disappear. One by one the spirits vanished, along with their canoes.

He thought they had not noticed his presence, or could not see him, but as the last of the canoes reached the shore, a ghostly young woman seated in the back turned and waved goodbye to him. And Luther could see a smile upon her lips, for she had finally come home. That smile was the last thing the old man saw as she faded from sight.

Pulling his paddle from the water, he allowed his canoe to come to a slow stop. He drifted there, bobbing gently on the water, looking where the woman had disappeared. He pulled a handkerchief from his pocket and gently wiped away a tear. He was crying, but they were tears of happiness. And he knew that one day he might again see the young woman, for he was an old man and would soon be making his own final journey across the sacred waters.

But he would not be making that journey today, for his destination lay in a different direction than the one taken by the spirits. Dipping his paddle back into the water, he turned his canoe and traveled parallel to the shoreline until he reached the mouth of a wide stream. According to Bonepicker, the stream led to a portal between the two worlds—a portal that would take him closer to his daughter than the doorway he could open using his own magic.

He was about to turn up the stream when he happened to look behind him.

Another canoe crossed Ataga'hi. Unlike the others, this one was not semitransparent but solid looking, and the person paddling it was not a spirit on a final journey. On the contrary, inside the canoe was the same orderly he had seen at the Willows Nursing Home, a shape-shifter who could wear his fur inside out.

"Trickster," Luther hissed, fear blowing a cold kiss down his spine. His heart racing, he turned and guided his canoe up the stream, paddling with all his might.

Coyote was right behind him, and closing fast.

CHAPTER 25

Raven stood perfectly still on one of many barrels on a flatbed trailer pulled by a bright red semi-truck. Like a tiny black statue, he braved the pounding wind and cold in order to read the road signs they passed. Below him, Mouse had curled into a ball on the floor of the trailer and slept soundly, no doubt dreaming of chocolate bars filled with creamy nougat.

He had stood guard on the barrel for hours, watching as the countryside of North and South Carolina, rolled past, and then Georgia. Raven thought about jumping ship when they reached the Florida border, but his wings were still tired and the wound between his shoulders quite sore. Instead, he had held fast, waiting and watching, allowing his furry traveling companion to continue sleeping.

Just south of Jacksonville, Florida, he saw the road signs he had been waiting for. The ancient city of St. Augustine lay somewhere off to the east.

Time to go.

Flying off the barrel, he landed on the trailer's bed beside Mouse.

"Wake up, little friend."

The tiny rodent continued to sleep, snoring softly.

"Wake up, Mouse. We must go."

Mouse murmured in his sleep, nuzzling his nose deeper into his fur.

Frustrated, Raven hopped closer to the sleeping rodent, pecking him hard on top of his head.

"Owww …" Mouse squeaked, coming instantly awake. "Owwww … that hurt." He jumped up and spun around, seeing Raven standing above him. "Owww … Why did you do that? Are you trying to kill me?" Mouse rubbed the top of his head. "Owwww … I'm dying."

"You are not dying," Raven replied.

"Yes, I am," argued Mouse. "Look. Blood."

Raven looked at the top of Mouse's head. "There is nothing there. You are not bleeding."

"But I feel something sticky."

"It is probably just caramel from the candy bar. You should try to be a little neater when you eat."

Mouse tasted the stickiness on his foot. "Hey, you're right. It is caramel. Mmmm …"

Raven clicked his beak, annoyed. "If you are done playing around, we must go." He turned around, offering his back to Mouse. "Climb on, and don't get my feathers all sticky with your feet."

The little rodent did as he was told, climbing on the back of Raven and holding onto his shiny black feathers. Raven flew back onto the barrel, again buffeted by the wind.

"Hang on," he shouted, squatting slightly and tensing his leg muscles.

Mouse hunkered even lower, holding on for dear life.

Taking a deep breath, Raven launched himself into the wind. He flapped hard to clear the truck, veering sharply to get away from the highway and to keep from being hit by the speeding vehicles behind them.

They narrowly missed being smashed against the windshield of a pickup truck, which had chosen that exact moment to pass the semi. Mouse screamed in fright, and may have peed himself, because Raven felt something warm and wet running down his back.

A few moments later they were clear of the interstate and flying over the countryside west of St. Augustine.

"Whew. That was close," squeaked Mouse, a quiver of fear in his voice.

"Yes, it was," agreed Raven. "Did you pee on me?"

Mouse cleared his throat. "Pee? Me? I don't know what you are talking about."

Raven flapped to gain altitude, following one of the main roads leading to the historic city, dripping tiny droplets of rodent urine from his back as he flew.

The old section of St. Augustine was not nearly as large as the historic districts of other well-known American cities, like New Orleans, Charleston, or even Savannah, but what it lacked in size it made up for in importance. Here was the oldest European settlement in the New World, carved out by the Spanish and later occupied by the British and Americans. It was here the white man started his conquest of a new frontier, and where the first nail was set into the coffins of the native people.

St. Augustine was a city where hardship and suffering went hand-in-hand with hope and dreams, where European settlers longed for their native Spain and refused to be buried in the soil of a foreign land. It was a city that had witnessed native villages, conquistadors, pirate invasions, widespread sickness and disease, and many corrupt politicians. It was a place filled with shadows, and many secrets, where visitors and tourists often felt a chill on even the warmest day. It was a city filled with ghosts.

Following the aptly named King Street from U.S. 1, Raven flew over the sprawling ornate buildings of Flagler College. Built by Henry Flagler as a resort for the very rich, it now served as dormitory and classrooms for young people seeking a Bachelor of Fine Arts degree.

"What's that?" Mouse asked, peeking over Raven's shoulder at the scenery below.

"Flagler College," Raven replied.

"How do you know?" the rodent asked, never satisfied with a simple answer.

"I have spent much time here," Raven replied.

"College means young people," Mouse said. "They are messy. There will be much food to be found: pizza, bagels, hotdogs, even beer."

"We will eat later."

"I like beer," Mouse said. "It tickles my nose, and makes my head feel funny."

Raven could only laugh.

Leaving the college behind, he flew over a tiny park and traveled down St. George Street. Below them, dozens of tourists walked along the narrow avenue, pausing to inspect the window displays of little stores and restaurants. Raven realized he had made a mistake in following St. George when they were suddenly assaulted by the smells from numerous restaurants, fudge shops, and even the Spanish Bakery.

"Food, food, food." Mouse wiggled on Raven's back, trying to get a better look. "Pizza, chocolate, fresh bread. So much food, so many smells. It drives me mad."

"Hold your breath and ignore it."

"I cannot." Mouse wiggled forward, putting all his weight on Raven's right side.

"You must move back," Raven warned. "You are going to fall."

"We must stop. I am starving."

"Get back!" Raven cried. "I cannot flap my wing with all your weight on my side."

Mouse reluctantly returned to his original spot in the center of Raven's back. As he did, his right foot stepped squarely on Raven's wound, causing a bolt of pain to shoot through the shape-shifter's back.

"Owww ... You did that on purpose."

Mouse giggled slightly. "Did not."

"Be more careful, or I will drop you down a restaurant chimney and make you someone's lunch."

Mouse giggled even louder. "I will be very tasty."

They were halfway down St. George Street when Raven lowered his left wing and veered to the west. They passed over several blocks of stores, historic inns, and old homes, finally reaching their destination of the Tolomato Cemetery.

The Tolomato was located just south of the Old Drugstore, about a block from the ancient City Gates. The final resting place for Catholics, it was no longer open to the public nor had there been a burial on its property for many years. It was now mostly a visiting place for tourists and ghost hunters, for it was said that the Tolomato was very haunted with many claiming to have encountered—or captured on film—a spirit or two during the late hours of the night.

The cemetery was definitely spooky, even in the bright light of day. Towering oaks heavy with Spanish Moss stood like silent sentinels over the ancient graves and above-ground crypts, whispering secrets in a language all their own.

Raven flew over the front gates of the Tolomato, making a beeline for the mausoleum at the back of the cemetery. The mausoleum was the final resting place for Augustin Verot, the first Bishop of St. Augustine. Or it should have been, for the bishop's body had been secretly removed years ago and reburied elsewhere. The mausoleum now stood empty, unused except by a feathered shape-shifter who had found the building vacant years earlier.

Landing on the roof of the mausoleum, Raven surveyed his surroundings to make sure he was not being observed. Expect for a pair of tourists standing just outside the front gates, the graveyard was quite empty. After hopping down to a marble sill, he pushed open a small, unlocked window and entered the building.

There, he shook Mouse off of his back and then reversed his skin and transformed back into a man. He stood in the center of the room, naked, stretching his muscles to ease the pain of too much flying.

Mouse giggled. "I have never seen a human naked. You look funny."

"No funnier than you, my little friend," Raven retaliated.

"You have no feathers, no fur." Mouse giggled even louder.

Raven glanced down. "I have a little fur."

"Very little," Mouse laughed even harder. "Doesn't your baby-maker get cold?"

"Yes, it does," Raven replied. "That is why humans wear clothes."

He crossed the room, retrieving a laundry bag he had hidden in the corner on a previous journey. He opened the bag and removed a pair of blue jeans, underwear, socks, a shirt, leather jacket, and pair of work books. The bag also contained a leather wallet with money and a driver's license with the name of Michael Blackwing.

Despite being a shape-shifter, Raven had spent much of his life in the New World. Therefore, he had done what it took to move freely and unnoticed in the world of humans, including learning a skill and having a job. Money was the key to living in the New World, and he did whatever necessary to earn it.

He put on the clothing, then slipped the wallet into his pants and placed Mouse into the breast pocket of his leather jacket. The little rodent squirmed around for a moment, then poked his head back out of the pocket so he could see.

"Comfortable?" Raven asked, smiling.

"Very."

"Good. Then we must go, before someone sees us and calls the police. They do not like people sneaking into the graveyards here in St. Augustine."

Raven jumped up and grabbed the windowsill, pulling himself through the tiny window and dropping lightly to the ground on the outside. He crouched in the shadows for a moment, making sure his actions had not been observed. But there were no longer any tourists at the front gates, or standing along the fence.

After sprinting to the back of the cemetery, he quickly climbed the fence, then hurried across the parking lot of the neighboring business. He slowed his pace to an unsuspicious walk as he reached the sidewalk, traveling west along Orange Street.

Four blocks later, he turned north on Ponce De Leon Boulevard, walking to the U-Lock-It Storage Facility. He removed a key from his wallet, unlocked the padlock on unit #215, and raised the roll-down door.

Inside the fifteen-foot by twelve-foot storage unit was an antique leather hunting pouch, with a beaded shoulder strap containing two hand-forged tomahawks. There was also a jet-black Harley Davidson motorcycle.

"You have a motorcycle!" Mouse cried out, excited. He climbed out of Raven's pocket and ran down the front of his body, scurrying across the room to the big bike. "How did you get a motorcycle?"

"I worked for it," Raven replied. "I've spent much time in the New World as a man. I had a job."

Slipping the strap of the hunting pouch over his head and shoulder, so it hung snugly on his side, he scooped Mouse off the floor and put him back into his jacket pocket. Climbing on the Harley, Raven raised the kickstand and started the engine. He twisted the throttle a few times, allowing the engine to warm up, then shifted into first gear.

He left the storage facility, picking up speed as he moved out into the street. He turned onto Ponce De Leon Blvd., opening up the big bike as they headed back toward the interstate.

Mouse stuck his head farther out the jacket pocket, enjoying the ride. "Weeeeee ..."

CHAPTER 26

Greenwood history tours were always held on the Friday closest to the full moon, starting at nine p.m. and lasting around two hours. Jack had been leading the tours for almost five years, never charging a dime for his time and effort. He actually enjoyed doing the tours, for they gave him a chance to share his acquired knowledge of local history and show off his graveyard a little. It also gave him a chance to be in the spotlight, and polish his performance skills.

He guessed that somewhere deep down inside of him was an actor dying to get out. He had a few small parts over the years in various movies, all of them filmed at Greenwood. Jack knew he would never be a real actor, or make it to Hollywood, not that he really wanted that sort of thing, but he did like to perform and cut up in front of a live audience, and meet new people, and his tours were the perfect opportunity for him.

Of course, he rarely took center stage without a little liquid encouragement to help kill the jitters. Keeping a watchful eye on the clock in his office, he opened a bottle of rum and dumped a healthy shot in a plastic cup filled with cola and ice. Sarah sat on the other side of the desk, sipping a drink of her own.

After draining half his drink in a single gulp, he wiped his mouth with the back of his hand and smiled at his wife. "Ah, much better."

Sarah giggled. "It's hot out tonight. You're going to feel that when you walk outside."

He shrugged. "So? I'll sweat a little. No one will notice. If they do, they'll just think I'm working hard." He glanced again at the clock. "Almost nine. Guess it's time we wander down to the front gates and start letting people in."

Sarah finished the rest of her drink. "I'm ready."

They left his office, Jack turning off the lights and locking the door behind him. Leaving the office building, they walked up the road to the front gates of the cemetery.

Summer Johnson stood just inside the locked front gates, talking with some of the people on the other side. Summer was a college student living in a city-owned house on the east side of the cemetery. She got free rent in exchange for closing the front gates at night. Of course, she had to patrol the property before locking the gates, making sure she wasn't accidentally locking someone inside for the evening. Not surprisingly, few people ever wanted to spend the night in a graveyard.

"Hi, Summer," Sarah said, calling out to the young college student. Both women were good friends, and had occasionally partaken in a "girls' night out."

Summer turned away from the gates, flashing Sarah a warm smile. "Hey, Sarah. How's it going? Jack said you were here when he called earlier. You staying for the tour?"

Sarah gave her a hug. "I was thinking about it. How about you?"

Summer shook her head. "Can't. I have an exam on Monday, and I need to study."

"Too bad. Tests suck."

"Yes, they do." Summer turned to Jack. "If you don't need me, I'm going to take off."

"No. You can go," Jack replied. "Thanks for warming up the crowd."

Summer smiled, and started walking up the hill toward the office.

"Where's your car?" Sarah called after her. "I didn't see it."

"It's at the house. I walked. Figured I could use the exercise."

Summer's back fence had a gate, allowing her easy access into the cemetery. It came in handy on certain occasions, mostly weekends and holidays, when Jack would call and ask her to assist someone on property.

Jack watched for a moment as Summer walked up the hill, then turned his attention to the crowd waiting outside the front gates. There were about fifty gathered for the tour, and he could see several more coming down Greenwood Street toward the cemetery. There would probably be more late arrivals, because finding a parking spot along the narrow cobblestone street could be a bit tricky, especially on tour night.

He flashed Sarah a smile, then stepped forward and removed the padlocks and chain from the gates. He only opened the gates wide enough for him to slip through to the other side, because he wanted to address the crowd before allowing them entrance into the cemetery. Sarah remained inside, watching the show.

"Howdy, folks." He smiled, raising his voice to be heard. "I'm Jack Reynolds, sexton for the city of Orlando. Welcome to Greenwood Cemetery's full moon history tour. It's really nice to see so many people here tonight."

As Jack talked, he surveyed the people standing in front of him, singling out those he might need to keep an eye on during the tour: elderly people who might have trouble keeping up with the rest of the group; individuals toting cameras who were more interested in hunting ghosts than learning about history and who might be tempted to wander off on their own.

While he didn't have anything against ghost hunters, he knew from past experience that they could sometimes be a pain in the ass. He had been interrupted on numerous occasions by such people, who would shout out that their cameras had just captured an apparition or orb, or that they had just seen the ghost of someone wandering through the graveyard. They were annoying, and their constant camera flashing always played hell on his retinas, especially when they aimed directly at him while taking photos.

He also tried to size up who might have had a few too many drinks before coming to Greenwood. It was amazing how many people used the tours as an excuse to get drunk and party. The drunks were far worse than the ghost hunters, because they had no respect whatsoever for their surroundings, or for what was being said. On several occasions, he had to stop his tour to escort an intoxicated guest off property.

And then there were the Goth kids. Often outlandishly dressed, they could be intoxicated or high on drugs, or both, looking for a chance to party in a graveyard. Even the ones that were well-behaved often freaked out the elderly members of the tours, offending those who had family members buried at Greenwood.

But luckily he saw no Goths among the people standing outside the gates. Nor did he see anyone that appeared intoxicated, high on drugs, or mentally deranged. Once, about a year ago, he had stopped a woman from bringing a shovel along on the tour. She claimed the shovel was needed to help liberate the dead in the name of Jesus. Jack had taken the shovel away from her three times that night, finally escorting her out the front gates and threatening to call the police if she returned.

Looks like a good night. No weirdoes.

He was just starting to breathe a little easier when he spotted some late arrivals coming down the street. Three young men, probably in their early to mid-twenties, dressed alike in tight blue jeans, black T-shirts, and worn leather jackets. They had sharp, angular features and unkempt hair, like punk rockers or reform school dropouts. They looked dangerous.

The three men stopped before reaching the rest of the group, keeping to themselves and talking in whispers. They paid little attention to Jack or the others waiting for the tour, instead sneaking glances at something inside the cemetery. He turned to see what they were looking at and a chill danced down his spine when he realized the object of their attention was Sarah.

Why are they looking at my wife?

He didn't like the looks Sarah received from them, but there wasn't anything he could do about it. Looking at someone was not a crime, and he certainly could not bar them from entering the cemetery or taking the tour because of it. If he did, they could file a complaint at City Hall and there would be hell to pay. No. All he could do was keep an eye on them, and hope there wouldn't be any trouble. His wife was the best-looking woman there tonight, so he really couldn't blame them for staring.

Jack cleared his throat to get everyone's attention. "Okay, folks, we're about to get started. How many of you have gone on this tour before?"

A few hands went up.

"Great. Now, how many of you have relatives buried here at Greenwood?"

A few more hands.

"Okay, then you've probably been here before."

He pushed open the front gates, explaining that they would be closed for the tour, not locked, but held together with a wide rubber band. That way, if anyone got tired of walking, they could leave early.

Stepping aside, he allowed the crowd to enter Greenwood.

"Our first stop of the evening will be the office building up the hill. There are restrooms inside, and I encourage anyone who needs to use them to please do so now. It's a big cemetery, and we've got a long walk ahead of us tonight."

"How big is it?" asked a middle-aged man wearing a Hawaiian shirt.

"The cemetery itself is right at a hundred acres, and we have an additional twenty acres next door in the wetlands."

The man whistled in surprise. "Wow. That's really big, and so close to downtown. Who would have thought?"

"Well, we are Orlando's oldest gated community." Jack smiled, happy to use one of his favorite lines. He threw a quick glance at Sarah, who only shook her head.

The crowd mingled in front of the office for a few minutes, waiting while members of the tour used the restroom. As he waited, Jack spoke with some of the other guests. Among the visitors that night were several schoolteachers, a retired police officer, a fire marshal from Maitland, and a novelist.

The three young men in leather jackets continued to distance themselves from the others, but Jack was grateful to see that they no longer focused all their attention on Sarah.

The last person to use the restroom rejoined the group, allowing Jack to start the tour. He led everybody up the hill between sections L & M, past the Wilmount mausoleum, pointing out the headstones belonging to some of Orlando's notable citizens. They were heading to the oldest section of the cemetery, traveling back in time to the late 1800s and the founding of The City Beautiful, to a period long before the arrival of Mickey Mouse and Walt Disney World.

The night started off quite cloudy, but as they reached the historic section the clouds parted and the cemetery was bathed in the bright illumination of a full moon. Thousands of headstones suddenly seemed to glow, giving an eerie carnival quality to the graveyard. If there were such things as ghosts, then it surely must be a night for them. Jack could almost imagine a horde of spirits holding a midnight waltz among the grave markers.

Sarah sided closer to him, looking down the hill to the area known as the diamond. "It really is beautiful, isn't it?"

He nodded. "Yes. It is."

Despite all the headaches that came with being a city sexton, he really did love Greenwood Cemetery, especially on such a beautiful night. He was pleased to note that the caretakers had put in an extra effort during the week to make sure all the bushes in the historic section had been trimmed in preparation for the tour.

A slight breeze suddenly sprang up, making the leaves in the oak trees whisper and their long beards of Spanish moss move like shimmering gray ghosts. He stopped and admired the scenery for a moment, then turned his attention back to the task at hand.

Leading everyone down the hill, Jack ignored the numerous flashes going off at his back. Let the ghost hunters have their fun; at least they were waiting until the group moved on before taking pictures. So far, he had not been blinded. But the night was still young, and he was quite sure he would be seeing double before it was through.

Stopping before the section belonging to members of the Grand Army of the Republic, he again addressed the crowd. "The men buried here fought for the Union during the War of Northern Aggression ..." His joke got a few laughs. "... and you'd be surprised to know that these residents are actually buried backward, with the headstones at their feet."

"Why are they buried like that?" someone asked.

He smiled. "Well, that's what we call 'southern justice.'"

From the final resting place for members of the Grand Army of the Republic, they proceeded to Section J, and the burial spaces for those who had fought for the Confederacy during the Civil War. And instead of an American flag flying above those brave southern boys was the Bonnie Blue.

And even though the Confederate section was quite small, it had been an area of contention and argument over the years. Once a year, a group of Civil War Re-enactors, and descendants of Confederate soldiers, gathered at the site to celebrate Confederate Memorial Day. They would give speeches, march in formation, acknowledge their ancestors, fire a volley with historic rifles, eat a Sunday meal featuring southern fried chicken, and decorate all the graves with the Stars and Bars.

It was the only day of the year the Confederate Battle Flag was allowed to fly on city property, and there were some who thought that even one day was too much.

The local chapter of the NAACP had been threatening for years to gather at Greenwood to protest Confederate Memorial Day, but luckily that threat had never been carried out. The last thing Jack wanted was bad publicity.

From the Confederate section, he led his tour group to Sections C, D, E, and F, which were arranged to form a large diamond. Situated near the original entrance into the cemetery, on Gore Street, the diamond was the burial place for many of the city's founding fathers and former mayors. It was veritable who's who, with many of the dead buried in the diamond having city streets named after them.

Among the distinguished residents to be found in the diamond was Francis J. Eppes, the grandson of President Thomas Jefferson. There was also Cassius A. Boone, great-grandson of the legendary pioneer

Daniel Boone. But perhaps the most interesting story associated with the diamond was that of Fred Weeks. According to legend, Mr. Weeks had been tricked into buying a worthless piece of swampland by four Orlando businessmen. Seeking revenge, old Fred had purchased a cemetery plot near the original front gates. There he had erected a large headstone with the Biblical verse: "*A man from Jerusalem went down to Jericho and fell among thieves.*" And at the end of that line he had carved the names of the four men who cheated him. Word quickly spread about the headstone, and the four men gave Fred his money back. They also purchased that burial space, removing the scandalous headstone.

But Mr. Weeks wasn't through with the scoundrels. He built himself a nice mausoleum in the diamond, and on the door he again carved the Bible verse about the man going down to Jericho and falling among thieves, and he again added the names of the men who had cheated him. Those names remained on the door until Mr. Weeks died. Shortly after his death, someone sneaked into the cemetery late at night and chiseled the names off the mausoleum door.

From the diamond they headed to section H, an area of few headstones but many bodies. When Greenwood became the official city cemetery, all the other graveyards in the city limits of Orlando were closed and the bodies relocated to section H, most becoming nameless and forgotten over the years.

As Jack explained Section H, a young lady in the group asked the question he had been expecting to hear all evening.

"Have you ever had any weird experiences here at Greenwood?"

He smiled. "Weird experiences? Meaning?"

"Have you seen any ghosts?" asked an older man, adding to the young woman's question.

Jack wondered when the question would come up on the tour, and was surprised it had taken so long. He personally never had any ghostly encounters, but former caretakers claimed to have had such experiences. One even refused to work alone in Section J, claiming he had been tapped on the shoulder in that section by someone, or something, that could not be seen.

Of course, even if he had witnessed an apparition or two, Jack knew better than to talk about it. The city took a dim view of those who told ghost stories about their cemetery. Such talk only encouraged people to sneak into the graveyard at night, hoping to have an eerie encounter of their own. Ghost stories about Greenwood could also offend families with relatives buried on the property. How would they feel knowing that grandma was residing in a "haunted" cemetery?

He also didn't dare talk about the man buried on the property, who—rumor had it—was killed by the infamous Lake Clinch monster, located in the nearby town of Lake Wales. Jack had heard the story from a well-known cryptozoologist, who researched the story for an article he wrote for *Mysteries* magazine.

And then there was the mysterious black fingerprints which had appeared overnight on a gravestone in Section I, looking as though the woman buried in that spot had reached up and smeared her hand down the front of the marker. Perhaps she was upset someone had misspelled her name, or that no death date had been carved on the stone, despite her being dead for nearly eighty years. A trusted caretaker discovered the fingerprints while making his morning rounds, a caretaker who swore they had not been there the previous day.

No. Ghosts, spooks, apparitions, voodoo offering, or anything else weird that happened in the cemetery were taboo to talk about, and could never be part of a city-sanctioned tour. Like Jack had said many times to his staff, "What happens in Greenwood stays in Greenwood."

"Nope. I've never seen any ghosts here in Greenwood," he replied. "Nor have I ever had anything weird or unexplainable happen to me."

"My sister came on a ghost tour last year," said the young woman, obviously not wanting to lay the subject of spooks to rest, "and she caught several orbs on film. One of their group also heard a man whisper 'get out.'"

Jack bit his lip to keep from laughing. He couldn't count the number of people over the years who had shown him orb photos, claiming they were ghosts when in reality they were probably nothing more than specks of dust, light reflection, rain drops, or lens flare.

As for the ghost tours that occasionally took place at Greenwood, always given by an outside source and not an official city tour, they were usually made up of people with overactive imaginations. They came with cameras, EMF meters, and other high-tech equipment, looking like rejects from a paranormal television show. The last tour to visit the graveyard included a woman who claimed to be psychic, who insisted she had a seven-foot Indian for a spirit guide.

"I really don't know much about orbs," he said, wanting to change the subject, "or electronic voice phenomena. I leave that sort of thing to the experts. But again, I have never experienced anything weird in Greenwood and I have spent many a night out here, including Halloween."

It was an annual ritual for him to spend Halloween night in Greenwood standing guard against people sneaking into the cemetery. On those nights, he would sit on top of the hill by the Wilmount Mausoleum, enjoying a rum and Coke, or two, and wait for the sound of someone climbing the fence along Gore Street. The top bar was deliberately missing from the wire fence to make it loose, and the rattling sound of someone climbing over it could be heard halfway across the graveyard.

When he heard an intruder coming over the fence, Jack would sneak up on them and shine a flashlight in their eyes, scaring the hell out of them. Once caught, they rarely gave him any trouble, knowing he could call the police and have them arrested for criminal trespass. Most he would simply escort out the front gates, but some would take off running, climbing the fence to get back out a hell of a lot faster than they had climbed it to get in. One young lady he had caught sneaking into the cemetery had gotten so scared that she completely forgot about the fence and ran face-first into it.

Not wanting to answer any more questions about ghosts, Jack shined the flashlight at his wristwatch. "Well, folks. That concludes tonight's tour. I hoped you all enjoyed yourselves, and maybe even learned a little bit of history. The office is still unlocked if any of you need to use the restroom before leaving."

He led the group back over the hill to the front side of the cemetery.

Sarah moved closer to walk beside him.

"Ghosties and orbs," she whispered, giggling. "You knew that was coming."

He nodded. "Yes, I did."

Standing outside the office, he did a silent headcount as everyone filed past, walking toward the front gates. As the last person left, he realized the three young men who had shown up late were no longer with the group. Come to think of it, he hadn't seen them for some time. No doubt they were not really interested in Greenwood's history, and had wandered off to do a little exploring on their own.

"Great. Just great," he mumbled.

"Something wrong?"

"The three young guys on the tour, the ones dressed alike in leather jackets—"

"The punk rockers?"

He nodded. "They didn't leave with the rest of the group, not unless I missed them."

"I didn't see them either."

"They must have wandered off, and I definitely don't want to leave them in here by themselves. No telling what they'll do." He pulled his truck keys out of his pocket. "Listen, go ahead and lock the front gates. I'll take a ride back through the cemetery to look for them. They might have gotten bored and already left, and we just didn't see them leave."

He gave Sarah a quick kiss. "I won't be long."

"Good. This is cutting into my Friday night drinking time," she teased.

"Mine too," he replied. "I'll be back in a minute."

He walked around to the back of the office and climbed into his truck, starting the engine. After turning on the headlights, he shifted into gear and started up the hill to the backside of the property. If the leather-clad trio were still inside the cemetery, they were probably in the old section. The historic section was darker and spookier than the rest of the graveyard, and always attracted the oddballs like moths to a flame.

Reaching the bottom of the hill, he turned past the diamond and the Weeks mausoleum. He turned again, cruising slowly north along section A and the oldest part of the cemetery. He was just passing an area where the state of Florida had buried patients from the Sunnyland mental hospital when he spotted two of the young men. They stood in a clearing on the south side of Unit 8, about twenty yards off the road. Both were completely naked.

"What the hell?" Jack slammed on the brakes, bringing his big Ford pickup to a screeching halt. He couldn't believe what he was seeing. "Oh, hell no. Not in my cemetery."

Neither man seemed concerned that they had been caught doing something they shouldn't. They never even looked in his direction, nor did they make any move to put their clothes back on. Jack suspected they were on drugs of some kind, or they were simply fucking nuts. Either way, he didn't want to challenge them without a little backup.

He grabbed his cell phone, thumbed the numbers for the Orlando

Police Department. He didn't dial 9-1-1, because he wasn't sure that what he was seeing constituted an emergency, and knew calls to 9-1-1 were considered public record and didn't want it to end up on the local news.

He had only entered half the numbers when one of the men ripped open his own chest, stepping out of his skin as if it were a one-piece jumpsuit.

"Holy shit," Jack exclaimed, the cell phone slipping from his fingers and falling unnoticed to the floorboard of his truck.

The young man turned and looked in Jack's direction, his body a skinless mass of bloody muscle and tissue. And then, with an almost casual air, he shook his skin and turned it inside out to reveal a side covered in thick gray fur.

"What the fu—" Jack tried to speak, but his voice came out as a soft hissing of air.

He watched in horror, spellbound, as the young man stepped back into his skin with the fur side out. As he did, his body began to magically reshape itself, transforming into a large gray wolf. No sooner had the first man changed when his partner did the same.

As Jack watched the transformation of the two men, he suddenly remembered there had been a third in their party. He also thought of his wife standing alone outside the office, waiting for him, unaware of the strange things going on in Greenwood.

"My god, Sarah ..." He stomped on the accelerator and jerked the steering wheel, heading back toward the office at full speed.

CHAPTER 27

Luther paddled with all his might, his muscles quivering, sweat pouring down his face. He guided his canoe upstream, steering around large rocks and avoiding the shallows. He couldn't afford to get stuck, not with Coyote breathing hot and heavy down his neck.

Casting a quick glance over his shoulder, he saw that the Trickster was closing in and would probably overtake him in no time.

"Foolish old man," Coyote called out, licking his lips. The gesture was frightening, even though the shape-shifter wore his fur side in. "Do you hope to outrun me?"

He knew he couldn't outrun him. Even in human form, the Trickster was incredibly strong. Luther Watie was nothing but an old man burdened with an ailing body. Nor could he stand and fight, for he was weaponless, save for a tiny pocketknife and the wooden paddle clutched tightly in his hands. And he doubted if either would do much good against an opponent who could quickly transform into a beast of fur and fangs.

No. Luther could not outrun Coyote, at least not for long, and he couldn't stand and fight—not unless he wanted to end up as dead as the residents of the Willow Nursing Home. But all was not lost, for up ahead was a shimmering green glow, a portal between Galun'lati and the New World—the same portal Bonepicker had told him about.

But the portal was a good hundred yards away, if not farther, a nearly impossible distance for an elderly Cherokee struggling against fatigue and a strong current. His muscles were already on the verge of giving out completely. If he didn't have a heart attack from the stress and strain, he would tire out before ever reaching the portal.

What then? Probably certain death, and maybe even painful torture. Would Coyote eat him after killing him, or simply cast aside his lifeless body like a worn-out play toy? Did the Trickster play with his food?

Luther was about to give up completely, throwing his hands up in despair and allowing Coyote to take his life and end his suffering, when he suddenly had a plan. Coyote may be the Trickster, but Luther still had a few tricks of his own.

Bringing his wooden paddle tight against the side of the canoe and turning the blade, he veered sharply toward the shore. Coyote saw what he was doing, the old man perhaps intended on making a run for the safety of the forest.

"Run, rabbit. Run," Coyote called out behind him. "Go ahead, run for the forest. I am much faster on land than I am on the water. On land, I will again have four legs. You will have but two."

He ignored Coyote's banter, concentrating on what he needed to do. Two more strokes with the paddle brought him to the shore.

Not wanting the canoe to run aground, fearful it would get stuck in the mud, Luther jumped out while still in two feet of water. He reached back into the dugout vessel, grabbed his medicine bag, and quickly untied it.

"Wait right there," Coyote called. "I'm coming."

Luther's hands shook as he struggled to open the leather bag, pouring some of the powders into the bottom of the canoe. Quickly mixing the powders with his fingers, he reached into his pants pocket for the Zippo lighter.

"Come on. Come on. Where is it?"

His fingers were numb from gripping the paddle so tightly, his hands shaking with fatigue. It took a few moments of fumbling before he could locate the lighter. A few more seconds elapsed before he could pull it from his pocket.

The lighter almost slipped from his grasp and fell into the water, but Luther managed to hold onto it. Opening the lid, he struck the tiny wheel with his thumb.

Nothing.

Panic shot through him as he thumbed the lighter. No flame. No spark. He wondered if the flint had fallen out somewhere. Perhaps the fluid had leaked out, or evaporated.

"Don't do this to me," he said aloud, nearly having a nervous breakdown. He wasn't a well man; his heart couldn't take the stress.

Coyote was only about sixty feet away and closing fast. The Trickster grinned, already tasting victory. Or maybe it was human flesh he tasted.

Luther thumbed the lighter again, and got a spark. Not a flame, but a spark. The flint was still good. He closed the lid and shook it hard, hoping to spread around any remaining fuel that might be inside of it. He whispered a prayer, "Please, Great Spirit, let it work. Please help me. Spirits, I need you."

Coyote was now only forty feet away. The shape-shifter leaned forward in his canoe, splashing the water with powerful strokes of his paddle, aiming straight for him.

A prayer still upon his lips, Luther opened the lid of the lighter and thumbed the striker wheel.

"Please ..."

He nearly fainted with joy when he saw a tiny flickering flame. Fearful it would die out at any second, he quickly reached down and touched the flame against the powders in the bottom of the canoe.

The powders ignited with a whoosh and a great cloud of white smoke, the gunpowder in the mixture causing the other ingredients to catch fire.

Coyote was only twenty feet away. Perfect.

Luther shoved the canoe back out into the stream, sending it on a course that cut directly across the Trickster's path.

As the dugout canoe crossed in front of Coyote, the burning powders opened a doorway between Galun'lati and the world of men. The Trickster saw the doorway open and tried to stop his canoe, but he had too much forward momentum and there wasn't time. He vanished from sight. The powders in Luther's canoe burned out quickly, and the door closed with the shape-shifter on the other side.

Luther stood on the shore, breathing hard. He felt exhilarated and a little dizzy watching Coyote disappear, not sure if he wanted to cheer or pass out. It was an exciting moment, and to celebrate he pulled out his penis and urinated into the stream.

Feeling much better having relieved himself, he waded out into the water and caught his canoe, dragging it to shore. Climbing back aboard, he pushed off and paddled back into the middle of the stream. He steered toward the strange green glow of the portal to the New World.

The portal was actually a large whirlpool in the middle of the stream, its churning waters casting off an eerie green light. Luther paddled up to it, then hung on for dear life as the swirling waters caught the wooden canoe and sucked it straight down.

And as he was sucked down, Luther thought hard about his daughter, Sarah, and where she lived back in the New World, for this was Bonepicker's instructions to him, the little man promising that the portal would take him where he needed to go.

Down, down, down he went, deeper and deeper, the greenish glow growing ever brighter. Luther's ears popped and his ancient lungs screamed for air. And just when he thought he would surely hit bottom and drown, his canoe shot out of the water and landed upright on the surface.

Luther coughed and choked, spitting water. He wiped wet hair from his eyes and looked around in surprise. Instead of a small stream with a glowing green whirlpool, he found himself in the middle of a wide river. Nighttime had also fallen, the sky illuminated with the glow of a full moon. Still trying to get his bearings, his canoe drifted beneath a large bridge of concrete and steel. Such things did not exist in Galun'lati, so Luther knew he was once again in the New World.

He was so busy looking at the bridge that he neglected to look behind him, and didn't see the large riverboat until it was almost on top of him.

The shrill blast of the riverboat's whistle startled the old man, nearly causing him to capsize his tiny canoe. Seeing that he was in danger of being run over, he paddled hard to get out of the way. He steered clear of the boat, hanging on for dear life as the wakes caused by the passing riverboat slapped against the side of the canoe. As it passed, Luther could see the name, *Riverboat Romance,* painted on the side. Dozens of people were inside the vessel, seated at tables and enjoying dinner. He wondered if anyone saw him as he nearly capsized, his canoe tossed about like a cork in the choppy water.

The riverboat continued on its way, and the water again grew calm. Not wanting to run the risk of being run over by anything else, he got his bearings and paddled for the distant shoreline, and about fifty feet from it noticed a log on the surface of the water—not floating, but swimming, moving against the river's current. Curious, he slowed as the log passed in front of him, noticed that it had eyes that glowed in the moonlight.

At first he thought it might be something supernatural, but quickly realized the log was actually an alligator, its powerful tail pushing it silently along. Luther quickly doubled his efforts to reach the shore, fearful of being capsized in a river inhabited by gators. He also realized he was somewhere in the south, for only a few southern states contained alligators.

Hope fluttered in his heart. Florida had alligators, and that's where Sarah lived. Bonepicker had promised that the whirlpool portal would take him very close to where he wanted to go. Could he have been so lucky as to end up in the same state as his daughter?

Luther was about twenty feet from shore when he heard a man yelling at him.

"Hey, what the hell are you doing?"

Looking around, he spotted a black man standing on the shore fishing.

"Get away from there," the man yelled. "You're going to cross my line."

"Sorry," Luther called back, using his paddle to turn sharply. He reached the shore moments later, climbing out of the canoe and pulling it onto dry land.

Straightening up, he found the black man standing behind him.

"You must be plumb crazy," he said, shaking his head. "Don't you know better than to be out canoeing at night, and without a light? You're going to get yourself run over."

"I almost did," Luther said and smiled.

The man also smiled. "That you did. Put on quite a show. Thought for sure you were going to be gator bait."

"Me too."

The man offered his hand. "I'm Siler Lock."

He shook hands with him. "Luther Watie. Pleased to me you." He looked around. "Could you tell me where we are?"

Siler cocked his head slightly, looking at him funny. "You don't know where you are?"

"No, sir. Not exactly. You might say I've traveled a long way."

Siler nodded toward the canoe. "In that thing? You're either very brave, or very stupid. But to answer your question, you're in Deland."

"Deland, Florida?"

"Of course, Florida. Where in the hell did you think you were?"

Luther nearly jumped for joy at learning he was in Florida. "Have you ever heard of a town called Sanford?"

"Sanford's about twenty miles from here."

The old Indian could barely contain his excitement. He never dreamed the portal would deliver him so close to the town where Sarah lived. Twenty miles. He could be there in less than an hour, if he only had a ride. At the very least, he could look up the number of her funeral home and call her. He fidgeted nervously, anxious to continue his journey.

"Listen, I'm not from around here, so I really don't know the area. I need to call my daughter. It's important. Is there a gas station nearby, or a convenience store, someplace where I might find a payphone?"

"No gas stations around here, but you can use my cell phone." Siler pulled a smartphone from his pocket, handing it to Luther. "Signal's not the best, so you might have to move around a bit until it comes in clear."

Luther accepted the phone with eager fingers. Reaching into his back pocket, he took out his billfold and removed a folded piece of paper with Sarah's phone number, the ink faded and barely readable in the dark. He had obtained the number almost a year ago after sneaking a peak at his medical records.

Hands trembling, he entered the number on the cell phone. A few seconds passed, then he heard ringing as the call went through.

Pick up. Pick up. Please be home.

There was a click, then an answering machine came on with a recorded message. It was a woman's voice he assumed was Sarah. Just hearing her voice made his heart ache.

"You have reached the William Powell Funeral Home. Our hours are nine a.m. to five p.m., Monday through Friday. Please leave a message at the beep, and we will return your call as soon as possible …"

Luther cleared his throat, preparing to leave a message. But Sarah's voice continued talking, "And don't forget that this Friday, March 12th, is the Full Moon History Tour at Greenwood Cemetery in Orlando. See you there."

The beep sounded, but Luther did not speak; instead, he thought about the message he had just heard.

Full Moon History Tour at Greenwood Cemetery in Orlando. This Friday, March 12th. See you there.

He closed the phone, handing it back to Siler. "What's the date?"

Siler slipped the phone back into his pocket. "You don't know the date either?"

He shook his head. "No. Please, tell me."

"It's the eleventh … No. No. It's the twelfth. Friday the twelfth."

Luther's heart jumped into his throat. His daughter was at Greenwood Cemetery. He knew where to find her.

"How far are we from Orlando?"

"About forty miles," Siler replied.

He looked around, desperately trying to come up with a plan. He needed a ride, but didn't know where he could find a bus. He didn't have enough money for a taxi. As a matter of fact, he didn't have any money at all. The staff at the nursing home had stolen it from him."

He turned to Siler. "Do you have a car?"

The black man shook his head, casting out his line. "Nope. I've got a pickup truck."

"Listen, Mr. Lock. I'm desperate. I need a ride to Greenwood Cemetery in Orlando. It's a matter of life and death."

Siler looked at him funny. "You want to go to a cemetery, at night? You are crazy. Not me. No way. You won't catch a black man in a graveyard after dark. Besides, you can't get into Greenwood at night. That's a city cemetery. They close at sundown."

"It will be open. They've got a tour there tonight," Luther argued. "Please, my daughter is there. She needs my help. It's a matter of life and death."

"I've heard that before." Siler laughed. "It's always a matter of life and death." He slowly reeled his line back in, looking Luther over. "Listen, I don't even know you. And I'm sure as hell not going to drive all the way to Orlando just because you need a ride. I'm fishing, and I don't get to fish that often nowadays. The wife and kids always got something for me to do."

"Please," Luther pleaded.

"No. Now piss off, you crazy fucking Indian. Leave me the hell alone. This is my night off, and I'm going to enjoy it."

Desperation showed in Luther's voice. "I'll pay you."

Siler stopped reeling. "How much?"

Luther again pulled out his billfold, looking through it, hoping to find some folded money the nursing home staff had overlooked. But he came up empty-handed, and flat broke.

Siler grinned. "That's what I thought. You don't have any money, do you?"

Luther shook his head.

"And you don't have any ride either." Siler hooked a thumb over his shoulder. "Orlando is about forty miles that way. I suggest you start walking."

"I'll give you my canoe," he said, thinking quickly. "It's sturdy … handmade. Imagine how many fish you'll be able to catch with a canoe. You can go after the big ones, get right up next to them."

Siler scratched his chin, thinking over the offer. "That thing's not stolen. Is it?"

"No. It's not stolen." Luther raised his right hand. "Honest Injun."

"And all you want for it is a ride to Greenwood Cemetery. Nothing more?"

"That's it. Just a ride."

"Help me load it into my truck?"

"I'll help you load it."

"Ah, hell. I wasn't catching anything tonight anyway." Siler reeled in his line, setting his fishing pole down. "Chief, you've got yourself a ride. Let's load that canoe; looks like I'm going to Orlando."

CHAPTER 28

Sarah sat on a granite bench across the road from the office, waiting for Jack's return. It had been a long night, and an even longer day, and she wanted nothing more than to slip into comfortable clothing, curl up on the couch, and watch an old movie with a good glass of wine.

"Make it two glasses," she said aloud, giggling to herself. She turned and looked around, but saw no sign of Jack's pickup, not even the flash of the truck's headlights bouncing off the headstones or illuminating the branches of trees. He was probably on the backside of the cemetery, and couldn't be seen from where she sat.

She considered climbing the hill behind her to try to see him, but that seemed like too much trouble. She was tired, and had already done way too much walking for one evening. He would be back in a minute, with or without the three young men for whom he was searching.

Truthfully, she thought Jack was on a wild goose chase. The three men had probably left the cemetery earlier in the night, bored out of their minds with the history tour, and drinking themselves into oblivion in a downtown bar or club. But her husband was very protective when it came to Greenwood, and would not call it a night until he was absolutely certain there was no one inside the cemetery.

Not that he really needed to be concerned about such things. In the years he had been the sexton, there had been little vandalism at Greenwood, despite it being only a few blocks from the heart of downtown Orlando. And the local transients who inhabited the area rarely wandered into the cemetery, even when it was open to the public. They knew it was a sure trip to jail if caught trespassing on city property at night, and kept to the parks and wooded lots.

Sarah glanced at her watch. It was almost midnight, the witching hour. She smiled, thinking how many people went out of their way to avoid being in a graveyard at night, but such things didn't bother her. But then again, handling dead bodies didn't bother her either.

You're definitely a strange girl.

Nope. Graveyards and dead people didn't bother her. Waiting did.

"Come on, Jack." She said, talking to herself. "They went home already."

She stood and looked around, again debating if she should climb the hill to search for Jack. Or maybe she should just go on home. She had her car, and the gates were still unlocked. She could call him on her cell phone and let him know she was leaving.

But she didn't like the thought of leaving her husband alone in the cemetery, even though he had spent the night in Greenwood by himself on numerous occasions. What if the men for whom he searched were still on property, and dangerous? What if he got jumped? She wouldn't be able to live with herself if she left and he got hurt.

She sighed and sat back down. Leaving was out of the question. She would have to wait, no matter how long it took.

Sarah had just sat down when she saw movement out of the corner of her eye. It startled her, causing her heart to skip a beat.

She spotted one of the missing men coming around the far end of the caretaker's barn. As he walked out of the darkness into the yellow glow cast by a security light, she saw that he was completely naked.

She jumped up, shocked, not knowing what to think or exactly what to do. It wasn't everyday she saw a nude man walking toward her.

Wanting to put something a little solid between herself and the man, she hurried across the road to the office and tried to open the front door. But Jack had already locked the office for the night, and she didn't have a key.

"Fuck."

She backed away from the door, her gaze focused on the approaching man. He moved with an odd fluid gracefulness, as if completely comfortable being nude, his muscles rippling. But it was the man's eyes that scared her most, for they reflected the light like those of a wild animal, glowing a bright amber.

Sarah grabbed her cell phone and started to call Jack, but then she noticed the man's shadow cast upon the front of the caretaker's barn by the bright security light. It was not the shadow of a man, or even a person. Instead, it was the shadow of a rat, or some other large rodent, blown up to man size proportions and cast in black across the front of the building.

Seeing the shadow caused something to flutter and stir deep down inside her memory. She had seen something similar a long, long time ago.

he man must have noticed her expression of shock, because he stopped and looked behind him, seeing his shadow cast in black on the building. He turned back toward her, an evil grin unfolding upon his face.

"Ah, I see my shadow has given away my true identity."

Sarah swallowed hard and found her voice. "Who ... What are you?"

"Just a warrior, nothing more. Someone Coyote sent to find you."

Again, the moth wings fluttered deep inside her mind, stirring memories long suppressed and forgotten. The name Coyote was something to be afraid of, but she did not know why.

The young man was still grinning as he placed both hands on his chest and pushed inward with his fingertips, tearing flesh with his nails. Blood flowed, running in tiny rivulets down his naked body. And then he pulled his hands apart, parting his skin from forehead to crotch and stepping out of it as one would shed a jumpsuit.

Sarah tried to scream, but only a soft whimper escaped her throat. The cell phone slipped unnoticed from her fingers and shattered on the pavement. And deep down inside her mind another memory floated to the surface, bursting like a bubble.

She had seen a skinless person once before, long ago. She had run screaming from that person, seeking safety in the darkness of a forest. Sarah wanted to run screaming now, but her legs had gone all rubbery and refused to move.

The man shook his skin, as one would shake the wrinkles from a pair of pants or cotton shirt. And then he turned the skin inside out, like a reversible jacket, revealing a lining of dark brown fur. He stepped back into his skin, first slipping into the legs and then the arms, resealing the opening by pushing the two sides together with his hands. And as the opening again closed, he began to change in shape and size, from a man into a large rodent. A rat.

Fuck.

She stared in horror, too scared to even think about running, mesmerized by what was happening before her. The young man might have shrank to the size of a normal rat, but as the transformation took place, he reopened the wound in his chest a fraction of an inch, stopping the change in mid-phase.

What stood before her now was neither man nor rat, but a demented combination of the two. Towering over her in height, it was like something out of a Lon Chaney Jr. werewolf movie, only rodent-shaped. A wererat.

Sarah threw herself against the office door, kicking madly and twisting on the doorknob, but the door refused to budge. She turned and ran for the safety of her car, but only took a couple steps when Rat rushed forward and grabbed her by the hair, jerking her backward and slamming her against the front of the building.

Pain exploded white hot through her brain, shooting down both sides of her body. She almost passed out, but a little voice in the back on her head told her to stay conscious, to stay on her feet and keep fighting. If she passed out, she would be completely helpless … she would be dead.

Digging his clawed hand into her shoulder, Rat picked her up and held her at arm's length. His whiskers twitched as he examined her, his eyes shining with reflected light. And then his lips pulled back in a hideous rodent grin, revealing teeth that were pointed and razor sharp.

Rat pulled her closer, perhaps intending to plunge his teeth into the unprotected flesh of her neck. But she had other plans and lashed out with a vicious kick to the creature's groin, causing him to squeal in pain and release his hold on her.

Sarah stepped back. She was about to kick out again when the roar of a truck engine got her attention. Jack's big pickup barreled down the hill at high speed, heading straight for them.

The truck's horn blew, splitting the night and sounding like the howl of an angry demon. Rat straightened and turned his head in the direction of the noise, the truck racing toward him. Sarah spun on her heals, sprinting to get out of the way.

The truck reached the bottom of the hill and launched across the road, nearly going airborne. It slammed into Rat and carried him backward, smashing like a runaway freight train into the front of the building. Wood, glass, and concrete blocks exploded as the pickup crashed, completely destroying the front door and knocking a huge hole into the wall. Blood and pieces of shape-shifting rodent splattered in all directions as the truck came to a halt in the middle of the lobby. The wailing horn and roaring engine fell silent, replaced by the metallic ticking of heated metal parts as they cooled.

A moment passed, the dust slowly settling, and then the driver's door opened and Jack climbed out of the vehicle. He was bruised and banged up, but not seriously hurt.

He stepped away from the pickup, surveying the damage to both the office and his truck. Finally, he saw what he had done to the rodent shape-shifter. Pieces of Rat clung to the front of the truck and were splattered across the walls.

His head ringing from the impact, Jack staggered across the lobby and out the gaping hole in the front wall, stumbling over broken cinderblocks and pieces of the door.

His wife stood in the middle of the road, her eyes wide with fright. She collapsed when she saw him, as if someone cut the cords holding her up, and sank to her knees on the pavement.

"Sarah!"

Jack tried to hurry to her, but he moved in a daze, staggering, unable to walk in a straight line. He wondered if something inside of him had been damaged in the collision, causing him to lose control of his body, but there was not time to think of such things. He could get checked out at a hospital later; right now, he had her to worry about.

"Sarah," he called again, reaching her side. She was still on her knees, slumped forward and staring at the ground. He grabbed her by the arms, helping her to her feet. "Are you okay?"

She raised her head, studying his face, the light slowly coming back into her eyes.

"Oh, Jack. I was so scared." She touched his arms, his chest. "Are you hurt?"

He shook his head. "I'm okay, just banged up a little."

"Thank God." She threw herself into his arms, hugging him. "I was so scared. What was that thing?"

"I don't know," he replied. "But it's dead now."

She stepped back, looking past him. "Oh, Baby. Your truck. I'm so sorry." Tears formed at the corners of her eyes. The truck was his pride and joy.

"It's okay. I'll get a new one."

"But what about your office? The city will have a fit. You'll get fired."

"Stop worrying. Everything will be okay. I'll work it out."

He stepped forward and they embraced again, holding each other for strength. He turned her slightly so that she was no longer looking at the office and the bloody remains of the creature he had run over. What the hell was it anyway? In the bright beams of his headlights, it had looked like a giant rat.

Sarah was right about the office. The city would have a fit. There would be some serious explaining to do, and would anyone believe a story about a monstrous rodent?

"Jack …"

But he would worry about that when the time came; right now he was just happy his wife was safe.

"Jack …"

"Shhh … don't worry," he whispered, comforting her. He tried to hold her tighter, but she pushed away from him, screaming.

"Jack …"

Sarah pointed up the hill, her eyes wide with fright.

He turned to see two large furry shapes moving toward them at great speed.

Wolf and Fox were coming.

CHAPTER 29

Raven slowed his Harley Davidson as he turned onto Magnolia Street, bringing the big bike to a stop and parking next to the curb. Across the street sat a stately gray, two-story Victorian house. The sign in front of the house identified it as the Lewis Powell Funeral Home.

Lowering the kickstand, he leaned the bike but did not dismount. Instead, he remained seated, studying the house. Mouse also studied the funeral home, his head poking out the left breast pocket of Raven's leather jacket.

A light could be seen through the tiny windows set high in the front door, but it was an interior hallway light no doubt left on for security. No light shone from any of the windows on the second floor, where Sarah and her husband lived. They were either not home, or had gone to bed early.

Not sure what he would say to the woman he had never met, or if his warning would even be believed, Raven climbed off the motorcycle and walked across the street. Chances were she would think him deranged, or high on drugs, and call the police. But it was a chance he had to take, the future of mankind in the New World at stake.

Walking up the narrow sidewalk, he climbed the three steps to the porch. He started to ring the doorbell, when he detected a slight scent upon the wind. A faint musky odor.

Mouse also picked up the scent, wiggling his nose and sniffing.

"Coyote," Mouse squeaked, worried. He climbed out from the pocket and scrambled up the jacket to sit on Raven's shoulder.

"Yes, but not the Trickster. One of his kind." Raven sniffed. "The odor is faint. It has been many hours since they were here."

"Not long enough," Mouse said and wiggled his nose, whispering in Raven's ear. "They might return."

"Do not worry, my little friend."

"Easy for you to say," Mouse replied. "You are not in danger of being eaten."

Raven pushed the button and the sound of a doorbell rang deep within the house. He waited a minute, then pushed it again. Stepping back from the door, he looked up at the windows on the second floor.

The doorbell was loud, and would have been heard upstairs. But no lights came on.

"No one is home," Mouse said, giving a worried look back toward the street. "We should go."

"Where?"

"Someplace safer," said the little rodent.

Raven laughed. "With Coyote and his followers on the prowl, no place is safe."

He stepped back up to the front door and tried the knob, surprised when it turned easily in his hand. He pushed, and the door opened with a squeak.

"This is not good."

"Maybe they forgot to lock it," suggested Mouse.

"Doubtful. Funeral homes have chemicals some consider valuable, especially to crack heads and drug dealers. This door should have been locked, and the alarm set."

"What is a crack head?" Mouse asked.

He ignored him, not wanting to get into a long explanation. After all, how do you explain such things to a rodent?

Raven entered the building, closing the door behind him but not locking it. He stood there, motionless, listening to the sounds around him. The building was quiet, except for the soft *tick-tick* of an antique clock coming from the waiting room. No noise to indicate anyone else was there but them.

He inhaled, his nostrils searching for telltale signs that danger was nearby. But there was no scent of Coyote or any of his followers inside the building. But there were smells associated with death inside the home: the pungent odors of decomposing flesh, like a flower garden gone bad, the chemical stink of formaldehyde, the coppery smell of blood accidentally spilled on a tile floor. But these were smells associated with the business of a funeral home, and not those of violent death and murder.

"Let's look around," Raven said, starting down the hallway.

"But no one is here," Mouse stated.

"True. But maybe we can find out where they went. Blue Sky Woman is in danger, and Coyote is on the hunt."

"We should start in the kitchen," Mouse suggested. "I can look in the cabinets."

Raven laughed. "She will not be hiding in the food cabinets."

"It does not hurt to look," retorted Mouse.

They started their search on the first floor, beginning with the office and chapel. Finding nothing, they proceeded on to the storage and embalming rooms.

"It stinks in here," Mouse said as they entered the embalming room.

"Yes, it does," Raven agreed.

In the center of the room were two stainless steel tables, both empty, surrounded by equipment for draining blood from lifeless bodies and replacing it with preservative chemicals.

"What is this place?" Mouse asked.

"It is a place for preparing bodies for burial."

Raven looked quickly around the room, then stepped back into the hallway. "There is nothing here."

"Just sadness," said Mouse.

Turning off the lights, they left the embalming room and headed upstairs.

They searched the living quarters on the second floor, but also found them empty. Nor did they find anything to indicate where the occupants had gone. Raven was just about to call off the search and go back downstairs when he noticed the answering machine sitting on an end table next to the sofa.

He pushed the button to play the recorded message: the voice of Sarah Reynolds telling callers about the Moonlight History Tour at Greenwood Cemetery.

Raven had been to Greenwood on several occasions, watching Sarah and her husband from afar, so he knew how to get there. He was fearful that Coyote and his followers might be snapping at the young woman's heels, perhaps even following her when she left the funeral home, so he knew there was no time to spare.

"Let's go," he said to Mouse.

After heading back down the stairs to the first floor, Raven hurried down the hallway and crossed the lobby. He was about to leave, when he noticed that the front door now stood slightly ajar. He had made sure to close the door when they entered the building, so someone must have entered after them.

There was a soft squeak as one of the interior doors behind them opened. Raven turned just as a neatly dressed man wearing a suit and tie stepped into the hallway. He held a Glock semi-automatic pistol, pointed at them.

Raven froze. Mouse squeaked and ducked back into the leather jacket's breast pocket, shivering in fear

"Michael Blackwing, I presume?" Keeping the gun pointed at the shape-shifter, the man reached inside his suit and removed a photograph, tossing it on the floor in front of Raven. "Go ahead." He gestured with the gun. "Pick it up."

Raven picked up the photograph. The grainy black and white image, obviously taken by a security camera, showed him entering the Willows Nursing Home.

"My name is Special Agent Kelly, FBI, and you're under arrest for murder."

"I didn't do it."

"There will be plenty of time to explain that to a judge. In the meantime, I want you face-down on the floor. Put your hands behind your back. Any sudden movements and I *will* shoot you. You got that?"

The shape-shifter nodded. Moving very slow and deliberately, he lowered himself to the carpeted floor and put his hands behind his back. He was careful to keep his weight on his right side, because Mouse was still in his left pocket and he didn't want to squish him.

Keeping his gun trained on Raven, Agent Kelly reached behind his back and pulled a pair of handcuffs from underneath his suit jacket. "You know, I didn't even come here looking for you. I came to talk with Mrs. Reynolds. You called her the other night. Didn't you? That was your mistake. That, and coming here. Funny we should show up at the same time, don't you think? I'll probably get a promotion."

Agent Kelly kneeled next to Raven.

"I don't suppose you'll tell me what you did with her father?"

Raven didn't reply.

"Yeah, I didn't think so." The agent leaned forward, and started to put the handcuffs on Raven's wrists, when Mouse darted out of the jacket pocket and scurried around to his back. The little rodent jumped onto the back of the agent's right hand, racing up his arm.

"Hey!" Agent Kelly jumped back. "What the hell."

The agent slapped at Mouse, but missed. The gun went off, the bullet striking the floor. Mouse avoided several more slaps, and after reaching the agent's shoulder, he jumped up and clamped a set of sharp teeth onto the man's earlobe. Mouse bit down hard, drawing blood, his body hanging like a furry earring.

Agent Kelly screamed in pain.

Raven leaped up from the floor and threw himself at the agent, grabbing the gun and taking him to the ground. Mouse let go of the ear and ran for safety as Raven struck the FBI agent once, twice, and then three times, knocking him unconscious and tearing the pistol from his grip. Flipping him over and onto his stomach, he pulled Agent Kelly's arms behind his back and handcuffed his wrists.

Raven tucked the pistol into his pants, scooped up Mouse, and placed him back in the jacket pocket. "Time to go, my friend." Leaving the funeral home, he crossed the street and climbed onto his Harley.

Mouse resumed his riding position, with his head sticking out of the leather jacket's breast pocket.

Raven fired up the big motorcycle and made a U-turn in the middle of the street and headed toward downtown Orlando. Next stop: Greenwood Cemetery.

CHAPTER 30

With fangs bared and murder in their eyes, Wolf and Fox raced full speed down the hill, passing the Wilmount mausoleum and heading straight for Jack and Sarah.

Jack looked around for a weapon, frantically searching for anything he could use to fend off the attack about to happen, but there was nothing to be had—nothing but broken pieces of cinderblocks, and he didn't think he'd be able to throw more than one before the beasts leaped upon them.

These were no ordinary animals that raced down the hill to attack them. He had seen them change shape, from human to creatures of fur and fang. They were supernatural monsters, a werewolf and a werefox, and no doubt possessed strength and powers far exceeding that of the animals whose skins they now wore. Forget cinderblocks, he needed a fucking bazooka.

He cast a quick glance to his right, hoping they could escape in Sarah's car. But she had parked too far away from the office, and there was no way they could make it to the car, unlock the doors and climb inside before being set upon. Even if they could, one of them would have to get out again to unlock and open the front gates of the cemetery. It would be suicide.

Jack studyied the building that stood a mere twenty feet from the office. The caretaker's barn was also built of concrete blocks, strong and sturdy, and it contained landscaping tools that could be used as weapons: shovels, pitchforks, even some power tools. It was their only hope.

"Come on. Hurry!" He grabbed Sarah's hand and pulled her away from the demolished office building. She resisted at first, pointing at her vehicle.

"My car."

"No time. We'll never make it."

She must have realized the wisdom in his argument, because she didn't resist. Instead, she gripped his hand even tighter, and together they raced for the caretaker's barn.

Jack already had the key in his hand when they reached the front door. He unlocked and opened the door and pushed Sarah inside, quickly following behind her. He had just closed and bolted the door when something slammed into it from the other side. He stepped back, listening as an animal sniffed around the door to find a way inside.

"What the hell are those things?"

"I don't know," Sarah replied, breathing hard, "but they can change shape from human into animal ..."

"I know. I saw one change."

"... and into something in-between."

"But that's impossible," he said. "Isn't it? I mean, shape-shifters ... werewolves ... that's something out of Hollywood. They can't really exist."

Sarah looked away from him, staring at the door. Something was still sniffing around on the outside. "After this week, I'm not sure what's possible and what isn't anymore. Weird phone calls in the middle of the night, corpses that sit up and talk ..."

He remembered what he had seen the other night. "And coyotes trying to open the front door of the funeral home."

Fear caused the corner of Sarah's mouth to tremble. "My god. Do you think it's all connected?"

"Like you, I don't know what to think anymore. I'm baffled."

"And frightened."

He nodded. "And frightened."

"But if the animal you saw the other night ... if it really was trying to get in, then it might have been one of these things. That means—"

"It means they followed us here," he said, completing her thoughts.

"We're being stalked."

"Or hunted."

"But why, Jack?"

He shook his head. "I don't know, but I'm not waiting to find out." He looked around, searching for possible weapons to defend themselves. At the opposite end of the room, just inside a large rollup door, sat a small backhoe and a four-wheel drive John Deere Gator.

The caretakers didn't dig the graves at Greenwood—that was contracted out to a private company—but they used the backhoe to remove azalea bushes and other shrubbery planted by families of the dead, neglected over the years. The backhoe wasn't used often, but it was well-maintained and very useful when needed.

The Gator was used daily, providing transportation for the caretakers to various gravesites where work was needed. Sitting next to the Gator was a green golf cart, with the words *Greenwood*

Cemetery painted on it in white letters. Jack and Anna relied on the golf cart when showing potential customers different sections of the cemetery.

Crossing the room, he looked in the bed of the Gator delighted to find an assortment of tools that could be used as weapons, including a shovel, pitchfork, and a machete.

He picked up the shovel first because it had the longest handle, and felt along the edge of the blade. The caretakers had always kept the edges of their shovels sharpened, because they often had to cut through roots when digging, but it had been a long time since this particular shovel had been sharpened and its edge quite dull.

"Nope. No good."

The machete was sharp, and could easily cleave through flesh and maybe even bone, but its blade was only about two feet long and he didn't want to get that close to the creatures outside, especially if they could transform into beasts even more frightening and dangerous than an ordinary wolf or fox.

The pitchfork was probably the best weapon of the bunch. The four steel prongs were sturdy and sharp, and the handle long enough to keep an attacker at bay. Jack lifted the pitchfork from the bed of the Gator and stabbed at the air a few times to get the feel of it.

"Is that all we've got?" Sarah asked, watching him.

"This should put a nasty hurt on those things," he replied. "And if they get past the pitchfork, then there's the machete."

"What about gasoline?" she asked. "We could light them on fire, maybe."

"Afraid the gasoline is locked up in the tool room, along with all the power tools."

"Don't you have a key?"

"In the office, not on me."

She frowned. "What kind of supervisor are you?"

"One who sits behind a desk for most of the day. My caretakers use the tools, so they carry keys to the tool room. Even if I had the key, we would have to go back outside to get to the tool room."

Sarah shook her head. "Forget that. We're not opening this door."

Jack smiled. "I thought you'd see it my way."

She pointed at the backhoe. "Maybe you could siphon some gas out of that."

He shook his head. "I'd need a hose, and I doubt if there is anything to put the gas in. We'll just have to make do with what we've got." He grabbed the pitchfork and machete. "They're primitive, but effective."

He started back across the room to her, but then spotted something sitting on the other side of the Gator. "Hello. What's this?"

"What?"

He leaned the pitchfork against the wall and picked up a gas-powered chainsaw with a twenty-inch blade. "I should be madder than hell that my guys forgot to lock this in the tool room, but right now I could kiss them."

"Does it work?"

"It had better work. We've got three chainsaws and all three have to be maintained in case the city gets hit by another hurricane."

Jack laid the machete on the floor before setting the chainsaw's safety brake and priming it with a few quick pulls of the rope. He moved the switch to the Start position and pulled the rope again. The chainsaw started with a roar.

Releasing the brake, he squeezed the trigger, causing the cutting chain to spin. He revved the motor a few times, then turned off the saw. "I'd say it works."

"Thank God," she said, relieved.

A chainsaw could be a formable weapon, and might even keep a shape-shifting creature at bay. Grabbing the chainsaw and other tools, Jack walked back to where his wife stood. He handed her the machete, but kept the chainsaw for himself.

"I'd rather have the chainsaw," she said, trying to get the feel of the machete. "This feels kind of puny."

"Think you can start a chainsaw by yourself?"

She thought about it a moment. "No. I guess not."

"Then you get the—"

A wolf's howl sounded just outside the door, deep-throated and loud. A second howl followed, sharper and higher pitched than the first. Jack suspected the second howl was that of a fox, but he had never heard a fox howl and couldn't be sure.

"What are they doing?" Sarah asked, a chill dancing down her spine.

He listened for a moment, then turned to her. "I could be wrong, but I think they're calling for help.

Jack stood on an aluminum stepladder, looking out the windows on the west end of the caretaker's barn. Sitting about ten feet from the building, halfway between the barn and the office, was a red fox. Not just an ordinary red fox, but a supernatural creature, a skin-walker, with the ability to transform from human into animal.

Fox had been sitting there nearly motionless for over an hour, watching the windows and front door, standing guard to prevent their escape.

Jack hadn't seen the other shape-shifter for quite some time, but suspected that Wolf stood guard at the other end of the building, watching the large roll-up door.

During the past few hours, the howls of Wolf and Fox had been answered by the cries and arrivals of other animals.

First to show up was a great horned owl, which had perched on top of the office roof like a sentry on guard duty. A score of rats had joined the owl, attacking the rubber hoses and electrical wiring on Sarah's car. The car now sat on four flat tires, and it was doubtful if the engine would even start.

"What's it doing now?" Sarah asked. She sat on the golf cart, her forehead resting on the steering wheel.

"It hasn't moved," Jack replied over his shoulder. "It's just sitting there, watching the windows."

"Persistent fucker," she said, her voice fatigued.

He smiled, but when he turned to her his smile faded. Sarah looked drained, nearly sick with worry and fear. He needed to do something to keep her spirit up, but he didn't know what to do. They were trapped, cut off from the rest of the world by creatures apparently out to get them. And for the life of him, he didn't know why.

The situation was absurd, insane, and if he wasn't seeing it with his own eyes, he never would believe it. He never believed in the supernatural, not even ghosts, but after tonight he was willing to accept just about anything. Monsters? Most definitely. Bigfoot? For sure. Little green men from outer space? Why, of course.

"What time is it?" he asked.

Sarah raised her head wearily and looked at her wristwatch. "Almost three a.m."

"Another three hours and it will be light outside." He tried to sound cheerful, but it wasn't working.

"What time does Summer open the gates?"

"Gates open at seven, but she may open them a little earlier."

Sarah suddenly sat up straight, her eyes widening in fear. Jack thought she saw something in the windows behind him, turning around quickly to look.

"Jack ..."

"What is it? What did you see?"

"Nothing. I didn't see anything." She shook her head. "But you said Summer is opening the gates at seven. She always walks from her house through the cemetery. If those things are still here, they might attack her."

"You're right," he agreed, "but what can we do?"

"We have to do something. We have to warn her."

He shook his head. "We're in no position to warn anyone."

"We have to try," Sarah argued. "We can't just sit here and let her walk into this mess. They'll attack her ... kill her. It will be our fault. Her blood will be on our hands."

She started to cry, tears streaming down her face. She wasn't crying out of fear for herself and Jack, but for the safety of the young woman who might soon be in mortal danger—tears of compassion for another human being.

Jack descended the ladder and hurried to his wife's side, holding her and whispering words of comfort into her ear.

"Everything's going to be okay, you'll see. We'll get out of—"

Something struck the door hard from the other side, causing both of them to jump.

"Jack, what's going on?" She wiped the tears from her face.

"I'm not sure," he said. "Wait here." He got off the golf cart and hurried back to the ladder, quickly climbing it to look out the window.

Fox was still guarding the building, but he was on his feet and wagging his tail. Something was definitely going on.

"What is it?" she asked.

"I don't know. I think something is happening."

Just then Wolf came around the building. The shape-shifter had transformed into a terrifying creature, half man and half wolf, walking upright on its two hind legs and towering over seven feet in height. He carried a triangular piece of gray granite, a chunk of headstone that probably weighed two hundred pounds. And though he was still thirty feet away, he hurled that chunk of stone at the windows as easily as one would throw a baseball.

"Look out!" Jack yelled, jumping off the ladder.

The piece of gravestone struck the framework between the two windows, breaking through the wall and shattering the glass into a thousand pieces.

He hurried to the golf cart and grabbed the chainsaw off the floor, frantically pulling the rope handle to start it. "Come on. Come on, you bitch. Start!" He pulled the rope again, and again, but the chainsaw only sputtered.

"Jack, hurry!" Sarah stood near him, watching the broken windows.

Outside, a bloodcurdling howl split the night.

Jack pulled on the rope again, and the chainsaw roared to life. He slapped the safety brake, allowing the chain to spin freely.

"Got it!"

Wolf leaped through the glassless window and landed in their midst. The creature quickly spotted them, its lips pulling back in a snarl to reveal deadly fangs.

Sarah screamed and backed away, not even bothering to grab the machete off the golf cart's seat. She knew the puny blade would be of little help against such a creature.

Wolf paid little mind to Jack, his attention focused entirely on the woman backing away from him, tracking her every movement with amber eyes. It was the female he was after, not her mate. Muscles tightening for the attack, he licked his lips in eager anticipation.

"Get back!" Jack rushed forward to position himself between Sarah and the monster. He swung the chainsaw in a wide arc, the spinning blade severing the two smallest fingers on the creature's right hand.

Wolf howled in pain, blood spurting from his wound. He turned and fixed Jack with a murderous gaze, a roar of anger sounding deep within his throat.

"Sarah, get out!" Jack shouted over his shoulder, not daring to take his eyes off his opponent. "Take the backhoe and go."

Jack had taught her how to drive the backhoe on a quiet Sunday about a year ago, and knew the caretakers always kept the keys in the vehicle. It was her best means of escape, if only he could keep the werewolf occupied until she got safely away.

He cast a quick glance across the room.

Sarah had not moved. She stood frozen in terror, her eyes wide.

"Sarah, goddamn it, snap out of it. Move your ass!"

He must have gotten through to her, because Sarah suddenly

blinked and shook her head, as if coming out of a hypnotic trance. She looked at Jack, hesitant to leave him. Her gaze went to the machete on the golf cart, and she started forward to grab it.

"Sarah, no—"

With a furious roar, Wolf lunged forward and swung at Jack, black claws slicing the air with a whistling sound. Jack tried to raise the chainsaw to block the attack, but wasn't fast enough. The claws struck him high on the left cheekbone, cutting him open to the bone and splattering blood across the room.

The force of the blow spun Jack like a top, turning him around with his back to the monster. Grabbing him from behind, Wolf bit down on Jack's unprotected neck with razor sharp fangs, severing his jugular and crunching through vertebras.

Sarah staggered back in horror.

Blood spurted from Jack's neck, He tried to scream, but only a wet gurgling escaped his lips. Wolf bit down again, and Jack's head fell away from his body and rolled across the room.

"Nooo!" Sarah screamed. With her brain sending out a thousand messages at once, her legs finally received the signal needed to get moving. She turned and sprinted for the backhoe at the other end of the room.

"Oh, god ... oh, god ... oh, god ..."

Wolf held onto Jack until he stopped kicking, then cast aside his headless body like a child tossing away an unwanted toy. He turned and started across the room, stalking Sarah.

She reached the backhoe, climbing quickly into the seat and starting the engine. She shifted into reverse and stomped down on the gas pedal. The big back tires spun wildly on the concrete floor and then got traction, the backhoe hurling backward into the big rollup door. The door exploded, tearing free from its mounting, the backhoe shooting out into the night.

Sarah kept the accelerator floored until she was free of the building. Slamming on the brakes, she brought the backhoe to a screeching stop and struggled to shift into first gear. Wolf emerged from the barn and came after her. He moved at a slow trot at first, then quickly picked up speed when he realized she was having trouble.

"Come on, come on, come on ..."

She stomped the clutch and shifted gears again, finally able to get it into first. The backhoe chugged forward, gaining speed.

She cut across the southern end of section K, knocking over two headstones before reaching the street. Jerking the steering wheel, she shot past the caretaker's barn and the office as she headed down the hill to the front gates.

Wolf rounded the buildings, racing to catch her.

Sarah spotted a pair of headlights ahead of her, a vehicle stopped at the cemetery gates.

Help had arrived.

"Over here. Help me!" she screamed, waving madly.

She had just passed the office building when dozens of nocturnal creatures rushed out of the darkness to stop her: mice, rats, raccoons, bats, an owl, and a very large fox. The owl flew at her face, causing her to duck and steer wildly, several of the smaller creatures dying beneath the crushing back wheels of the backhoe.

Sarah had just made it through the pack when she heard the sound of heavy footfalls behind her. Turning, she saw black claws reaching out to grab her.

CHAPTER 31

Siler Lock brought his pickup truck to a stop at the entrance to Greenwood Cemetery. He started to get out to see if the gates were unlocked, but hesitated when he heard a loud crash from inside the graveyard, followed by the roar of an engine, and the metal on metal grinding of gears.

"What the hell is that?" he asked.

A backhoe suddenly appeared out of the darkness, being driven erratically at high speed by a young woman. Its headlights swung left, and then right, piercing the night and illuminating creatures of fur and feather hurrying from the darkness, apparently attempting to stop it.

"Look!" Luther pointed through the windshield.

Sarah screamed and waved, trying to get their attention. A hideous creature chased after her, half man and half wolf, its gray fur wet with the bright crimson of fresh blood.

"Sweet mother of—"

"Move!" Luther stomped down on Siler's foot, mashing the accelerator. The pickup shot forward with a lurch, crashing through the double gates and roaring into the cemetery. The wooden canoe slid unnoticed out of the back, bouncing across the street.

Siler gripped the steering wheel tightly, desperately trying to keep control of the speeding truck. "Glove box!" he shouted. "Open it."

Luther opened the glove box, fumbling to remove a large revolver. The pickup ran over several rats and struck a large owl that stood in the middle of the road with its back to them. Feathers flew everywhere. Siler steered to intercept the monster that was now only a few feet behind the backhoe.

"Shoot that damn thing!"

Luther removed his foot from the top of Siler's. He stuck the revolver out the window and fired three shots at Wolf, but missed. He was about to pull the trigger again when a snarling, snapping Fox leaped in through the open driver's window and attacked Siler.

Siler screamed and let go of the wheel, trying to protect his face and neck. The truck veered wildly, slamming into an oak tree. The impact threw all three occupants forward, with Fox bouncing off the windshield and laying stunned on the dash.

"Get out!" Luther reached across and opened the driver's door, pushing Siler out the truck. He followed him, slamming the door behind him.

Fox got groggily to his feet.

As they staggered away from the truck, Wolf leaped over the vehicle from the other side. He grabbed Siler by the back of the neck and shook him like a rag doll, the tiny bones in his neck snapping like dried pieces of chalk.

Wolf gave Siler a final shake, then tossed aside his limp and lifeless body. He turned and advanced slowly toward Luther. But the old man was ready, the big revolver clutched tightly in both hands.

"You chose the wrong side to fight on."

Luther slowly squeezed the trigger, and the big revolver roared with a flash, the bullet slamming into the center of Wolf's chest and knocking him back. He quickly fired twice more, the second and third bullets also striking dead center of the creature's chest. Wolf gasped in pain and sank to his knees, toppling over on his side. He took two raspy breaths and then went still, his tongue rolling limply from between fangs.

Luther stood over Wolf and squeezed the trigger once more, but the pistol was empty and the hammer only clicked on an empty cartridge. Tossing aside the revolver, he turned to his daughter.

Sarah still sat on the backhoe, clutching the steering wheel in a death grip, her gaze focused on the dead Wolf. Luther resisted the urge to run to her, for he was a stranger to the young woman. She was obviously traumatized by what had transpired, and he didn't want to frighten her any more.

He stopped a few feet from the backhoe, looking up at her. Luther had not seen Sarah since her childhood, yet he knew the woman was indeed his daughter. The gift he had been given as a Council member told him that she was flesh and blood, family.

"Sarah ..."

She did not respond, her gaze still fixed on the dead shape-shifter.

"Sarah Reynolds," he said, raising his voice. But the young woman on the backhoe remained motionless, and he worried that her mind had become unhinged with fright. The medicine he carried in his bag could cure certain illnesses, but it could do nothing for afflictions of the mind. Stepping closer, he cleared his throat and tried again. "Sarah Reynolds, I am your father."

She stirred then, her head slowly turning in his direction. She blinked and her gaze focused upon him, perhaps seeing him for the first time.

"I know," she said, her voice flat and emotionless.

"You know?" he asked, surprised. "How?"

She shook her head. "I'm not sure, but I knew it was you as soon as you got out of the truck."

He nodded, realizing that other powers were at work. Perhaps a spirit had whispered in her ear, telling Sarah that her father had arrived to help. The spirits often took an interest in what transpired in the New World, especially when the safety of a Council member—or future Council member—was at stake.

She turned to Wolf, a tear leaking slowly down her face. "That thing killed my husband ... tried to kill me. Why?"

Luther saw her shoulders slump, and knew she was about to succumb to emotions. There wasn't time for such things, not when she was still in danger. Wolf had obviously been sent by Coyote. Others aligned with the Trickster might also come.

The old Indian took a step forward, wanting to comfort his daughter, but wanting even more to quickly explain what was going on so she would be aware of the dangers.

"Sarah, we have—"

A loud, threatening growl sounded from behind him. He turned just as the driver's door of the pickup slowly opened, and something large and furry emerged to stand on two legs.

He had completely forgotten about Fox, thinking the creature had been injured or too stunned to fight. But Fox had recovered, transforming into a form that was half human and half animal. While not nearly as big as Wolf, the shape-shifter was much larger than Luther.

Fox studied the two of them, swaying slightly on his feet. Hoping the shape-shifter might still be a little dazed, Luther lunged forward and grabbed the wooden leaf-shaped paddle out of the pickup's bed. Backing away, he gripped the paddle in both hands like a cricket bat.

"What you are doing is wrong," he said to Fox. "It is forbidden to harm a member of the Council."

"What are you doing?" Sarah asked, her voice strained with fear. "That thing can't understand you."

"Yes he can, only he chooses not to listen. Coyote has poisoned his brain."

He turned to her. "I want you to know that what they said about me isn't true. I never molested you, or did anything to hurt you. Not once."

She nodded. "I know. I'm starting to remember."

Luther looked away from her just as Fox attacked. The shape-shifter closed the distance between them in a single leap, avoiding the swing of the paddle, and landing on top of him.

"Daddy, noooo!" Sarah screamed, helpless to do anything to stop the frenzied attack.

Fox bit and clawed like a creature gone mad. Luther managed to roll over and get to his hands and knees, managed to get out from underneath the shape-shifter, desperately trying to crawl away, only to be grabbed by the creature and dragged back beneath his murderous rage.

His clothing ripped to shreds as he bled from a dozen ghastly wounds.

The old man reached a trembling hand out to a daughter he barely knew, and silently mouthed the words, "I love you."

It was the last thing he ever said, for Fox did not stop until Luther was horribly mutilated, the ground littered with puddles of blood and tiny pieces of flesh and fabric.

Screaming in terror, Sarah jerked the steering wheel and stomped on the gas. But she let the clutch out too quickly, causing the backhoe to lurch and die. She turned the ignition key, but the engine refused to start.

Frantic, she jumped down off the backhoe and ran for the front gates, seeking safety in the neighborhood beyond the cemetery. Behind her sounded a growl, and she knew that Fox chased after her.

"Help me!" she screamed at the top of her lungs, but there was no one around to hear her cry. "Heeeelp!"

A light suddenly appeared at the far end of the street, moving at great speed toward the cemetery—the single white headlight of a motorcycle. Hope fluttered in her heart, for here was possible help and maybe even salvation. But from behind her came the sound of rapidly gaining footfalls, and the raspy breathing of the beast hurrying to overtake her.

Fox or the motorcycle. Which would reach her first?

It was a race, and it was going to be a close one.

CHAPTER 32

Raven pulled out the Glock pistol as the big Harley roared through the gates of Greenwood Cemetery, but he dared not shoot for fear of hitting Sarah.

He tucked the pistol back into his pants and removed one of the tomahawks from the hunting pouch he wore, gripping it tightly.

"Get out of the way!" he yelled at her, steering the bike to intercept Fox.

He swung the tomahawk and struck the shape-shifter in the shoulder, cutting through flesh and bone. The back end of the bike spun around in an arc as he brought the motorcycle to a screeching halt. Fox stood less than twenty feet away, one arm hanging limp at his side. Blood gushed from the tomahawk wound in his shoulder.

Lowering the kickstand, Raven quickly dismounted the bike. He glanced at Sarah to make sure she was safe. The young woman had stopped running, and stood watching what was about to transpire. He turned his attention back to Fox, smiling.

"I bet that hurts."

"Not as bad as what I am going to do to you," Fox answered in animal speak.

"Threats. Nothing but threats," Raven mocked, laughing. "Are you going to just stand there barking, little doggie? Or are you going to bite?"

Fox howled in rage and charged at full speed, running low to the ground.

Raven hesitated a moment, then pulled the Glock and fired in rapid succession.

The first two bullets hit Fox in the chest; the third hit him in the head, blowing his brains out in a pretty, pink spray. Fox took two more steps and died, his body collapsing in a furry heap.

Slipping the pistol back into his belt, Raven hurried to the body lying near the pickup truck. Even though the body was terribly mutilated, he knew it was his old friend, Luther Watie.

"Goodbye, my friend. I promise songs will be sung about you at Council fires."

Sirens sounded in the distance. The gunshots had probably been reported, and the police would be showing up in force at any moment.

Raven grabbed Luther's medicine bag, and then pulled the Zippo lighter from the dead man's pocket.

Sarah still stood a few feet away, watching him. He walked over to her, handing the young woman the bag and the lighter. "These are yours now. Take them."

She hesitated, eyeing the bag suspiciously. "What's in it?"

"Your father's medicine. It is *your* medicine now."

She hesitated a moment longer, then accepted both items.

The approaching sirens grew louder.

"We must go. There isn't much time." He grabbed her hand and started to lead her to the motorcycle.

Sarah planted her feet and pulled from his grasp. "Go? Go where? I'm not leaving. The police are coming ... I've got to stay here. My husband is dead."

"I am sorry, but the police cannot help you. Your husband is dead, but it is *you* they are after. Please hurry, your life is in danger."

She shook her head. "I don't even know who you are."

Raven quickly explained that he was a friend of her father's, and was there to help her. He reached into his breast pocket and removed a small black feather.

"I sent you a warning."

Her eyes went wide. "Oh, my god. The feather at the funeral home ... that was you?"

"Not me, but a spirit messenger acting on my behalf. A guide."

"And the corpse of Ray Talmage, it did sit up and speak to me. I wasn't imagining it."

"Yes, it sat up and spoke. I'm afraid the spirits are often overly dramatic. It's their nature. Now we—"

Just then Mouse poked his head out of Raven's jacket pocket, wiggling his nose at Sarah. "Is this Blue Sky Woman? Wow. She's pretty. I'd like to ride in her pocket."

Sarah took a step back, shocked, pointing at Mouse. "He spoke. I heard him. That mouse can speak ..."

"They can all speak," Raven said. "Only you couldn't understand their language until now. The gift of animal speak is bestowed upon all Council members, passed down through the bloodline. Your father's gift was passed on to you at the moment of his death."

The sirens grew louder. Flashing blue lights appeared at the end of the street.

"I will explain everything to you," he said, "but we must leave now."

"How can I trust you?"

"Deep down inside, you know I am telling the truth. You can feel it. It's part of who you are."

She studied his face for a moment, then nodded. "Okay. Let's go."

They hurried to the motorcycle and climbed on, Raven raising the kickstand and starting the motor. He glanced toward the open gates, but knew they could not leave that way.

"Is there another way out of this cemetery?"

"There's a back gate, on Gore Street," she replied. "It's locked, but I have a key." She pulled out a set of keys from her pocket.

"Gore Street it is." He revved the throttle and shifted into first gear, taking the road that led to the old section of the cemetery.

They had just disappeared over the hill, when several Orlando Police Department patrol cars roared into the cemetery with lights flashing.

At the back gate, Sarah jumped off the motorcycle and quickly removed the padlock and chain. She opened the gate and waited for Raven to drive out of the cemetery, then jumped back on the motorcycle. She hung on tight as he shifted gears, the big bike picking up speed.

"Where are we going?" she asked, shouting to be heard above the Harley's engine.

"I don't know," he shouted back. Someplace where we can talk. Someplace safe."

The Harley Davidson headed west on Gore Street, passing through the quiet streets of downtown Orlando. Neither one of the riders paid attention to the scenery flashing by, for they knew somewhere in the darkness behind them Coyote was snapping at their heels.

CHAPTER 33

Bear was terribly upset. He paced the great chamber of his cavern home, shaking his head in worry. Coyote had promised to be discreet in his dealings with Luther Watie and his daughter, but the Trickster had gone and enlisted the aid of others and they had made a mess of things.

Word was quickly spreading through Galun'lati about the murder of the old man and the attempt on the life of Blue Sky Woman. Allegiances were being formed among some of the tribes, angry words spoken. Some had even painted their faces and struck the war pole.

War had not been known in Galun'lati for over a thousand years, but now there was a tension in the air and the sound of distant drums. What should have been a simple assassination had turned into such a mess.

"Stupid Coyote. I should have known better than to trust you."

He walked to the far wall and took down his elm wood bow, bending it across his knee to attach its string. If war did come to the sky world, he would be ready for it. He would lead his people into battle. And if he had to do so in order to save his position as leader of the Great Council, then he would gladly put an arrow through the heart of Blue Sky Woman.

CHAPTER 34

Following Sarah's directions, Raven left downtown Orlando and headed west on Colonial Drive, putting distance between them and Greenwood Cemetery. Traffic was almost nonexistent at that time of night, so he was careful to keep the motorcycle under the speed limit. The last thing he needed was to get pulled over for speeding, and a big Harley traveling fast down an empty road would definitely get a cop's attention.

Passing strip malls, shopping centers, and numerous car dealerships, all closed for the night, they turned onto a little used dirt road leading to a lake on the back side of the Central Florida Fairgrounds.

It was more of a path than an actual road, and he was hard-pressed to keep the bike upright while avoiding the numerous potholes, ruts, and broken beer bottles. After skirting an open field on the south end of the lake, they finally parked in the inky darkness beneath a strand of trees.

Raven turned off the motorcycle and sat in silence for a few minutes, looking back the way they had come to make sure they weren't being followed.

Sarah remained on the bike behind him, also looking around, perhaps fearful that something might rush out of the darkness to attack her.

"I think we'll be safe here," he said. "We have outrun Coyote's followers, at least for the moment."

"But they'll find us again?" she asked.

"Yes," Raven said and nodded. "But we'll worry about that when the time comes. For now, we will rest. Talk. I'm sure you have many questions."

"One or two."

He lowered the kickstand and dismounted, stretching the muscles in his back. Sarah also got off and stretched, but her actions were due more to nervousness than stiffness.

He lead her away from the motorcycle, and they took a seat on a bare patch of ground. Speaking in a voice barely above a whisper, he told her about Galun'lati, the Great Council, and why her father had been killed. Mouse also helped with the explaining, climbing out of Raven's pocket and sitting on his knee.

As the story unfolded, bits of forgotten memory floated to the surface of her subconscious.

"So that night when I was a child, when they found me ... hysterical. My father was trying to teach me medicine?"

He nodded. "Luther wanted you to be ready to take over at the Council, but I think you were not ready for what he showed you that night. That is why you ran away.

"But why was I naked?"

"I wasn't there, so I don't know what ceremonies he performed. Perhaps you had gone through a sweat, or a cleansing, and lost your blanket when you ran away. Maybe he was about to perform a scratching."

"A scratching?"

"An ancient ceremony used more often for young men, sometimes boys. The medicine man takes a bone comb and scratches a series of seven lines into the skin, first the arms and then the legs. I have seen it done for those seeking the warrior path, even for stickball players before they entered the ballfield—for their games are often more like battle than play—but I have never heard of it being done on a girl. But your father and I are from different tribes, and I do not know all of his ways."

"But it wasn't something sexual?" she asked.

Raven looked shocked. "Never. Why would you think such a thing?"

"The authorities took me away, said my father had tried to sexually molest me. That's why I was naked."

"It is not true," he said, angry. "I have known Luther Watie for many years, and he would never do such a thing. His medicine was strong; he would not do anything to lose the gift, or bring dishonor upon himself or his family."

Sarah quickly wiped away a tear. She was dealing with painful memories from her childhood, dredging up images from the dark recesses of her mind.

"But he never said otherwise. Not a word. He allowed the authorities to take me away, and put me in a foster home ... an orphanage. Do you have any idea what hell I went through in that place? First, I lost my mother, and then my father. I was all alone. I had nobody."

"You were never truly alone."

"How do you know?" she argued. "You weren't there."

"Yes. I was."

"Yes. You were what?" Sarah asked, angry.

"I was there," Raven replied, calmly. "Watching you. Your father asked that I keep an eye on you, because he could not be there to protect you, so for many years I watched from afar."

"Bullshit." She shook her head. "I would have noticed you if you had been watching me, even from a distance. There weren't that many long-haired Indian types around."

"He's a shape-shifter," Mouse blurted out, giving away Raven's secret.

Sarah's eyes widened. "A shape-shifter? Like the others ... at the cemetery?" She shrank back in fear, started to get to her feet.

Raven reached out and put a reassuring hand on her arm. "Please, don't be afraid. I am not like them. But yes, I can turn my skin inside out and change forms. There are more of us than you think in this world, even more in Galun'lati. It is a gift, and sometimes a curse."

She studied him, trying to read his face in the darkness, searching for a lie. "What do you change into?"

He again pulled the black feather from his pocket. "You already know the answer."

"Show me."

He put away the feather. "You will see soon enough, but not now. Changing one's skin uses energy, and that can draw the attention of those looking for us ... looking for *you*."

"But I—"

Raven's hand shot out like a snake, his fingers covering her mouth and silencing her words. He leaned closer to her, whispering in her ear. "Shhh ... be still. We have company."

He removed his hand from her mouth, but she did not speak ... and dared not move.

Sarah sat still as a statue, barely breathing, listening to the sounds of the night.

The shape-shifter also sat motionless, his muscles tense and his head cocked slightly as if listening to something only he could hear. A few moments passed, seeming like an eternity to Sarah, and then he visibly relaxed.

"It's okay," he said. "We have nothing to fear."

"What was it?" She looked around, but saw nothing.

"Just a local resident in search of food."

"Where? I can't see anything."

He laughed.

She turned to look at him, annoyed. "What's so funny?"

"Humans rely so much on sight alone, ignoring their other senses … and their gifts."

"I don't understand."

"Can you see in the dark?"

"No."

"Then forgot about your eyes, and what you can't see. Use your ears. Use the gift your father passed on to you. Listen. What do you hear?"

Sarah sat still, slowing her breathing and focusing on the sounds around her. She listened carefully, instantly becoming aware of a chorus. There was the wind, whispering through the trees and causing the waters of the lake to lap at the sandy shore. Hundreds of insects could also be heard, communicating with a melody of chirps and strange songs. There was also a rustling noise as something crossed the field, moving in their direction, its tiny footfalls soft but distinct.

A chill touched the back of her neck. She remembered the animals back at the cemetery rushing from the darkness to stop her escape.

She listened to the creature coming toward her, quickly becoming aware of the sounds of its movements, its rapid breathing, even its voice: *Where? Where? Tasty. Tasty. Hungry. Must eat. There. Yes. There. Dig. Dig. Dig. Yes. There. Got it. Juicy. Delicious. Find another. There. There. Dig. Dig.*

It was as if her mind and the mind of the unseen animal touched, merged, and became one. For just a brief instant, she saw what it saw, felt what it felt, and knew what the creature was and that it posed no threat.

"It's an armadillo," she said, relaxing, "searching for grubs."

And then the connection was gone, the armadillo moving on in search of tasty treats, disappearing into the night.

She looked at Raven, amazed, barely able to believe what she had just experienced. "I understood everything it was saying, what it was thinking."

Raven nodded. "In Galun'lati, all creatures speak the same tongue, but here, in the New World, mankind has lost the ability to understand animal speak."

"But why?"

"Because humans kill their brothers and sisters of the forest for fun and sport, and not for food. Animals understand what it is to hunt to stay alive. But they do not understand why the two-legs hunt for sport, taking pleasure in just the kill. Entire tribes have been wiped out by the weapons of men, so the Great Council decided years ago to punish mankind by taking away his ability to understand the birds and animals of the forest. Mankind now stands alone, outcasts in a world of his own making."

He looked at her for a moment before continuing, perhaps waiting for his words to sink in. "Like your father, you have the ability to understand because you are now a member of the Great Council, and must be able to understand the other members seated beside you. And since you are a representative of the Council, the gift will be with you no matter where you go."

"I'm a regular Doctor Dolittle."

"Who?"

"Forget it. Bad joke," she said and smiled.

Sarah's smile faded as she looked around at the darkness surrounding them, a shudder of fear passing through her. "Are you sure Coyote is still looking for me?"

He nodded. "You are the only human to sit at the Council. Eliminate you and mankind will lose power in this world. Coyote will continue looking until he finds you."

"But you have a gun. You can shoot him if he shows up, like you did the other one at the cemetery."

"Coyote will not be as easy to kill. He is one of the Old Ones, and has strong medicine. That is why we run from him now, rather than stand and fight. If we have to fight the Trickster, then it is better we do so in Galun'lati. There we have friends, those who will stand and fight beside us. Here we have no one."

"You have *me*," Mouse spoke up, annoyed that he had been left out of the equation.

Raven smiled. "Yes. We have *you*, my brave little Mouse."

"Is he a shape-shifter too?" Sarah asked.

"No. He is just a mouse," replied Raven.

"Hmmp ... just a mouse," Mouse repeated, ruffling his fur in anger. "You did not think I was so small and insignificant when I was saving your butt back at the home of Blue Sky Woman."

"You were at my house?" she asked, surprised.

Raven quickly told her about their encounter with Agent Kelly, who was probably already free from the handcuffs and looking for them. It was another reason they could not stay in the New World.

Finished with his explanation, he laid down and put his hands behind his head. "But I am tired, and must rest for now. You should do the same. We will leave here before first light."

Sarah also laid down, closing her eyes and shedding more tears for the death of her husband. But her sobs eventually turned into snores as she fell into a troubled sleep. She didn't notice Raven sit back up, unaware that the shape-shifter stood watch over her.

CHAPTER 35

Sarah awoke with a hand clamped firmly over her mouth. She struggled and tried to scream, but couldn't.

"Shhh … be still. They are looking for us." Raven removed his hand from her mouth, pointing at a pair of owls circling in the night sky. "Coyote's spies."

"What can we do?" she whispered.

"We need to leave this world, find a doorway to Galun'lati." He nodded toward Luther's medicine bag, lying on the ground beside her. "Your father could open a doorway whenever he wanted. That is how he escaped Coyote back at the nursing home."

"Here. Take it." She picked up the bag, offering it to him.

Raven smiled and shook his head.

"That is your father's medicine. Not mine. He could create a doorway out of thin air. I cannot. I must find one that already exists. There is a portal in St. Augustine, but that is too far away. We must find one closer."

"What does a portal look like?" she asked, looking around at the darkness.

"They look like every other place, but they are always spots where strong energy can be felt. The doorways between the two worlds are often considered special places, even by those who cannot open them. They feel the power; it draws them like moths to a flame. These places of power were once used as gathering places by the ancient peoples. They are sacred."

"Gathering places? You mean like Stonehenge?"

He nodded. "Stonehenge is a doorway to Galun'lati. The people who built it circled the standing stones around the portal."

"You mean the Druids?" she asked.

"The Druids did not build Stonehenge, but they held their ancient ceremonies there. They could feel the power, but did not know how to open the doorway."

"What about Devil's Tower in Wyoming? Is that also a portal?"

"It was," he replied, "but that passageway closed a long time ago. Even if it was still open, Wyoming is a long way from here. We need something closer."

"You said there is one in St. Augustine. What about *that* one? It's only a few hours' drive."

He looked up at the circling owls above them. "We may not have a few hours. We need something closer."

"But there's nothing around here," she argued. "This is Orlando. It's a new city, not some ancient holy site."

"What was here before the city?"

"Not much. Orange groves mostly, and swamps."

"What about Indian tribes? And villages? Were there any native people living in this area?"

"Not around Orlando. They were found mainly along the St. John's River, east of here. There were a lot of tribes along the river, but they were scattered. I don't know of any sacred gathering spots ... just some old shell mounds, and those are nothing but glorified trash heaps."

"Are you sure?"

Sarah nodded. "I live in Sanford, just a few blocks from the river. I've studied the history of the area. There is nothing special there, certainly nothing considered sacred."

"Still, with a lot of tribes living along the river, there may have been be a portal."

"Should we go look?"

Raven considered it a moment, then shook his head. "The portal could be in the river, and we do not have a boat."

"But there's no place—" She paused, her eyes growing wider. "Oh, my gosh. I just remembered something ... a place where Indian tribes used to gather."

"Where?"

"There's a cypress tree in Longwood, Florida called the Senator. It's older and bigger than all the other cypress trees in America, about thirty-five hundred years old ... older than Jesus. I've read that it was a place where Florida Indian tribes gathered to perform ceremonies at certain times of the year. Could that be the location of a portal?"

"Very possible," Raven said, hopeful. "How far away is this tree?"

"Not far. Maybe twenty miles."

He looked up again. The sky was clear, no sign of the circling owls. "They're gone, but probably not for long. I think we should go before they come back."

He stood, offering Sarah his hand.

The two of them quickly gathered their belongings.

"Hey, don't forget me," Mouse called from the tall grasses where he had been hiding. Raven kneeled and scooped up the little rodent, dropping him in his jacket pocket. Mouse squirmed around, quickly poking his head out so he could see.

"Where have you been, my little friend?" Raven asked. "I thought you had run away."

"I was hiding," Mouse replied. "Owls are very fond of eating my people."

Double-checking to make sure the sky was still clear, they hurried to the motorcycle and climbed on. Raven started the Harley, and they made their way back down the bumpy road to Colonial Drive. Turning on Colonial, they headed toward Longwood.

North on Highway 17-92 they passed through the towns of Winter Park and Maitland, finally reaching Longwood, Florida. It was quite late and the streets empty, and Raven was careful to stay within the speed limit. Still, he held his breath as they twice passed police cars parked along the side of the road.

Sarah tapped Raven on the shoulder, pointing out the sign for Big Tree Park. Slowing the motorcycle, he turned off of the highway onto a blacktop road leading to the giant cypress tree.

He parked well away from the security lights and turned off the engine. The big black motorcycle was nearly invisible in the darkness, and shouldn't draw the attention of anybody driving by the park.

Sarah slid off the back while Raven lowered the kickstand and climbed off the bike.

"This way," she said, leading them across the parking lot to a wooden boardwalk.

They hurried down the elevated boardwalk to the Senator. The giant tree stood about twenty feet from the boardwalk, surrounded by a four-foot-high wrought iron fence.

"Wait here," Raven said. He climbed down off the boardwalk and circled the Senator several times, studying it from top to bottom. He rejoined her a few minutes later.

"Is there a portal?" she asked.

"Yes. But it will not be easy to reach."

"Why? Where is it?"

He pointed at the very top of the tree. There, among the branches, was a large hole in the trunck, about three feet tall and two feet wide.

OWL GOINGBACK

It looked black in the moonlight, like a gaping toothless mouth.

"How the hell are we going to reach that?" she asked. "Unlike you, I can't sprout feathers out of my ass and fly."

"We climb."

"Climb? Are you out of your freaking mind? I can't climb that."

"Then you will hold onto me as I climb."

"There's no—"

An eerie howl sounded from back down the boardwalk. Loud and long, and bone-chilling, it caused the skin at Sarah's temples to pull tight. A second howl sounded from the forest to their left, followed by high-pitched yips and the sound of movement through the underbrush.

"Coyote's followers have found us. They must have been guarding this place." Raven pulled his pistol, checking the magazine. He only had only a few bullets, not nearly enough.

"Look!" Sarah pointed back down the boardwalk.

Dozens of shadowy shapes rushed toward them, running on four legs, eyes bright in the moonlight.

"Hurry. There are too many to fight." He quickly tucked the pistol back into his waistband, helping her down off the boardwalk, and together they raced to the giant cypress tree.

Raven grabbed Sarah around the waist and lifted her over the fence. He was about to climb over himself when a large red wolf charged out of the darkness and tackled him from behind.

"Raven, no!" she screamed, backing away in terror. The wolf attacked with a snarling, savage frenzy, tearing at the leather jacket in an attempt to sink its fangs deep into Raven's flesh.

With a frightened squeak, Mouse jumped out of Raven's pocket and raced past Sarah, scurrying up the Senator for safety.

The wolf tried to bite the back of Raven's neck, but the shape-shifter covered himself with his hands. Rolling over, he jammed the muzzle of the pistol under the wolf's jaw and pulled the trigger. The gun roared and the top of the wolf's head exploded.

Raven tossed the dead wolf off him and quickly stood. He fired at the other animals racing toward them, then tossed the empty gun away and leaped over the fence. He pulled the two tomahawks from the hunting pouch he carried and struck the tree with them, burying the forged metal blades into the wood.

"Climb onto my back and do not let go," he instructed.

Sarah quickly did as she was told.

199

Raven grabbed the wooden handles and pulled the two of them upward with the strength of his arms, using the tomahawks like a mountain climber would use a pair of ice axes. It would have been an impossible feat for a normal man, but the shape-shifter possessed greater than human strength.

Higher they went, Raven moving first the right tomahawk and then the left, sticking the forged iron blades deep into the wood of the ancient cypress tree. The muscles in his arms quivered with the effort; sweat ran down his face and stung his eyes.

Beneath them, a pack of wild animals circled the base of the tree, looking up with hungry eyes, waiting for them to fall.

"Keep going," Sarah cried, seeing the creatures below them.

They were thirty feet off the ground, but Raven could go no more. He was exhausted. But there was no place to rest, for all of the tree's branches were at the very top.

The assorted animals crowded around the tree must have sensed he was tiring, for a chorus of yips and barks suddenly filled the night.

Seeing that his friends were in trouble, Mouse came running down the tree to help.

"Why are you stopping?" cried the little rodent. "You must climb."

Mouse urged Raven to keep moving, but his words fell on deaf ears.

"I give up," Raven said, his voice strained. "I can climb no more."

"Nonsense," Mouse said. "You can do it."

"Go away," Raven's said, his grip slipping on the wooden handles of the tomahawks.

Sarah hung onto the shape-shifter, unable to do anything to help, her additional weight making the climb that much harder.

Frustrated, Mouse jumped onto Raven's head and bit his left ear.

"Owwww!" Raven screamed, shaking his head.

Mouse hung on and bit down harder.

"Owww ... stop that!"

"Climb, or I will bite it off." Mouse chomped down again on the ear.

"You little bastard, I'll make a tobacco pouch out of you." Raven pulled the tomahawk in his right hand out of the tree and stuck it back in at a higher location. He did the same thing with the left one.

Sarah held on for dear life.

Mouse's attack did the trick. Raven was moving again, climbing faster than ever before, determined to reach the top and rid himself of the pain being inflicted.

They reached the fifty-foot mark when an unearthly howl echoed through the forest. A second howl sounded, louder and closer than the first.

All the animals at the base of the tree fell silent.

Looking below her, Sarah saw a dark shape coming down the boardwalk. It moved upright like a man, but was at least seven-foot-tall and completely covered in fur. And though she had already seen a wolf-man and a fox-man, she knew this was something far more dangerous.

"Coyote," Mouse whispered, speaking out the corner of his mouth.

The Trickster jumped off the boardwalk and closed the distance to the tree in a single running leap. He launched himself straight up, far into the air, claws barely missing a grab at Sarah's leg.

"Move!" she yelled, terrified.

Raven worked the tomahawks, climbing the tree at an unbelievable rate.

Mouse let go of Raven's ear and scurried back up the tree, seeking shelter.

Coyote jumped again and grabbed Sarah's ankle, trying to drag her down to the ground. She screamed and hugged Raven tighter, choking him.

"I have you now, Blue Sky Woman," Coyote hissed through deadly fangs. "Time to die."

"Hang on!" Raven shouted.

The Trickster jerked and twisted like a trout on a fishing line, determined to tear her from Raven's back.

Sarah held on for dear life.

"Let go, you bitch!" snarled Coyote, his claws sinking into the flesh of her ankle.

Sarah shrieked in pain; her grip on Raven slipped.

Remembering that her father's medicine bag hung from her belt, she removed her arm from around Raven's neck and quickly unhooked the bag and opened it. She turned the bag upside down and shook it, a cloud of powdered ingredients falling down on Coyote.

"Eat this, mother fucker!" Sarah cried.

She let go of the empty bag and jammed her hand into the front pocket of her jeans, pulling out Luther's Zippo lighter. She flipped open the lid and thumbed the wheel, a tiny blue flame illuminating the night. Taking aim, she dropped the burning lighter on Coyote.

Instantly, the magical powders covering the Trickster's head and shoulders ignited and burst into flame. Coyote howled and let go of her ankle, slapping at the tiny fires that singed his fur and burned his flesh. He fell straight down, continuing to slap at the burning embers.

"Climb, climb, climb ..." she yelled.

Raven worked the tomahawks like a mad man, not slowing until they reached the opening at the top of the tree.

Sarah squeezed through the opening first, followed by Raven.

He put the tomahawks back in his pouch, then scooped up Mouse and dropped him in his jacket pocket.

"This way, hurry," Raven said.

Taking her by the hand, they descended what appeared to be a sloping tunnel leading down into the tree, a passageway large enough to walk upright with walls that glowed a faint green. This was no ordinary tunnel, but a magical doorway from one world to another that could only be used, and seen, by ancient tribes, shape-shifters, members of the Great Council, spirits, and an occasional mouse with the gift of gab.

The tunnel widened and leveled out, and they soon found themselves walking uphill.

Sarah saw light up ahead, brighter than the glow given off by the surrounding walls. She caught a glimpse of a night sky with a horizon touched by the colors of an early morning sunrise.

They emerged on a hillside overlooking a land that had never seen a skyscraper, parking lot, highway, or shopping center. Here ancient tribes and animals still spoke a common dialect, existing side by side with spirits and supernatural beings. It might not be Heaven, but it was where mankind and all animals had originated from, and to where many had returned.

Sarah felt her breath catch, for there in the deep purple sky of early morning were twin moons, sister satellites in orbit around an alien world, and she realized she had just fallen farther down the rabbit hole than she ever dreamed possible.

She also realized that this strange and wonderful place was where she truly belonged, for the often-painful longing that had been in her heart since childhood was suddenly gone, replaced by the feeling that she had finally come home.

And though Sarah knew that Coyote was snapping at her heels, and her life was still in danger, she allowed herself a moment to take a deep breath and marvel at the beauty that stretched before her, a smile unfolding on her face.

Raven saw the smile and squeezed her hand. "Welcome to Galun'lati."

ABOUT THE AUTHOR

OWL GOINGBACK has written numerous novels, children's books, short stories, and articles. He has also ghostwritten novels for celebrities. His novel *Crota* won the 1996 Bram Stoker Award for Best First Novel, and he was nominated for his novel *Darker Than Night* (1999). Owl's novel *Shaman Moon* was published as part of the omnibus edition *The Essential World of Darkness*. His books often draw on his Native American heritage to tell stories of supernatural suspense. His children's books *Eagle Feathers* and *The Gift* have received critical acclaim, and he was the recipient of the Storytelling World Awards Honor. His shorter works of fiction have appeared in numerous anthologies, and his story *Grass Dancer* was a Nebula Award Nominee. Among his other works: the collection *Tribal Screams* and the novel *Breed*. www.owlgoingback.com

LATEST BOOK RELEASES

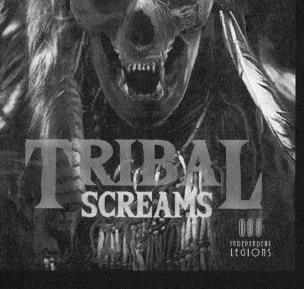

MONSTERS OF ANY KIND

DAVID J. SCHOW
RAMSEY CAMPBELL
JONATHAN MABERRY
EDWARD LEE
LUCY TAYLOR
OWL GOINGBACK
MONICA J. O'ROURKE
CODY GOODFELLOW
DAMIEN ANGELICA WALTERS
MICHAEL BAILEY
BRUCE BOSTON
ERINN L. KEMPER
MARK ALAN MILLER
JESS LANDRY
GREGORY L. NORRIS
GREG SISCO
SANTIAGO EXIMENO
MICHAEL G. BAUGHAN

INDEPENDENT LEGIONS

EDITED BY
ALESSANDRO MANZETTI
AND DANIELE BONFANTI

SPREE
AND
OTHER STORIES
LUCY TAYLOR

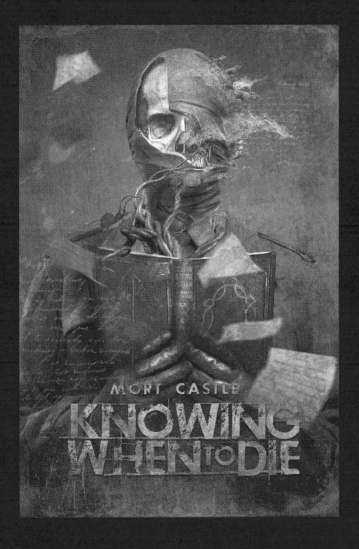

LATEST BOOK RELEASES

MORT CASTLE

KNOWING WHEN TO DIE

AVAILABLE BOOKS

Our publications are available at Amazon and major online booksellers. Visit our Website: **www.independentlegions.com**

BOTH PAPERBACK & DIGITAL PUBLICATIONS

FEARFUL SYMMETRIES
by Thomas F. Monteleone

DARK MARY
by Paolo Di Orazio

TRIBAL SCREAMS
by Owl Goingback

MONSTERS OF ANY KIND
Edited by Alessandro Manzetti & Daniele Bonfanti

KNOWING WHEN TO DIE
by Mort Castle

ARTIFACTS
by Bruce Boston

NARAKA THE ULTIMATE HUMAN BREEDING
by Alessandro Manzetti

A WINTER SLEEP
by Greg F. Gifune

SPREE AND OTHER STORIES
by Lucy Taylor

THE BEAUTY OF DEATH 2 – DEATH BY WATER
edited by Alessandro Manzetti & Jodi Renee Lester

THE LIVING AND THE DEAD
by Greg F. Gifune

THE CARP-FACED BOY AND OTHER TALES
by Thersa Matsuura

THE WISH MECHANICS
by Daniel Braum

CHILDREN OF NO ONE
by Nicole Cushing

THE ONE THAT COMES BEFORE
by Livia Llewellyn

ALL AMERICAN HORROR OF THE 21ST CENTURY: THE FIRST DECADE
Edited by Mort Castle

BENEATH THE NIGHT
by Greg Gifune

SELECTED STORIES
by Nate Southard

FORTHCOMING BOOKS

BOTH PAPERBACK & DIGITAL PUBLICATIONS

HORROR CALCUTTA
by Poppy Z. Brite (graphic novel)

DARK CARNIVAL
by Joanna Parypinski

THE MAN WHO ESCAPED THIS STORY
by Cody Goodfellow

CROTA
by Owl Goingback

THE DEMETER DIARIES
by Marge Simon and Bryan D. Dietrich

UMBRIA
by Santiago Eximeno

LOST TRIBE
by Gene O'Neill

DARKER THAN NIGHT
by Owl Goingback

NOT FADE AWAY
by Gene O'Neill

BREED
by Owl Goingback

INDEPENDENT LEGIONS PUBLISHING
DI ALESSANDRO MANZETTI
Via Virgilio, 10 – TRIESTE (ITALY)
+39 040 9776602

WWW.INDEPENDENTLEGIONS.COM
WWW.FACEBOOK.COM/INDEPENDENTLEGIONS
INDEPENDENT.LEGIONS@AOL.COM

ASSOCIATION
SPECIALTY PRESS AWARD RECIPIENT

Made in the USA
Columbia, SC
10 June 2020